Viking Warband

Book 19 in the Dragon Heart Series

By

Griff Hosker

Viking Warband

Published by Sword Books Ltd 2017
Copyright © Griff Hosker First Edition

The author has asserted their moral right under the Copyright, Designs and Patents Act, 1988, to be identified as the author of this work.

All Rights reserved. No part of this publication may be reproduced, copied, stored in a retrieval system, or transmitted, in any form or by any means, without the prior written consent of the copyright holder, nor be otherwise circulated in any form of binding or cover other than that in which it is published and without a similar condition being imposed on the subsequent purchaser.
A CIP catalogue record for this title is available from the British Library.

Cover by Design for Writers

Contents

Viking Warband	1
Prologue	4
Chapter 1	8
Chapter 2	19
Chapter 3	32
Chapter 4	44
Chapter 5	56
Chapter 6	66
Chapter 7	75
Chapter 8	84
Chapter 9	97
Chapter 10	105
Chapter 11	115
Chapter 12	126
Chapter 13	140
Chapter 14	150
Chapter 15	164
Chapter 16	178
Chapter 17	190
Epilogue	200
Norse Calendar	202
Glossary	203
Maps and drawings	209
Historical note	211
Other books by Griff Hosker	216

Prologue

My wife died a year to the day after the wolf, Úlfarr, sacrificed himself to save my great-grandson and grandson when the Saxon assassin tried to kill them. It was a year, to the day, after Sámr killed his first enemy and began his journey as a warrior. It was a year, to the day, since I had sworn vengeance on Æthelwulf, King of Wessex. I had always thought that I would be the first to go to the Otherworld. I had almost lost my life many times.

My wife, Brigid, had become ill almost as soon as we returned home to Cyninges-tūn. Kara, Aiden and Ylva, our healers, had put it down to the upset, the journey and the weather. It may have been. She worsened, day by day. She was dying. I could see that but she did not. Her faith in her god, the White Christ, made her believe that she would recover. The illness seemed to eat at her. I was so close that often I did not see how much she had worsened. When my son and his family visited they were shocked. When it became obvious that she was seriously ill my wife made a momentous decision. Rather than allowing Kara to heal her, she insisted on travelling to Whale Island. They had a church there and a priest. I loved my wife and I acceded to her demands. She seemed happier for her children and grandchildren were there but she still worsened.

I could not leave her. I could not do as I wished and that was to take my ships to Wintan-Caestre and sack it. I waited knowing, as each day passed, that she was closer to death. I watched as death took her body, slowly, gradually, painfully. The day she died it seemed almost a relief for she was free of pain. Her emaciated body looked like a woman twenty years older. Whatever had killed her had not been kind. Her god had not given her relief and she had refused the medicine of what she called, the pagans. She was buried in the small Christian cemetery near the church she loved. I had a stone carved with her name upon it.

I took comfort in my family during that most difficult year. I had Sámr, Ulla War Cry and my youngest grandson, Mordaf Gruffydson. We played and, while we did, I taught them. I gave them the skills I had been taught by Old Ragnar in Norway over fifty years earlier. I now knew, better than ever, why the old man had invested so much time in me. He lived through me. He had become the father I had barely known and liked even less. The Saxon who had sired me had taken my mother and beaten me. He was not a father to celebrate. Ragnar more than made up for him. He was strict and he was hard but he was also kind and patient. I tried to be all of those things with my young charges.

Sámr was the eldest. He had now seen ten summers and his body was filling out. In that moment when he had used the fruit knife to slit the Saxon's throat he had changed. After that, he laughed less and took his training more seriously than Ulla War Cry. Ulla became almost a big brother to Mordaf Gruffydson. The three of them got on well together but Sámr was closer to the time he would go to war with his father and his great-grandfather. For that reason, he seemed to be closer to me than the other two. If I am honest I was the one he wished to raid with. The reason was simple, I was old. Brigid's illness made him realise that my time in the land of the Wolf was limited. He wished to raid with me before I went to the Otherworld. I did not feel old. We were not a vain people and we had none of the shiny mirrors my servant, Atticus of Syracuse, had told me about. Nonetheless, when I caught my reflection in the water I saw a greybeard. I had not gone to fat but I was losing my teeth and my hair was growing thin.

The day that we buried my wife, in the small Christian cemetery by the church I went alone to look out towards the south. My wife had been born there in the south of the country they called Dyfed. I had become a jarl and a warrior on the island that was Man and my enemy, Æthelwulf lived even further south. I mourned my wife but I was relieved that she was now free from pain. I would now begin to plan my raid on Wessex.

I saw the drekar bobbing on the water. Which ones would I take and who would be the warriors I would lead? My thoughts were interrupted by the arrival of my son, Gruffyd, and grandson, Ragnar. My nearest kin sat next to me. "How are you, grandfather?" There was concern in Ragnar's voice.

I looked at Ragnar. He was older than my son and was now the leader of the clan. He still deferred to me on most matters but my plan had been to enjoy a quiet life in Cyninges-tūn. The Norns and the Saxons had ended that dream.

"How am I? I have buried two wives, a son and a grandson yet I am still alive. I am sad and I feel an emptiness inside that grows. If it were not for Sámr, Ulla War Cry and Mordaf Gruffydson then I would be the hollow man."

"We would not have you sad."

"I know, my son, and yet I am. Nothing that you can do or say will end that sadness. Time alone will make the pain lessen."

There was silence broken only by the sea breaking on Whale Island and the cries of the gulls. Some said the cries were the dead who had not died with a sword in their hands.

"You still think of vengeance."

My grandson's words had startled me. "Of course. Your sons were almost killed."

"But had we not raided Lundenwic and Essex then Æthelwulf would not have sent those killers. It must stop sometime."

I looked at them both. "All of us married Christians. That changes a man. Perhaps I am luckier than you two. Erika was my first wife and she was not only Viking, she was a volva. We cannot change our nature. The wolf that hunts sheep and lambs cannot stop hunting and cannot stop killing. If that were not true then Úlfarr would still be alive and Sámr and Ulla War Cry dead." I saw that my grandson was battling with himself. I smiled, "I do not ask you to come with me when I take my vengeance. I will offer oars on my drekar. I had planned on taking all of them but it may be that others feel as you do. There are easier targets than the Saxons. The Hibernians, Welsh and the Picts are easy to defeat."

"You make it sound as though we are afraid!"

"I know, Ragnar, that you are not. You have a family. Your family is larger than my own ever was. Your wife fears for your safety. All of that is perfectly clear to me. I ask you to understand that I have a wolf inside me. If you hurt me or my family I will have vengeance. If you threaten me or my family then I will punish you. Egbert knew that and his son does too. We will not be safe just because we do not raid Wessex. So long as I live then killers will come for me. I have lived too long and been a thorn in the side of the Saxons for more than forty years. When I am gone they may forget the Land of the Wolf but that is your curse. You live with Jarl Dragonheart. You live in the Land of the Wolf which is guarded by the Wolf Warrior. I am sorry if you find that hard."

Gruffyd shook his head, "We just worry about you. You are no longer a young man, father."

I laughed, "And that makes me unique. Haaken One Eye and I are the last of the warriors who came from the land of snow to take Man and build this home here in the Land of the Wolf. When we are gone we will be just stories told to make the young wonder if they were really true and, eventually, they will become just fragments, legends which are not truly believed."

Ragnar shook his head, "But they are real and we know them!"

"They have changed already. Haaken and I were the only ones who were there when my sword was touched by the gods. Aiden, Haaken and I were the ones who fought with the Norns. When we pass what then?"

We had returned to the hall for the warriors of the stad would celebrate Brigid's life in ale. That was the way of the Viking and I would drink, close my eyes and see the young girl I had saved and made my wife.

Part One
Queen Osburga's Crown

Chapter 1

I sent word to all the warriors who lived in the Land of the Wolf that I would be leading a raid on Wessex. I gave them a moon to join me. That gave me enough time to work with Erik Short Toe and ensure that '***Heart of the Dragon***' was ready for sea. It also gave Aiden time to make new maps for me. He was now aided by the Greek I had rescued from Lundenwic. Atticus of Syracuse was a clever man. We had found maps in Lundenwic and he also had knowledge of the wider world. The two of them spent days poring over the documents we had found and the maps we had discovered. The writings were just squiggles and marks to me. Aiden had realised that and he used colours on the map to help Erik and I find the targets we sought. The new maps were unique for they were made for me.

Many men came to join my warband. Of my Ulfheonar only Olaf Leather Neck, Rolf Horse Killer, Haaken One Eye and Rollo Thin Skin chose to raid. Aðils Shape Shifter had a new wife and family and Cnut Cnutson's old wound was giving him trouble. Beorn the Scout sent a message that he felt he would slow us down. I smiled when I heard that. I was twenty years older than Beorn. There were many others who chose to join me. Most were untried. They saw the chance of glory. They would raid with the Dragonheart. If they survived they would come back rich and if they died then they would be remembered forever in one of Haaken's songs. They were largely single men. Some had seen just fifteen summers. They each had a sword and a shield.

When I realised that I would not have large numbers of experienced warriors I changed the target. I had planned on raiding Wintan-Caestre. It was the home of Æthelwulf. I wanted to hurt him. That was not possible with an untried crew. I needed something which would be a punishment yet which would give my warriors who had neither mail nor helmet, a fighting chance. It was Atticus who supplied the solution.

"Lord, the Queen of Wessex, Osburga is the mother of Æthelwulf's children. She had the fourth last year." I cocked my head to one side and looked at him. He smiled. "I listen to the news which traders bring, lord. I met Queen Osburga when I served in Lundenburgh. She is a well-read woman. She is known to like books and she is deeply religious. Had she not become the queen she would be a nun. One of the ships which traded last year had called in at a port on the island of Wihtwara. That was where her father had lived. The captain said that the Queen had ordered a new monastery to be built there in honour of her latest son, Æthelberht."

Aiden said, "That makes sense. Egbert had but the one son. I think that when Elfrida was taken his new wife was not as fertile. Or he was not. If the Queen has four sons then that bodes well for the Saxons."

"That makes sense but how does it help us?"

"The monastery is on the island. The Queen likes to spend time there. If you wished to reap rewards and punish the King then you can do this by raiding Wihtwara."

I nodded. We had fought a sea battle near there and Eystein the Rock had died close by. "I know the island. It is the one the Romans called Vectis. Knowing it is on the island and finding it are two entirely different things."

Atticus beamed and took one of the maps which Aiden had made. He pointed to the one of Wihtwara. He jabbed his stylus at the north of the island. There was a blue line. I knew that Aiden used blue to indicate rivers. "This is the River Medina. There was an old Roman villa here. They have used the stones from the Roman villa to make a monastery." He dipped his stylus in the red ink and put a blob at the end of the river. "There is the monastery. You can sail up the river, raid and be out at sea before they know."

Atticus hated the Saxons. It was not just that he had been ill-treated by them but he had also found them both dirty and unpleasant to be around.

Aiden nodded his agreement. "If the Queen has endowed it then it will be filled with rich objects and, as she is literate then there will be books for us to sell. Now that Dorestad has dried up the port of Bruggas is a good market for us. The Empire's grip on that land is tenuous."

It seemed like a good plan. "Then make the maps. I shall assemble the crew."

Atticus said, "Lord, there is one thing…"

"Yes?"

"Young Sámr wishes to voyage with you." He cocked his head apologetically, "I am sorry lord but young people have good memories and, when you were recovered from your wound you said that when he was as tall as his pony he could be a ship's boy."

I remembered the promise, "Is he that tall already?"

Atticus saw him every day for he was the tutor to the boys. They would be able to read and write. They would be able to understand both Latin and Greek. "He is lord; taller."

"Then I will have to keep my promise."

"Perhaps his mother or father will refuse permission."

"No Atticus. Ragnar would never do that for he was younger than Sámr when he first sailed to war."

I went to see Ragnar as soon as I had left the others. He was with his wife, Astrid. She was nursing their new daughter, Anwen. Ragnar knew something was awry when I entered. My grandson knew me well. "What is amiss, grandfather?"

"I go to raid soon. Atticus reminded me that I had promised Sámr that he could come with me when he was as tall as his pony."

Astrid's hand went to her mouth and then she looked down at her daughter. She knew better than to interfere. She might object but her husband would speak. Ragnar said, "He told me your promise. Perhaps you should have asked his father first."

"Perhaps but you raided with me when you were younger."

I saw him reflecting on that, "You are right but…"

"But this is your eldest son and he came close to death once because of his grandfather and you would not risk him a second time."

Ragnar laughed, "By the Allfather! Are you a galdramenn?"

I shook my head, "I know my children, and my children's children and…"

Ragnar held up his hand, "Spare me."

"Besides he will be a ship's boy. Erik Short Toe will watch over him. You know that."

"I do but it does not make it any easier."

"You can say no."

Ragnar nodded, "And he will hate us." He looked at Astrid and then back at me, "He will be safe?"

"As safe as I can keep him. This will happen one day."

Astrid laid the sleeping bairn in her cot and said, sadly, "I would that it was not yet."

Haaken and Olaf arrived the next day. Both were keen to raid but for different reasons. Olaf was single. Haaken lived in a house full of women. Two of his daughters were married but he still had a wife and two daughters at home. A raid was preferable. Both were now much older. Haaken had lost most of his hair and his beard was white. He had long ago stopped wearing a patch and the scarred eye gave him a frightening appearance. Olaf had been scarred and cut by the many battles we had fought. Some of his wounds had not been cleaned as effectively as others and the scars looked like tattoos on his cheeks and forehead.

"I see we take virgins with us, Dragonheart!"

I shook my head. Olaf Leather Neck had ever been outspoken, "We all had to have our first raid. This one does not require veterans." Even as I said it I regretted the words for the Norns were spinning and the web they spun would trap us.

Haaken only had one eye but it missed nothing. He saw Sámr swarming up the mast with the other ship's boys, "And Ragnar's son comes with us?"

"I promised him last year and he remembered the promise."

He took his chest off his horse. "We have taken them all now: your son, Wolf Killer, Ragnar your grandson, and now Sámr, your great-grandson. Has any other Jarl ever taken three generations raiding?"

Olaf hefted his own chest on his back. "You write the stories, Haaken, is there another like the Dragonheart? Long after we are dead and forgotten he will still be remembered." He looked at me. "Do any other Ulfheonar sail with us?"

"Just Rolf and Rollo. The men we take are keen to impress. Do not terrify them too much Olaf."

He adopted an innocent expression. "Me?"

Ulla War Cry and Mordaf were both unhappy to be left behind. "Can we go next time?"

This time I was wary. "You can go when your mothers say that you can." I saw the relief on the faces of Ebrel and Astrid. Sámr was looking pleased with himself. "And you, Sámr Ragnarsson will be treated just like any other member of the crew. But you will have the added responsibility of every eye watching you. Your father is a great leader. Your grandfather had a reputation too."

"I know."

"And while we raid you will call me Jarl as do the rest of the crew. You will be at the beck and call of Erik Short Toe. When you are not reefing and furling the sail you will be fetching food and ale to the rowers. You will be tightening stays and sheets. You will be peering into the distance to spy our enemies." He nodded and I turned to the other two. "Does that sound like something you would like to do?"

To my dismay, they both nodded and grinned.

Whale Island was a safe anchorage but that very safety made it hard to get in and out. Úlfarrston had been easier but Raibeart ap Pasgen's home had been raided many times. The rowers had to edge us out to sea. We could not use a chant for they were listening to the orders being barked out by Erik. In many ways, it was useful for the rowers had to think and they became used to the voice of their captain. Then we were beyond the land and Erik shouted for the ship's boys to scurry up the stays and mast and unfurl the sail.

The wind was from the west. It was not an ideal wind but it meant we did not need to row. There was no requirement for us to reach our destination at a precise time. We had beaches and bays on the way where we could shelter. We would raid at night but it mattered not which day. As we headed out to sea I saw the island to the south which was Man and the distant coast of Hibernia. My granddaughter lived in Dyflin now with Thorghest the Lucky. Moon Child, their son, would almost be ready to raid soon. My offspring were growing. Veisafjǫrðr was also ruled by one of my jarls, Siggi Finehair. There had been times when the Vikings of Hibernia had been our enemies and a threat now it was not so. The men of Man, on the other hand… We were too strong for them but as *'Heart of the Dragon'* beat south the older warriors and crew kept a wary eye on that treacherous land.

When we neared the Welsh coast and the island of Ynys Môn I clutched my wolf amulet. My life was bound closely with that mountain. One of my ancestors was buried in a cave now covered in a rockfall. I had been to the bottom of an underground pool and felt the hand of the Allfather. I had died and come back. Each time we passed I felt that much older and closer to death. The crew had to row. Erik would not risk the passage between the land and the island with a westerly. The crew rowed. Haaken chose a song that he particularly liked. For me, it brought back too many memories and I wished he had not chosen it. Sámr loved it. He and the other boys were reefing the sails and I saw his face light up as the crew chanted the story of the wolf snake.

> ***The wolf snake-crawled from the mountain side***
> ***Hiding the spell-wight in cave deep and wide***
> ***He swallowed him whole and Warlord too***
> ***Returned to pay the price that was due***
> ***There they stayed through years of man***
> ***Until the day Jarl Dragon Heart began***

He climbed up Wyddfa filled with ghosts
With Arturus his son, he loved the most
The mouth was dark, hiding death
Dragon Heart stepped in and held his breath
He lit the torch so strong and bright
The wolf's mouth snarled with red firelight
Fearlessly he walked and found his kin
The Warlord of Rheged buried deep within
Cloaked in mail with sharp bright blade
A thing of beauty by Thor made
And there lay too, his wizard friend,
Myrddyn protecting to the end
With wolf charm blue they left the lair
Then Thor he spoke, he filled the air
The storm it raged, the rain it fell
Then the earth shook from deep in hel
The rocks they crashed, they tumbled down
Burying the wizard and the Rheged crown.
Till world it ends the secret's there
Buried beneath wolf warrior's lair
Till world it ends the secret's there
Buried beneath wolf warrior's lair
Till world it ends the secret's there
Buried beneath wolf warrior's lair

By the time the crew had sung it eight times we were clear of Ynys Môn and Erik turned us south and east. The rowers could stop and we used the sails. Sámr slid down the backstay and stood close to Erik to receive more orders. I saw Erik smile. His own sons had been ship's boys and now they captained other drekar. He was remembering them. "Well done Sámr Ragnarsson. Now take ale to the rowers. They have earned it."

Lars Long Nose was the senior boy and the biggest of them. "I will carry the barrel for you." He picked up the firkin. I could tell it was not full.

Sámr said, "Jarl would you like some ale?"

"No Sámr, I have had the easy task. Give it to the rowers they deserve it."

Erik gestured with his arm to Sámr's back as the two boys began to ladle ale into horns. "He is a good lad, jarl. He works harder than any and he does not quibble about unpleasant tasks. That is why Lars offered to help. He likes him."

I knew what he meant. When Sámr was older he would lead warriors. It was important that they not only obeyed but they obeyed willingly. That would come if they liked him. I was under no illusions. My magic sword made men wish to follow me but they had followed me willingly before the sword had been struck. Ragnar was the same as was Gruffyd. The Allfather had given us that gift when we were born or perhaps it came from the Warlord. The line which linked us was a long one.

The wind veered a little and sped us on our way. We normally stayed at Ynys Enlli but there was still light in the sky when it hove into view. Erik looked at me. I said, "Push on. There is that fjord in Wales. It is a good place to land."

He nodded. We had raided the monastery which had been on the headland. After we had destroyed it they had moved it further east. It meant the beach beneath the headland was deserted. There were rocks for shellfish and it was sheltered. It also meant that we would be able to sail through the islands of the witches in broad daylight. None of us wished to sail those waters at dusk.

As we sat around the fire the Ulfheonar asked me for more details of the raid. We picked at the crabs we had caught and cooked while we spoke. "The monastery is new. It is supposed to be richly furnished by the Queen. We will see. We knew Egbert left his son wealthy. Perhaps he has enough burghs and now wishes to build churches. We know it is built of stone and that is not common. We know that they think the island is safe from attack and there will not be many guards. It is not on the coast."

Having finished sucking the meat from the crab Olaf tossed away the shell. "Then this new Saxon king is a fool. The only thing which can keep us out is a stout wall."

Rollo Horse Killer laughed, "When was the last time a wall kept you out?"

"True. It slows us down then."

"But the result is still the same."

Haaken stretched out on the sand, "And then we visit Bruggas. I wonder if it is as lively as Dorestad was."

"So long as they have a good market I care not. We sell whatever we find and buy that which we need."

As we ate I looked at the groups of warriors gathered around their fires. I knew many of them. Some of them had fathers who had served with me. I pointed to one giant of a warrior. He was a good head taller than the tallest of my men. I knew him not but there was something familiar about his features. "Who is that huge warrior?"

"That is Haraldr Leifsson. It is Leif the Banner's son."

"I did not know Leif had had a wife."

"He did not. When he was a youth he was out hunting. He came upon Haraldr's mother and laid with her. They were both young. He died not knowing that he had a son. The woman and her son lived in Lang's Dale. It was only when Aðils Shape Shifter moved there that he discovered the story. Haraldr lived with his mother and grandparents. Aðils worked with him to give him skills and to tell him of his father."

"His father was big but not as big as he." Leif had carried my banner into battle. He had been a rock.

"Aðils told me that the boy's mother is tall too."

I wondered at that. Leif had been an honourable man. If he had known then he would have married the woman and brought up his son to be a warrior. If Aðils had not chosen to live in that remote valley he might have remained there not knowing his father's story. *Wyrd*. I had them take me through some of the other warriors I did not know. Haraldr's was the story I thought of as I went to sleep.

The next day we did not need to row for long as the wind was still from the west. Once we had cleared the headland we headed down the coast of Om Walum. I saw Haraldr looking at the land. If he had spent his life in Lang's Dale then the sea and all that lay along it would be new to him. I stood next to him. He was more than a whole head taller than I was. I saw that he had a leather jerkin on and he had a sword strapped to his waist.

When I approached he gave a slight bow, "Jarl."

I smiled, "You do not bow to me, Haraldr. We are not Franks. I understand that you only recently heard who your father was."

"I knew he was a warrior and my mother knew his name but that was all. Aðils Shape Shifter said he was a brave man."

"None braver. He carried my banner and that is the hardest task I can give a man for he cannot hold a shield and the banner." I pointed to his sword. "A good sword."

"Aðils gave it to me. He also gave me a shield and a spear. I have one of his wolf skin cloaks too." He smiled. "He offered me a helmet but, like the rest of me, my head was too big."

"Then when we return, rich and rewarded you must have Bagsecg make you one. A warrior needs a helmet, especially one whose head will stand above the shield wall."

He lowered his voice, "Jarl, Aðils taught me to use a sword and a spear. I can use a shield but I have not yet stood in a shield wall. I know not what to do."

"Do not worry. We will have time to teach you when we return. We should not need a shield wall on this raid." I should have waited to speak those words for we had not yet reached Syllingar. The witch who lived there would not have forgiven me. The Weird Sisters would spin. They liked to toy with warriors, especially one who had dared to take from them something they had wanted: Ylva!

Sámr came up to us with two horns of ale, "Here Jarl. This is the top of the new barrel."

"Thank you Sámr." I pointed to my great-grandson, "Haraldr Leifsson, this is my great-grandson Sámr. Like you, this is his first voyage. You have much in common."

They smiled at each other. Sámr was still a child inside and he blurted out, "I have killed a warrior. Have you?"

Rather than being offended which would have been the case with most warriors, Haraldr said, "But you are little more than a child! How did you do that?"

Sámr grinned and pulled out the fruit knife from his sea boots. "By being sneaky! I used this!"

I left them for Sámr was telling the story of Úlfarr and the Saxon killers. I did not need reminding about the brave wolf who saved my family.

We reached the waters of Syllingar just before the sun was at its highest. The new warriors just looked at the rocks and islands which seemed to dot the sea with interest. Erik and my older warriors clutched at amulets and invoked the help of Njoror to see us safely through. Our pleas must have worked for we were soon in the open water and flying as the wind was now from behind and our drekar was lithe and swift. When darkness fell we headed toward the coast of Om Walum. The Saxons had built towers and burghs but we knew places where there were sheltered bays. There was no need to land. We ran out two sea anchors and slept.

We did not sail at night unless we had to. Erik and his boys needed rest. A tired man makes mistakes.

The next day we headed out to sea. The Saxons had learned to fear raids from the sea. Most of the raids came from the east but their line of burghs and towers ran along the south coast of Wessex. Erik knew the waters well. We would sail due east until he estimated we were due south of Wihtwara. We hoped to reach the southern shores of the island at dusk and that would allow us to sail, unseen, around the coast and down the river. It meant that the crew would have to row at some point. As the wind had veered and was now coming from a south easterly direction that meant we began rowing.

The day was filled with grey. It was not raining but the air was filled with dampness. I now felt the cold more than I once had. I pulled my wolf cloak tighter about me. Just doing that brought back memories of Úlfarr. I stared to the south of us. A bank of either mist or rain was heading for us. Erik saw my look and nodded, "Lars saw it some time since. It is coming with the wind. It must be rain and not mist."

I nodded and went to my chest. I would need my seal skin cape. "The rain helps us." I put the wolf cloak in the chest and took out the seal skin cape. It was not as warm but I would be drier.

"It does, jarl. The men can stop rowing and we can head north. Njoror sends us a mizzle to cloak us and keep us hidden. The crew can rest and shelter from the rain. It is good."

Sure enough, as the squally rain hit us we turned. With the sail lowered and the oars stacked the rowers used their seal skin capes to make shelters on the deck. There they ate and drank. Older, wiser warriors like Olaf took the opportunity to sleep while the younger ones, like Haraldr, spoke excitedly of the raid. Once the sail was lowered and the stays and sheets tightened Sámr joined me at the steering board. Water dripped from him. I opened my chest and took out the wolf cloak. "Put this about you. You should have a seal skin cape. We will buy you one with the coins we take."

He sniffed the cloak as he draped it over his head and shoulders. He, too, was thinking of Úlfarr. I saw his hand clasp the wolf he wore about his neck. He turned to me. "I would rather spend my coin on mail."

I shook my head, "You are still growing. You need a cape more. When you are full grown then we look at a helmet, sword and mail."

"But how can I fight without a sword and mail?"

"Look at the young warriors. Few have any mail. They wear leather. They are young and they will use speed to defeat their enemies. Warriors like Olaf and Haaken do not move as quickly. They have to stand and endure blows. Younger ones do not. This raid you will need to do nothing but when you are called upon to fight then use your head. It is a weapon."

Erik said, "And now, Sámr, it is your turn to relieve Lars at the masthead. Take some dried fish and the water skin. You will be there until dark."

"Aye captain." He handed me back the wolf cloak. "Thank you for the cloak, jarl. I could smell Úlfarr. It gave me comfort. Is it wrong that I miss him?"

"No, for when you miss him you bring him back to life. I miss him too."

He went to the barrel with the dried fish; took some and grabbed one of the water skins. I did not envy him the climb up the mast. The rain had made everything slick and slippery. I held my breath until he squatted on the yard with his legs wrapped around the mast. The wind dropped a little but the rain did not abate. I sat on my chest and pulled my cape tighter about me. I almost dozed and then I heard Sámr's voice, "Land to the north!" We had reached Wihtwara.

Chapter 2

I stood and peered north. The light from the day was fading. The dying wind had almost cost us but the island could be seen as a darker smudge on the horizon. Erik put the steerboard over. It would slow us for a while but when we turned to sail along the eastern coast of Wihtwara we would pick up speed. Olaf and Haaken joined me. I saw that Rollo and Rolf both had clusters of younger warriors seated around them.

Haaken shook his head, "Times past I would have been the one they all asked about the battles we had fought. Now it is Rollo and Rolf!"

Olaf laughed, "We are old men, now Haaken. These young bloods think that we are past our best and will slow them up. Rollo and Rolf are younger." He turned to me. "Did you know that they both have sons now, jarl?"

"I did not but that is a good thing. We need warriors who have their blood. You should have fathered children. Leif did."

"And I too may have fathered bastards. When we raided I laid enough seed about. Whenever we visited Dorestad or Dyflin I expected to see someone as ugly as me."

"And the Allfather decided to make me the last of my line."

"You have daughters, Haaken. They may have sons."

He shook his head, "They have babies but all are girls. Your line will continue Jarl Dragonheart. I envy you that. There will be warriors, as yet unborn, who will have the blood of the most famous Viking coursing through their bodies. I envy you. We both began together, defending old Ragnar on that wall in the cold lands of the north. The Weird Sisters spun very different webs for us."

"Yet we have shared much."

"Aye, that we have and here is another tale that is yet to be written."

His face brightened and, amazingly, the rain abated. As Erik turned us so that the wind came from *'Heart's'* quarter our drekar seemed to leap through the water. We sailed into darkness. The ship's boys now took position along our larboard side and the prow to watch for rocks. We had never sailed this channel.

Lars ran down the centre of the drekar, after we had sped for a while north and west. "Captain, there is a river." That had to be the Medina. Atticus and Aiden had scoured all the parchments we had. They had only read of one river which emptied to the north of the island.

Erik nodded, "Then reef the sail. Rowers!"

I went to my chest and took out my mail. Wrapped in an oiled sheepskin it was free from rust. I slipped the byrnie over my head. I smiled as I watched Olaf do the same. He struggled. His girth was greater now than it had been. I took my sword from my chest and strapped that on. Ragnar's Spirit still protected me. With Wolf's Blood in my seal skin boot all that I needed was my helmet and I would be ready for war. I watched Haaken don his soft leather cap and then slip the mail hood over his head. Aiden had had to replace bone in Haaken's head with a metal plate. My oldest friend protected himself now when we fought our enemies.

They took their oars as the sail was furled and the steering board pushed over. The entrance to the river was wide. It was over a hundred paces from bank to bank. There was a tower at the entrance to the river and we saw the walls of a burgh. As lights flared from the walls and the alarm was given we sailed south. They knew the wolf was loose but we were now in the sheep pen. Atticus had marked the monastery four Roman miles down the river. Even if they sent a rider we would beat them. The river was wide all the way south. It was not like the Dunum and the Temese. It did not twist and turn. It felt more like a fjord than a river save that there were no mountains rising up like teeth along the sides. Atticus' map had indicated that the monastery was on a piece of high ground less than half a mile from the river. He had indicated that the river narrowed where we should stop.

Sámr slid down the backstay, "Captain, I see a glow on the hill."

Lars pointed to the river bank. "The river narrows, Captain."

I nodded, "Then we are here. Turn us around, Erik. I do not think we will need to leave in a hurry, these are just monks but let us be prepared."

"Steerboard oars, back water." The river was wide enough for us to turn easily. "Larboard oars in." With just the steerboard oars rowing we were sculled to the west bank of the river. I saw Lars and Sámr leap ashore and tie us up. I nodded to my great-grandson as I left the drekar. My shield was on my back and my sword was sheathed.

I waited until my men had all joined me. Gone were the days when Beorn the Scout would have raced ahead. I pointed to Rolf Horse Killer and Rollo Thin Skin. With their wolf cloaks to disguise them, they would lead us to the monastery. As we moved up the path from the river I wondered if we would find the priests and monks abed. I knew that they often rose in the middle of the night to say prayers to the White Christ. I could see the buildings above us. There was the glow of candles and lights. They were awake. Then I heard a shout, "Vikings!" They had watchers. The Norns had been spinning.

There was little need for secrecy and silence now, "Clan of the Horse!" I drew my sword and ran towards the buildings. I would not need my shield against priests.

Suddenly I heard the clash of swords. Rolf and Rollo had found the enemy. I saw a door open for there was a great deal of light and I saw armed men emerging. Some had mail! It was too late to regret not scouting out this, seemingly, easy target. I was attacking mailed Saxon warriors with untried youths. A Viking did not regret. I swung my shield around and, with Olaf on one side and Haaken on the other we bundled into the Saxons who had slain three of my men and surrounded Rollo and Rolf. I brought my sword high over my head to hack and slice down on the neck of a mailed Saxon. Even as he fell bleeding before me I took in that he had a fine byrnie. What were such warriors doing at a monastery?

As I slashed my sword into the shield of a second Saxon I saw why. There were men with horses and they were helping some women and two children onto them. I saw a crown. It was the Queen. We had the chance of capturing a greater prize than the holy books. If we could take Queen Osburga then we could demand a great ransom. The two young boys I saw were princes! The Saxon swung his sword against my shield. He only made a quarter swing and it did no damage. I slid my sword up behind his shield and it slid under his armpit. I saw the tip of Ragnar's Spirit as it came out of his neck. I punched another Saxon out of the way and shouted, "To me!"

I ran towards the horses. One of the women was struggling to climb on to the back of the skittish horse. She was terrified. Haraldr Leifsson and Siggi Einarsson, Einar Hammer Arm's son, ran with me. The men who were helping the women and children to mount suddenly had a dilemma. If they helped the women then we would reach them. The four of them left the women and ran to us. I saw the Queen's horse rear. She managed to control it but the crown fell from her head. One of the Saxons slapped the rump of her horse and she and the others galloped off. The woman who had been struggling with her mount fell and her skull was crushed by a hoof.

There were five men facing the three of us. Haraldr and Siggi were novices, "Flank me and guard my sides!" I would have to fight the five of them. Only two had helmets. They must have been abed when the alarm was raised. They were horsemen. They wore short byrnies and had smaller shields. A warrior who has fought as many times as I recognised such things quickly for they are the difference between defeat and victory; life and death. We had three shields facing them and they came at me piecemeal. I slashed my sword before me at thigh height. My blade tore through the unprotected thigh of one and into the knee of the second. I did not pause but raised my shield to punch it into the face of the third. I heard two cries from my side. The men I had wounded had been slain by Haraldr and Siggi. The man I had struck had no helmet and I saw that he was dazed. I tore my sword across his throat. The last two both wore helmets. They began to back away. They were heading for the open door of the church. If they reached it then they could delay us more and I knew not where the Queen had gone. Perhaps she would summon help.

"Flank them!"

We now had superiority of numbers for Erik Red Beard and Sven Svensson had joined us. I ran at the two men. My legs were not what they had once been but my mail, helmet and bloody weapon drew their attention to me. Haraldr and Siggi struck suddenly and swiftly. Haraldr's blow was so hard that his sword, short as it was, took the Saxon's head in one. Siggi brought his sword up under the short byrnie. Both Saxon warriors were dead. I looked around and saw shadows galloping north, along the river. We would not catch the Queen.

"Go into the church and find the holy books." There were still men fighting. I turned to go to the aid of Rollo and Rolf. I heard a gurgled cry and I saw a bloodied Rolf slay the last one. "Who is hurt?"

Olaf Leather Neck said, "We have lost six warriors. Rollo and Rolf are wounded."

"Get them back to the drekar. I wanted their hurts healed." Some of the young warriors were now standing around with open mouths. They had won but their friends lay dead. "Strip the enemy dead and take their mail and arms to the drekar. Then fetch our dead. We will bury them at sea."

I headed back to the church. The sky was becoming lighter. I saw the crown on the ground near the bodies of the bodyguards. I picked it up. It was made of gold and had one blue stone in the centre. This was treasure indeed. I put it inside my kyrtle and went into the church. I saw that the young warriors had slain some of the priests. Another three were about to die, "Hold! We do not kill priests! They are worth coin."

Haraldr looked appalled, "I am sorry, Jarl Dragonheart."

"It is my fault. I should have told you before we raided. Take the metal objects, the cloth and linen as well as the Holy Books." There were many of them. I had not seen so many gathered in one place before. "Put them in a couple of chests. Take them to the drekar and then return." They nodded and left. The three priests cowered. They had seen six of their number slaughtered. They had expected to die and now a fierce warrior dressed in mail approached them. I took off my helmet. I had not bothered with the cochineal and I looked less fearsome.

"When you built your monastery did you find anything left by the Romans."

The fact that I spoke to them in their language surprised them and my knowledge of Roman practices further confused them. One, the eldest of them said, "No lord. We just used the stone."

I nodded. It was as I had thought. The stones of the church were too small to have come from any substantial building. "And the woman who fled?"

"She escaped?" I nodded. "Praise be. That was the Queen and two of her sons. She has escaped the privations of the heathens."

I gestured to the door, "Whereas you have not. Tell me what she was doing here."

"She wished her sons, Æthelbald and Æthelberht, to learn more about our holy books. She sets great store by reading." That made sense. If she had endowed the monastery then the priests would do all that they could to accommodate her. "Tell us, lord, what happens to us?"

"You will be taken to Frisia. Perhaps someone may buy you as a scribe. You will live but we will sell you."

Their shoulders slumped in resignation, they left. I checked that all had been taken. My Ulfheonar would have cleared the sleeping quarters and the other buildings. As I emerged into the light I saw them carrying sacks of grain and hams. The monks ate well. So would we. Dawn had broken while I had been in the church. I saw the young warriors who had helped me defeat the last Saxons. I pointed to the dead warriors they had slain. "Take what you will from the dead. Their helmets, mail and swords will be useful. Their shields are piss poor."

They fell upon the dead and searched them. I saw Haraldr as he tried on helmet after helmet. None fitted. He found a long sword and look pleased.

"What about mail?"

"I am bigger than these, Jarl Dragonheart."

"Take the biggest one you can. You will be able to use it. Do not forget to search their purses for treasure. If they are Christian and have coin they may have a silver cross around their neck."

I wandered over to the dead woman. I saw that she lay at an awkward angle. I took the silver cross which hung around her neck. It was well made. It would fetch a better price than melting down the silver. I saw that she was an older woman. It explained why she had not been able to control the horse. I waited until the last of my men had begun the descent to the river. When I reached the drekar they were waiting for me. I boarded and I saw the relief on Sámr's face. The cloak-covered bodies would have been a reminder to him of how dangerous our life was. We rarely brought home our dead. The only ones who were aware of our losses were the families of the dead.

Erik shouted, "Loose the sail!" We would not need to row. The journey, however, was likely to be more dangerous than the one upstream.

I put my helmet in my chest. I left my mail on. I saw that the men who had acquired treasure stored it in their chests. They knew that we were not safe just yet. A couple of miles down the river I saw the Queen, her women and her sons. They were four hundred paces from the river and they had stopped. I remembered the crown and I took it out. In the daylight it was even more beautiful than I had thought. It was simply made but elegant. I noticed that the blue stone was the same as the one in my sword pommel. *Wyrd.* I put the crown in my chest. That alone would make the raid, even with the dead, worthwhile.

Lars Long Nose was the lookout. He shouted, "Captain, there are ships at the mouth of the river."

"How many?"

"Three. They have blocked the mouth."

I looked at Erik. He smiled, "Rowers, to your oars. Let us see if Bolli is a better shipwright than those who made these Saxon ships."

I went to my chest, "Ship's boys, get your bows! Let us see your skill!" The oars were run out and began to bite in the river. With the wind, the current, and the oars we were travelling as fast as I had ever known. I took the Saami bow and half a dozen arrows. As the ship's boys grabbed their weapons they followed me.

The three ships were all slightly smaller than ours. They had their sails lowered and were using those to hold them in position. The mistake they had made was in failing to tie their ships together. Had they done so then we might have been in trouble.

I nocked an arrow and pulled back. "When you think you can reach then send arrows at their sterns. Try to hit the steersmen. Even if you do not hit them you may make them panic."

I released. My bow had a longer range. It plunged down and hit a ship's boy who was standing next to the steersman on the middle ship. Immediately men ran for shields. I nocked another and sent that towards the ship. We were closing with them rapidly. One of my arrows managed to hit their rudder. Sámr and the other ship's boys were keen to emulate me. Their bows did not have the range and they had not the strength but their five arrows, falling on the Saxon decks had an effect. They were not watching our prow slicing through the water as my crew put all their efforts into the oars. They were watching for arrows descending from the sky. My men sang, joyously, as they rowed.

Haaken had chosen one of our victories over the Saxons. It seemed appropriate and inspired the men.

> *The Saxon King had a mighty home*
> *Protected by rock, sea and foam*
> *Safe he thought from all his foes*
> *But the Dragonheart would bring new woes*
> *Ulfheonar never forget*
> *Ulfheonar never forgive*
> *Ulfheonar fight to the death*
> *The snake had fled and was hiding there*
> *Safe he thought in the Saxon lair*
> *With heart of dragon and veins of ice*
> *Dragonheart knew nine would suffice*
> *Ulfheonar never forget*
> *Ulfheonar never forgive*
> *Ulfheonar fight to the death*
> *Below the sand they sought the cave*
> *The rumour from the wizard brave*
> *Beneath the sea without a light*
> *The nine all waited through the night*
> *Ulfheonar never forget*
> *Ulfheonar never forgive*
> *Ulfheonar fight to the death*
> *When night fell they climbed the stair*

> *Invisible to the Saxons there*
> *In the tower the traitors lurked*
> *Dragonheart had a plan which worked*
> *Ulfheonar never forget*
> *Ulfheonar never forgive*
> *Ulfheonar fight to the death*
> *With Odin's blade the legend fought*
> *Magnus' tricks they came to nought*
> *With sword held high and a mighty thrust*
> *Dragonheart sent Magnus to an end that was just*
> *Ulfheonar never forget*
> *Ulfheonar never forgive*
> *Ulfheonar fight to the death*
> *Ulfheonar never forget*
> *Ulfheonar never forgive*
> *Ulfheonar fight to the death*

We struck the stern of the middle ship so hard that Lars Long Nose fell to the deck. Erik shouted, "In oars. Even then he was not quick enough. Three oars sheered. The Saxon began to take on water. As I sent an arrow at a range of thirty yards into the chest of a mailed warrior I saw that she was down by the stern. We had sprung her strakes. The other two ships had a dilemma; did they pursue us or save their comrades? They chose, wisely, the latter. Had they tried to catch us and battle with us they would have lost. Erik put the steering board over so that we headed east. Once we had cleared the island we would head south and east. The wind would help us and we could stop rowing. When we were clear of the Saxon shore we would bury our dead. They had died with their swords in their hands and they would be in Valhalla. Their bodies would go to Njoror and he would guard them. When they were buried we headed due east. We would sail through the afternoon and the night. The wind would help us.

I watched the new men take out and examine the treasures they had collected. The coins and jewels were ignored. It was the weapons they pored over. I wandered towards Haraldr. He held the byrnie he had found before his body. It was obviously too small. "I told you jarl, it will not fit."

Olaf laughed, "Not like that. Give it here." He took his axe and held the shaft between his knees. Using a sawing action, he began to cut the links of mail in the middle. It took him time but eventually he had the byrnie split. He handed it to Haraldr. "Take off your leather vest and put it on."

The byrnie looked like a vest but it covered his arms and his back. The problem was that there was a gap down the middle. "I suppose it is better than nothing!"

Olaf snorted, "You young warriors do not have the strength you were born with! If you tried to use it like that then the first sword blow you took would rip the byrnie more. Put your leather vest on."

He did so.

"Now the leather will stop the mail which has been cut opening again. Your arms are protected and it gives you a little protection at the top of your legs. Until you have coin enough for Bagsecg it will do. When we land use a hammer to flatten the ends of the mail rings."

Haraldr looked delighted. He now had mail. All that he now needed was a helmet. With the coin he had taken he could have one made.

We sailed along the coast of Cent. We had camped at a beach close by Hæstingaceaster before now but I did not want to risk being attacked. With the wind behind we made good time. The sun began to set behind us, making navigation easier. It was completely dark when we were approaching the coast of the Frankish Empire. Since the raids on the coast of the King of the Franks they had begun to ally themselves with the men of Wessex. This would be the first time we had traded with them since the alliance. The effect would be interesting. It was a new harbour we would be entering and we had heard that it was tidal. Although we were shallow keeled it was not worth the risk and so we threw out a sea anchor and spent a night half a mile from the coast.

When dawn broke Erik and I consulted Atticus' charts. When we passed the small fishing village of Dunkerque we knew we were close. We lowered the sail and headed in under oars. We kept to the middle of the channel. I saw sandbanks and mudflats. Erik took us through as slowly and as carefully as he could. When Lars shouted that he could see masts we were relieved. There were no other drekar in the small port but there were knarr and other trading vessels. During the night we had taken our shields from the side. We told the world that we were there to trade and not to raid.

As we did not know the place I did not take off my mail. When we had finished tying up I said, "Erik, I will go ashore with the Ulfheonar. It will be better until we know how we will be received."

"Aye Jarl Dragonheart and I will examine our bows. We may have suffered damage. I will get the pine tar out and the sheep wool." The ship's boys would be kept busy.

This was part of the Empire; this was Flanders. The Emperor ruled. At the moment, so Atticus had told us, the sons of Louis the Pious was disputing with their father who ruled which parts of the land. The leader in Flanders was the Count. I was not certain how we would be viewed. Dorestad had always been on the edge of the Empire and a law unto themselves. We left our shields and helmets but took our swords. I carried the crown with me. Haaken had one of the Holy Books. We were greeted warily by the other sailors. We were pirates. If they met us at sea then they would expect us to try to capture them. Most had never seen us ashore and we were a novelty. A dangerous novelty but a novelty nonetheless. We smiled and greeted them as we passed. They answered us and that was a start.

I saw a hut. It was at the end of the quay. There were two armed men there and what looked like an official. They looked nervously at each other as we approached. The official spoke to me. I understood not one word. I guessed he spoke Flemish. I shrugged. He then tried Saxon.

"What is your business here?"

I smiled broadly, "We are traders. Have you a market?"

He nodded and looked a little relieved, "It is the day after tomorrow."

He looked nervously at the two men who were obviously his guards. They both looked intimidated. I did not blame them. Olaf, Rollo and Rolf were huge men with humourless faces. "Er, lord, there is the matter of port fees."

I nodded, "You shall have them… after we have sold our goods at the market." I paused and looked him in the eye, "You have my word."

He nodded. That was as good an answer as he was going to get. "Of course, lord. It is five silver pennies a day."

"And have you any decent alehouses?"

The man shrugged. I looked at the sentries. One said, "Freya brews a golden beer. She has the sign of the wheat outside her alehouse."

"Thank you, friend." I smiled and the man looked relieved. I led my men down to the ale house. We passed others. They were busy but not crowded. Before I let my young men loose I wanted to see the calibre of those who used the port. We had been ambushed before now in strange ports.

We had to stoop in the doorway. Frisians were smaller than we were. Inside there were just three tables. The chairs were overturned barrels. Just two drinkers stood at the wooden trestle table which passed for a bar. There was a man with a cudgel leaning close to it. He would be the one who kept order. He had gnarled hands. He looked like he could handle himself in a fight. He nodded at us. A buxom woman smiled as we entered. She spoke to us in Danish, "Things are looking up, Sven! With Vikings in port I shall make money!" The one she had called Sven walked to the door. He would watch from the outside now.

Olaf Leather Neck said, "Not if you insult us by calling us Danes!"

She put her hands on her hips, "You look like Danes." Then she smiled, "Never fear, you will enjoy my ale."

I held up my hand, "Before we drink. I have a crew who have coin in their purses. I have been recommended this ale house. I should warn you that if they are cheated or have their ale watered then the wrath of the Dragonheart will be visited upon you."

Her face became serious, "You are the Dragonheart?" I nodded. "Then I can promise you that your men will not be rooked nor robbed. It is an honour. I have heard of you." She gestured with her thumb, "I learned my trade in Dorestad. I was a young girl then but I heard tales of you and your men. You slew Rurik of Dorestad!" I said nothing although the snake had deserved death. She smiled, "And we have food. Well, we can have food when I will get those lazy whores off their backs. They can do an honest trade although I daresay you have lusty young warriors."

"We do." I turned, "Rolf divide the crew into two. Half now and half later."

"Aye Jarl." He stood and left.

"And now we will try your ale."

As she poured the golden ale into our horns she yelled over her shoulder, "Bertha, Hilde, Mathilde, work! Get a stew on!" I was interested that she spoke Saxon to the girls. That suggested they had been brought here as slaves.

The four of us drank deeply. I saw the ale wife looking nervously at us. It was good beer. Olaf quaffed all of his and shouted, "Another!"

Freya looked delighted, "I told you!"

We were on our third when Rolf returned with the crew. By then the three Saxon whores were busy fetching more upturned barrels. They were all naked from the waist up. It was hard to judge their age but none looked to be older than eighteen summers. They seemed cheerful enough. I saw that Sámr and Lars Long Nose were with the crew. Sámr looked nervously at me. Freya was ready with horns of ale. I gestured to the two boys, "These two have watered ale, Freya! We do not want them puking all night!"

"Very well but my ale will put hair on their chests and make men of them!"

Sámr looked a little wary of the three whores. He assiduously avoided looking at them. He took the horn proffered by Freya and said, "Thank you."

"He is a polite one. He has your looks Jarl."

Sámr looked at her and said proudly, "I am his great-grandson."

She laughed and pinched his cheek, "Keep your hands off this little one! Wait until he grows a little!"

Poor Sámr tried to make himself as small as he could. When she had gone I said, "That is what happens in these places. They mean no harm," He nodded. "Better not to mention it to your mother eh? She might not understand."

The two ship's boys enjoyed the night in the alehouse. Neither said much and they drank sparingly. The food was hearty and simple. Sámr and Lars had the healthy appetites of the young. They could not be filled. They listened to the young warriors talking about their first battle.

I stood after eight horns of ale, "First watch let us go and relieve our comrades. They have earned a night in this ale house too."

Freya came with the wax tablet on which she had marked our consumption. I did not look at it. I reached into my purse. The bodyguard, Sven, watched me. I daresay other customers had tried to leave without paying. I took one of the gold coins out. Queen Osburga had been protected by well-paid men. "This will do for all of my crew?"

"It is more than enough."

I nodded, "We will be in port for three days. We will get good service?"

She took the coin, reached up and kissed me on the lips. "You will get the service which a great warrior deserves."

Sven was leaning against the wall and bouncing his cudgel off the palm of his left hand. He bowed his head, "Good night, Jarl Dragonheart. I will see that your men get back to your ship safely."

"You know me?"

"When I was young I sailed with Jarl Gunnar Thorfinnson. I left him before he went to Raven Wing Island. I have paid for that mistake ever since."

I did not recognise the warrior. His story was not unusual. Some men, when they went ashore with coins to spend, forgot that they owed a duty to their oar brothers. It normally resulted from a meeting with a woman. They thought with their breeks. Their ship would sail and then they would be stranded.

I took a coin from my purse, "Here is coin to watch my men. We all make mistakes my friend. It is how we remedy them that make us what we are."

"You are right there, Jarl Dragonheart. I was lucky to find Freya. She has a kind heart."

As we walked back down the quay Sámr plagued me with questions about the young women we had seen. I was distracted for I was still thinking of Harald. Haaken One Eye laughed, "As much as I would like to hear the Dragonheart explain them, Sámr, I think that you should ask your father when you return home. Please do so when I am present!"

Chapter 3

We were moored in a strange port and Erik Short Toe was no fool. We had a good watch kept aboard. He had also rigged an old sail over the deck for we would be there for two days. Many of the crew had consumed too much beer. During the night I was awoken by the sound of men making offerings to Njoror over the side. It was ever the way with young men and they had earned the right for it had been a hard fight.

When I rose, early the next morning, it was to an overcast day which promised rain. I heard Erik, at the prow, barking out orders for the ship's boys. After I had made water and doused myself with sea water I strolled to the dragonhead. "You are up early, Erik."

He nodded. "***'Heart of the Dragon'*** is a strong ship but we struck that Saxon hard. It was well above the waterline where we struck but I am having the boys apply more pine tar and sheep's wool. It will keep them busy and out of mischief and I will sleep easier on the voyage home."

I nodded, "I will head into the town. I will put the word about that I have a crown to sell."

Erik looked concerned, "Do not go alone, jarl. We do not know this town yet."

I had no intention of doing so. I saw that most of the crew were still asleep. I had an old man's bladder. Haraldr Leifsson and Siggi Einarsson were both awake. I saw them talking. I waved them over, "You two, get your swords I have need of you."

Eager to serve they grabbed their weapons. I noticed that Siggi had the short mail byrnie he had captured and Haraldr wore the leather and mail. They were both different warriors already from the two who had left Whale Island. A Viking warband was something which was alive. It grew and it changed. You left home with one set of warriors. The battles, the voyage and the shared experiences made you something different from that which had begun the voyage. Women often complained that their men changed after a raid. With these young men that might mean they did not return to their mothers. They might take a wife themselves.

As we walked along the quay I asked, "Did you not drink as much as the others?"

Siggi laughed, "The girls in the alehouse offered Haraldr a lower price than the others. My friend here had little time for drinking."

Haraldr looked embarrassed, "They were nice girls."

I cocked an eye. It was rare to hear whores called nice girls. "We will call in at the alehouse and see if they have hot food." I nodded to Haraldr, "And hot food is all that we will enjoy!"

A place like Freya's never really closed. There were times when there were no customers but then one of the girls would be sleeping on the bar and I had no doubt that Sven or another like him would be on call in case there was trouble. The door was closed but it was not barred and I pushed it open. Bertha had been asleep on the trestle table. Her head jerked up as the door groaned. She saw Haraldr Leifsson and laughed, "Back for more!"

I shook my head, "Have you any food?"

She nodded but looked disappointed, "I can get you some. What would you have?"

"Something hot."

"I will fry some meat. It will not take long. There is pickled herring to be going on with. Ale?"

"Aye, whenever you are ready."

Sven ducked his head as he came from the back room, "Jarl Dragonheart, you are up early."

"I have business."

"I will get the bread. Baldwin the Baker makes good bread." He went out of the front door. I took that as a compliment. He trusted us.

I heard the hiss as salted pig meat was dropped into the pig fat. The smell made me hungry. Bertha came in. She had a platter in one hand and a jug of ale in the other. Her neck was festooned with horns. Haraldr stood and took the platter from her. She giggled. After she had poured our ale and he had sat down she kissed Haraldr on the cheek. "Thank you, Viking!"

Siggi smiled, "You have that one in the palm of your hand, my friend."

Haraldr was embarrassed. He changed the subject, "What do we do this morning, jarl?"

"I am going to make enquiries about the crown we took and the books. In Dorestad I knew where to sell such items. Here I do not. It is wise to be cautious in a new place. You can be robbed." We ate the pickled herring. It was not the best I had ever tasted but it served a purpose. Sven arrived with the hot bread. We smelled it before he even entered the alehouse.

"I have the bread, Bertha."

"Give them two loaves, Sven. I think the giant could consume one all on his own!"

Sven laughed, "The girls here have good hearts, jarl." He left two large loaves.

I broke off my favourite part, the crusty end. There were still herring juices on the platter and I mopped them up. Bertha brought in the steaming platter of fried, salted pig meat. She put the thick slices on the bread we tore. The juices would soak into the hot bread. When the meat was gone we would still have the taste when we ate the bread.

Sven had deposited the bread in the back room and he and Bertha also enjoyed bread and ham. I wiped my mouth with the back of my hand and washed down the bread with ale. I waved over Sven. He brought his horn over. "Sit, I would ask you questions."

We made room for him and he sat.

"I have some books we took from a monastery in Wessex and a golden crown. Who would buy then here in Bruggas? Is there a merchant we could trust?"

Sven finished off his bread and meat and wiped his hands on his breeks. "There are many who would buy them but whom could you trust?" He drank some ale. "If the treasures were mine I would go to Isaac the Jew. He knows gold and he is not afraid to handle the books you sell. There are others who fear the wrath of the White Christ. To Isaac it is just business. He also has Norse men to guard him. You can trust him."

When we had finished and paid I followed Sven's directions and headed for the house of the Jew. It was on the far side of the town. There were better houses that we passed and Isaac the Jew lived in what might be termed the poor part of town but that was deceptive. The door was strongly made and studded with metal. Eyes watched us as we approached. I knocked and waited. No one came although I knew we were being assessed from within. Siggi was impatient, "I could kick it in, jarl."

I shook my head, "You would break your foot before that door. Have you somewhere else you wish to be?"

"No, Jarl Dragonheart."

"Then let us be patient. This man risks death living in a land which worships the White Christ. My wife told me that they call them the Christ Killers. I would expect such caution. It bodes well."

Eventually, we heard bolts being slid back. At the same time, two warriors appeared from the side of the building. They were Vikings and they were mailed. Siggi and Haraldr were startled and their hands went to their swords. "Hold. I will tell you when you draw your weapons."

The two warriors said nothing and I waited. The door opened and a small, neat man with a skull cap smiled at us. He had a trimmed beard and fine clothes. In his belt, he had a dagger. He spoke to me in Danish, "Can I be of assistance to you warriors?" Behind him, I saw two more guards. These were not mailed and did not look like Vikings.

"I was told that you may be interested in buying some items we took from the Saxons."

"You are pirates then."

I smiled, "I prefer hunters. We hunt for treasure. I have a fine selection. I am Jarl Dragonheart."

The two Vikings recognised my name. The Jew looked at them. Their faces told him that they had heard of me too. "I believe I have heard that name. You may enter but you will forgive me if I do not invite in your two companions. I give you my word that you will be safe." He spread his hands apologetically, "My home is small and this giant would fill a palace."

"Of course. I have a crew of men in the harbour. I am certain that I will be safe." The implied threat made him smile. "Haraldr and Siggi, wait here. I will be out when my business is completed."

We entered. The outside was plain, almost run down, but the interior was opulently decorated. He had rugs on his floor although they were only in the centre. There were wall hangings to keep it warm in winter. The chairs were upholstered. He lived well. "I trust you will either take off your sea boots or stay on the wooden floor."

"Of course. This will not take long." I took out the crown. "I have some holy books. I believe that you might buy them." He nodded. "But this is something special. It belonged to Queen Osburga of the Saxons."

He looked up, "She is dead?"

"I told you we are hunters not women killers. She is alive but I think she will miss her crown."

"May I?"

"Of course." I handed it to him.

He examined it carefully and then handed it back. "It is worth more as a crown than melted down. I have a thought, Jarl Dragonheart. Let me sell it back to the King of Wessex and we will split the proceeds."

"I could do that myself. Why do I need an intermediary?"

He laughed, "I think not. It would be obvious that I had not taken it. I could negotiate without rancour. If I paid you what it is worth I would be out of pocket until the ransom was paid. This way we both benefit. You get more than you would if I offered you coin and I do not have to lay out money I could use to, let us say, buy your books."

"You are a clever man. I was told that I can trust you." I gestured at the four men who stood around us. "These men look tough but, believe me, I have tougher."

He laughed, "That I can believe. When can you bring me the books?"

"I can send my men back now if you wish. We intend to stay for your market tomorrow. My men have coins they wish to spend and we have other goods to trade." I went to the door. My two men looked relieved to see me. "Go the drekar. Have Olaf Leather Neck and some men bring the books we took from the monastery."

"Will you be safe, jarl?"

"I will be safe."

Once I was back inside one of the warriors asked, "Is that the sword that was touched by the gods?"

"It is, Ragnar's Spirit." I made no attempt to unsheathe it. Many men wished to touch it but I did not know these men.

The warrior nodded. He was not offended by my reluctance to show the weapon. He turned to the Jew, "Lord, as valuable as that crown is, to a Viking warrior that sword is worth much more. Men would sell a whole drekar just to own it."

The Jew smiled and spread his arms, "I am just a simple merchant. I know nothing of war but even I have heard of this sword. Many Danes and Norse seek me out to sell their goods. I am honest for Vikings do not try to kill me because of my religion. Often, they have spoken of this sword, you and your Land of the Wolf. I confess I have been intrigued." He waved to one of the warriors, "Fetch us wine while we wait." The man hurried off, "You do drink wine do you not?"

"I am well-travelled and I have been to Miklagård. I drink wine."

"Do not take offence, Jarl Dragonheart, but you are the oldest Viking I have ever seen."

I laughed, "I am not offended. I have been lucky."

The warrior who had asked me about the sword shook his head, "No, you are not just lucky. The gods favour you it is true but the men you have killed were all mighty warriors, Klakke Blue Cheek, Eggle the

Skull Splitter, Guthrum, Sigeberht the Saxon; the list is a long one. I have heard that so long as you wield the sword you cannot be killed."

"I have heard that too. I hope it is true."

"And that you went into the bowels of the earth, dived into a pool and recovered another sword, just as powerful as this one."

"I have a sword I found, aye. The Weird Sisters weave webs around me."

The wine was brought and I sipped it. It was red and it was unwatered. I saw Isaac the Jew watching me. This was a test. I smiled, "Good wine. A beaker will suffice. I do not wish to be dull witted when we negotiate for the books."

"Fear not, I will not rob you. This meeting is fortuitous. When I tell the other Vikings who come to me that you are one of my clients it will increase my esteem. I will make more coin from this visit."

We chatted about warriors he knew. I recognised some of the names. Most appeared to be Danes. Then there was a knock on the door. It was opened and Olaf Leather Neck and Haaken One Eye stood there with the two chests containing the books we had taken. Olaf glowered at the warriors who watched me. I smiled. Isaac thought he had hired the best warriors he could. Now he was seeing real warriors.

The old man might have been a Jew but he knew the value of the books and he paid us a higher price than I expected. He even purchased the chests we had taken. I stood to leave. I handed over the crown. "When can I expect a return?"

"It will take time. I would say six moons. I have to get a message to the King and then negotiations will take place. It will not be a speedy transaction." He looked nervously up at Olaf. "Is that satisfactory?"

"We will return in five."

"Five it is." The Jew held out his arm. "It has been a pleasure, Dragonheart."

As we headed back Olaf said, "Do you trust him?"

I nodded, "I trust him to make as much money for himself as he can. He paid more for the books than we have ever received. Tomorrow we see if we can sell the three priests. If not, we take them to Dyflin. There is a market there for such clerics."

Erik Short Toe and the ship's boys were cleaning themselves up as we returned. Erik looked pleased with himself. "The boys worked well, jarl. Tomorrow I will let them visit the market."

Sámr looked pleased and then said, "Jarl Dragonheart, where is our share from the books? We have empty purses."

Lars Long Nose looked shocked that Sámr had the effrontery to be so bold. I nodded seriously, "You are right to take me to task although we normally wait until we are at home to do so."

He looked crestfallen, "I am sorry. I did not know."

"No matter. Haaken, fetch the crew." I sat on the beer barrel and waved Haraldr over with the chest of coins we had been paid. I used the lid to divide it. A quarter went to me. I put that to one side. Then I took another quarter and, after dividing that in two, pushed it over to Erik. The remaining half I handed over to Haaken. He would divide it up. As Erik began to dole out the coins Sámr asked, "What is that half of a quarter for, Jarl Dragonheart?"

"The families of those who fell. They will also receive the same amount from that which we sell tomorrow and when we are paid for the crown." He was young but he was old enough to recognise the wisdom of such an action.

That night the crew went ashore again but I remained on board. I noticed that, as well as Haaken One Eye, Haraldr, Lars Long Nose, Sámr and Erik Short Toe also remained on board. As the others left I said to them, "We have enough to guard the ship. Stay as long as you wish…or can afford!"

I wondered why Haraldr stayed aboard and then I saw him take his byrnie and a hammer and go to the stone quay. He began to hammer flat the cut links. Haaken had bought some of the local sausages. He cut a slice off and washed it down with the beer. "He has done well for his first raid. Leif would have been proud of him."

Erik asked, "I wonder if those in the Otherworld can watch us here in this world. If not, Leif will have to wait until his son dies to discover what he has sired."

Sámr looked up at the stars. It was a clear night and it would be cold, "Does my grandfather know of me?"

I nodded, "He does for Úlfarr is in the Otherworld. The men who died protecting you are in Valhalla. He will know."

"What was Wolf Killer like?"

"He was a great warrior. He died protecting your father and he was trying to save your uncle. We slew his killers. Your father was lucky to have your grandmother. Elfrida was a strong woman. She kept you all together."

He was silent and stared at the stars. He had never known my son and that was sad.

Eventually, the crew came back aboard. It was late and they were noisy. Olaf smacked a few of the more boisterous ones and told them to be silent. I tried to get back to sleep but, as the last of them fell asleep, I found myself needing to make water. As I stood on the sheerstrake I saw a drekar slowly making its way to the quay. It had no shields along its side but it was a Dane. I finished making water and watched it tie up. They did not leave their drekar and so I returned to my sleeping blanket. It took some time to drift off to sleep. It was not a surprise that a Dane should visit Bruggas to trade but I was a little uneasy.

I was awake early. More ships had arrived and the quay was filled. Four ships had anchored in the harbour and were using skerries to ferry their men ashore. There were just two drekar and I was glad that we would be leaving in the evening when we had made our trades. Erik was awake. I pointed out the Dane. "Keep the ship's boys close and an eye on that one."

"I will. How long will you need to trade?"

"If all goes well we could leave in the early afternoon."

"I would prefer that, jarl. The waters can be tricky. If I do it now, in daylight, it will be easier next time we come."

The three priests had been closely watched. They knew their fate. I think they believed that the church might buy them back. I was not certain. Not all of our crew wished to trade. Many wished to spend their coin in the Land of the Wolf where we made better weapons than here in Flanders.

"Bring the captives and the trade goods." This was a Christian land. The religious artefacts would fetch a higher value here. The presence of the priests would only add to that value. The Empire did not approve of slave markets. All that had done was to drive them to the remote parts of the Empire. Bruggas benefitted and there were many slaves. I saw that the Danes had brought Saxons. They had been raiding Northumbria. Ours were the only priests. I left two men to watch them in the holding pen while I went with the Ulfheonar to sell the candlesticks and altar furniture we had brought. There were the dishes they used to place the bread upon and the goblets in which they served the wine. We could have melted them down but this would yield more profit.

I saw a stall which had poorer quality versions of our merchandise. Haaken opened the chest. "What price for these?"

Viking Warband

The trader had grubby fingers and I did not think that he would know their true value. Before he could answer a voice behind said, "Name your price heathen and the church will pay." I turned and saw a churchman. This was neither poor priest nor monk. He had jewelled rings on his fingers and fine clothes. He was also attended by two guards. They had short mail shirts and fine helmets. I just looked at him, "I am the Bishop of Lille. These are fine pieces and my church is a beautiful one. Name your price."

I did not like the man. He smelled of perfume but a sale was a sale. I made up a ridiculously high price. To my amazement he paid. I took his money and I smiled, "There are three priests too!"

He almost snarled at me, "We need no Saxon priests. And I would watch yourselves, barbarians. King Charles is now King of the Franks. He and his brother will search out your people from their rat holes and destroy your ships. The day of the Viking is at an end!"

His two men picked up his chest and he left. Haaken laughed, "The day has not been wasted then. We have made money and been insulted by a man who smells like a woman!"

We returned to the sale of the slaves. The lesser quality ones were sold first. Finally, there was just the three monks left. I looked for the churchman but he had gone. There were three nobles. Often a noble would buy a priest to educate his children or to write letters for him. Many Franks could not write.

When the bidding started I was surprised at how high it went. Eventually two nobles were left. The one who bought them was an older man. I asked a man nearby if he was from Flanders. The others had deferred to him. The man thought about refusing to answer my question and then realised that we were Vikings. He said, "He is the Count of Poitiers. He serves Lothair, the Emperor's son."

"I thought that was Charles?"

"He has three: Louis, Charles and Lothair. Louis and Charles just fought a war against Lothair and they won."

Suddenly everything became clear. That was why the Bishop had not made a bid. He would not wish to bid against Lothair; he supported Charles. I saw advantages to this port of Bruggas. We collected the coin. I turned to Olaf, "We will divide the coin when we are on the drekar. Tell the men they have until noon and then we sail on the high tide."

"Aye, Jarl Dragonheart."

Haaken and I walked back through the square and headed for the quay. A voice said, "I would like to buy you a drink, Jarl Dragonheart."

I turned and saw a Dane. He was not alone. He had a couple of hearthweru with him. He looked to be of an age with Rollo Thin Skin. He wore good mail and had a Danish war axe. I recognised him as being one from the drekar. I was going to refuse and then realised the futility of doing so. The Norns were spinning. "We sail on the afternoon tide. I can have one drink. We will drink at the sign of the wheatsheaf."

"You know your ale. Freya brews the best." I did not tell him that I also felt safer there. I merely nodded. "You have a fine drekar but I was somewhat surprised at the youth of your crew. I would have thought that the great Dragonheart would have mailed warriors who wear battle bands sailing with him."

Haaken One Eye smiled. It was not a pleasant smile. He was angry. "Battle bands are what the Danes wear to show that they have fought. The Dragonheart's crew let their deeds speak for them."

The hearthweru with the Dane bristled. "Peace. Haaken means nothing but do not insult my young warriors."

"I am sorry. I meant no offence. I have looked forward to meeting you for some time. I expected a different crew was all. Especially as you have just managed to steal Queen Osburga's crown."

I looked at Haaken. He had discovered that information quickly enough.

We had reached the alehouse. Freya greeted me warmly with another kiss, "I thought you were sailing on the afternoon tide and I did not expect to see you. Do you wish for food?"

I gestured at the Dane, "I have been invited for a horn of ale but I will buy a barrel of your golden ale for the voyage home." I took out a half-gold piece and gave it to her.

She smiled and said, "With any other warrior I would ask if he wished change but I know that you do not! You are something rare, Dragonheart."

The Dane sat opposite me. There were only three seats and so his hearthweru stood. "I am Hvitserk Ragnarsson. My father was Ragnar Lodbrok."

"I have heard of him."

Our ale came. The Dane lifted his horn and said, "I drink to the Dragonheart and the sword that was touched by the gods!"

Haaken raised his own, "I will always drink to that."

Hvitserk Ragnarsson said, "I will come directly to the point. I heard about your raid on Lundenwic. You took in a few ships and yet you came away with a fortune. The way you drew the Saxons to Essex was masterful."

I raised my horn and nodded.

He leaned forward, "Think what we could do if we took a fleet of three hundred ships to Wessex. It would not just be Lundewic, the whole of Cent, Essex and Wessex would be there for us to take."

I said nothing. I knew that Haaken was interested but he would wait for me to respond.

I saw that the Dane had expected a more fulsome answer. He spread his arms, "What can I do to persuade you."

"I have never sailed with Danes. The ones I have met, like Klakke Blue Cheek and the Skull Splitter were not men I would like to share the same air let alone a longphort."

"You would lead and it would not just be Danes. There are many Norse and those from the islands who wish to follow you. We would not need a longphort. With three hundred ships we could fill the Temese."

"And if we succeeded, what then?"

"We would be rich! We would rule the land of the Saxons."

"But I do not wish to rule any land. I am happy to live in the Land of the Wolf."

"Then one of us would rule it."

I drained the horn of ale. "And you would not rule it long. You would fight amongst yourselves for the right to rule and the Saxons would band together and drive you back into the sea." I stood.

"I beg you to think about it. Just lead us. You take your choice of the treasure and if we fight amongst ourselves then you will be gone. The sword that was touched by the gods can bring us victory. Especially if you lead us."

Haaken had stood too. "How long will it take you to gather such a fleet?" Haaken gave me a surprised look. I gave him the slightest shakes of my head.

The Dane also looked surprised. "In six moons I will know. We would raid at Einmánuður."

"Then I will be here in five moons. Leave word here with Freya."

"I said I would know in six moons, Jarl Dragonheart."

"If you do not have them in five moons' time then you will never have them."

He stood and clasped my arm. "I believe that we will succeed, Jarl Dragonheart."

"We will see." Freya had been listening and she came over to me as I left, "I am honoured that you trust me, Jarl Dragonheart."

"This white hair and beard are a testament to the knowledge I have gained over the years. I can judge people."

"I will not let you down."

As we headed back to the ship Haaken said, "Why agree?"

"Because if we had not then we would have made enemies of the Lodbrok clan. We have enough people coming to our land to try to hurt our families without inviting more Danes. He will not raise three hundred ships. When we see him next, he will come up with some excuse. Now let us head home. We have coin to share with our people."

There was a rustling in the air. I took it to be the breeze. It was the Norns.

Chapter 4

The voyage home was long but it was uneventful. The weather deteriorated but the winds were just precocious rather than dangerous. Erik's repairs held. We stopped frequently for we had lost rowers. That helped my men for they became even closer as a crew. We had left Whale Island with untried and untested boys and we had brought back men. It was *wyrd*.

As usual, the narrow entrance to our harbour meant that people had time to come down and to meet us. The quay was filled with a sea of fearful faces looking for loved ones. Only a handful would be heartbroken. Their pain would be lessened by the coin we would give as weregeld to their families. I thought that Sámr had grown on the voyage. I knew that he had changed. The hard work had broadened him and he would now have more strength when he practised with his sword. He and Lars Long Nose had become drekar brothers and that was good. Haaken and I were still oar brothers and it was more than fifty years since we had become so.

I saw Astrid and Ragnar, along with Ulla War Cry, waiting for us to dock. Astrid would not understand that Sámr would not be the first from the ship. He would be the last. He was not finished until the warriors had left and then the crew would put the drekar in some sort of order. The sail would be removed and the mast placed on the mast fish. Canvas would be rigged across the hull and all lines tightened. Only then would Erik Short Toe pay them off.

I turned to Haaken, "See to the treasure. I will go and speak with Astrid and Ragnar."

"Aye Jarl Dragonheart."

To my shock and embarrassment, the young warriors, who had been in the process of taking their shields from the side, began banging them with the hilts of their daggers and they chanted, "Dragonheart, Dragonheart, Dragonheart!"

I turned on the gangplank, drew my sword and roared back, "Clan of the Wolf!"

Those on the quay began to cheer. I sheathed my sword and strode down to meet my family. Ulla War Cry raced to me, "Next time I shall come with you!"

I hugged him. I was aware that I smelled of stale ale, salt spray and sweat. I needed to bathe. "Go aboard the drekar and fetch my shield." Delighted to be given such a responsibility he raced off. I smiled at Astrid, "Your son did well and came to no harm."

Astrid was one of the kindest people I had ever known. She was worried about her son as any mother would but she put her arms around me and hugged me. "He was with you; how could he be anything other? And you are unhurt?"

I realised that I had not even come close to a wound. "Aye. I am. Thank you." Clasping Ragnar's arm I said, "The raid went well and our young warriors acquitted themselves well. We almost captured Queen Osburga herself! We had to make do with her crown. We have much coin. There is wheat in our hold. We will take half back to Cyninges-tūn and leave the rest here." There were questions in his eyes. I smiled, "We will talk later. First I will bathe I must stink like a Saxon cesspit in high summer!"

When we ate I spoke at length to Ragnar and Gruffyd. I told them of Hvitserk Ragnarsson and his plans. Neither Ragnar nor Gruffyd trusted the Danes and they seemed relieved when I told them that I did not either. They were interested in the Jewish merchant. Such men were invaluable to pirates such as us. The treasures which we brought from the drekar made my son and grandson wish to raid. They decided they would make a joint raid on the Welsh and the Saxons who lived close to Wyddfa. They produced more grain on the tiny island than the rest of the land of the ones called the Welsh. Sámr, Ulla War Cry and Mordaf Gruffydson would sail with their fathers. Their mothers would worry but raiding the Welsh was usually less dangerous than raiding our other enemies. I left the next morning with those warriors who would be travelling to Cyninges-tūn and the places further north.

Haaken left us just north of the forest as did Rollo and Rolf. I rode with Olaf, Haraldr and Siggi. The two young warriors could not stop talking about the raid. For them, it could not have gone better. "I have bought some fine cloth for my mother and some pots for cooking. We have little in Lang's Dale."

"Your mother will be worried."

"I know jarl. When Aðils told me of my father I knew that it both pleased and pained her. It pleased her for she knew that my father had not left her with child deliberately and sad because she knew I would leave too."

"You have just over four moons to be with her and then we sail again. Unless, of course, you do not wish to raid. That would be your choice. There are warriors who raid once and decide that they would rather be farmers."

Olaf Leather Neck snorted, "Haraldr Leifsson is a natural warrior Jarl Dragonheart. You and I know that. When he becomes a farmer, it will be because someone has taken his arm or leg in battle!"

I could not help smiling. Olaf tended to speak plainly. It was always the truth but it could sound a little brutal.

Siggi Einarsson said, "Well I shall raid but first I will find a maid to wed and bed. My father made me when he was younger. I have a duty to the clan to give as many warriors as we can. Baldr, Jakaupr and Farbauti are in Valhalla now. They did not survive their first raid but they left behind no sons. Haraldr, we are shield brothers now. We should make a pact to father as many sons as we can."

"Aye, you are right. Life tastes sweeter for we are alive."

That was the way with young warriors. Their first test was always the hardest. We had lost more warriors on this last raid than we normally did. That was due to the lack of armour and the surprise of finding mailed bodyguards. The Norns had been spinning but I had been careless. Perhaps I was getting too old. I was making mistakes I had made few before.

As we neared the palisade around my home I felt sad. This was the first time I had returned from a raid in many years to an empty hall. My wife was dead and my children had left the nest. Mt son and grandson now lived at Whale Island. Atticus and Uhtric would make me welcome but I would sleep and eat alone. I had outlived my son and two wives. I had buried four dogs. I had lost more warriors than I could count and the thought of entering my empty hall sucked all the joy of the raid from me. Death in battle seemed attractive. There was a breeze from the Water and I looked over to the flower covered mound that was the grave of Erika. I seemed to hear her voice or perhaps it was the wind through the trees but I remembered that I had young warriors I wished to see grow into men. Sámr, Ulla War Cry and Mordaf Gruffydson needed the Dragonheart.

Atticus and Uhtric were waiting for me. My hall was apart from the others with a small palisade and gate. They stood by the gate. Uhtric was old and I was happy that he had the younger Atticus to help him. They were as different as one could imagine. Uhtric had been a slave we had captured when he was young. He had known no other life save serving me and my family. We had freed him many years ago but he had chosen to stay and serve. He was rough, unused to the world beyond our valley and hardworking. Atticus, in contrast, was genteel, well-educated but, he too, was hard working. They worked well together. I had bought items for both of them. For Atticus, it was wax tablets, styli and some spices. For Uhtric it was what the Romans called a mortarium. His teeth had long become rotten and he would be able to use it to mash up his own food. Atticus would also be able to use it to grind up his spices.

As Uhtric took my horse Atticus said, "A good raid, lord?"

"We almost captured Queen Osburga. She left so quickly that she left her crown."

Atticus clapped his hands. It was almost a female action. He had been ill treated by the Saxons and hated them. "Good news indeed, lord. And now you stay at home for a while?" He cocked his head to one side and reminded me of a blackbird looking for food.

"For five moons and then we go to be paid for Queen Osburga's crown." That seemed to satisfy the Greek. "Have Uhtric light the fire in the steam hut. I feel I need it. Sleeping on the deck of a drekar is hard on these old bones."

When I had bathed and been groomed by Atticus I contemplated visiting with my daughter and her family. When I had headed north the hall seemed to be somewhere which would be empty and cold. My two servants had made it warm and welcoming. Uhtric had cooked my favourite foods. Atticus had made sure there was wine and the fire burning in the centre of the hall made me decide not to visit with Kara, Aiden and Ylva until the next day. The food was good and the wine was heavy. I awoke in my bed not knowing how I had arrived there. The wine had driven dreams from my head but I guessed that the spirit of Erika had filled my thoughts for I woke calm and hopeful.

After breaking my fast I headed amongst my clan. Kara's home was on the other side and I passed the huts and halls of my men. Karl One Leg, whose men guarded my walls stopped me to ask about Olaf and the Ulfheonar. He had been one once. Bagsecg my blacksmith, now took life easier and, while his sons and grandsons laboured he enjoyed the pleasure of just being alive. He asked me about the raid and my great-grandson. Others asked me about the voyage. I spent a little time speaking with the parents of Jakaupr who lived in Cyninges-tūn. He had been one of the warriors we had lost. It took almost half a day to reach my daughter's hall. Ylva, grinning, greeted me. She hugged me,

"Grandfather, you are like an old gossip, talking to everyone in the stad!" Kissing me and taking my arm, she led me into the hall, "We have missed you."

"And have you dreamed?"

She laughed, "You are becoming galdramenn. We have. Mother will speak with you."

My daughter was growing old now. She had seen more than forty-five summers. She had flecks of grey in her hair but she did not look old. Those with malignant minds said it was because she was a witch and used spells. She did not. She was just content. She and Aiden were well matched and their daughter, Ylva, only added to that peace. As we walked towards the hall I said, "Do you know of the raid?"

She shook her head. "The spirits only said that our family was well. That is enough. Warriors worry about treasure. We do not."

I laughed, "And yet without the treasures then your hall would not have such fine pots, linens and furnishings."

She had the good grace to nod, "You are right, grandfather. I fear that sometimes I can be a little self-satisfied and arrogant."

"Do not disparage yourself, Ylva. You are the embodiment of your grandmother. She would have loved to see you growing into such a powerful volva."

Kara's hug was long and hearty. She whispered, "I have missed you father. I fear that you are too much alone. You should spend more time with us."

Shaking my head, I said, "Brigid was used to my ways. I am too old now to change the way that I act. I am content." We sat at her table. Aiden waited expectantly. Their servants came in with cheese, fresh bread and the dark ale they brewed. It was a favourite of mine.

"We know from the spirits that the raid went well. What did you get?"

I told them all. Unlike the warriors I led and my son and grandson, I told them all, including my innermost thoughts and fears. While I spoke, Aiden scribbled on a wax tablet. Kara nodded as I sat back. "You are right to worry. We dreamed of a sea filled with dragon ships. The Temese seemed to be made of wood and canvas. We saw the city burning. There was a great victory."

I sensed something more, "But."

She nodded, "But we also saw the same ships burning. We saw Viking heads on spears and we heard the bells of the churches of the White Christ ringing in celebration. It was clear to all of us."

I ate some bread and cheese and drank some of the beer while I thought. "But you did not dream my death."

Ylva put her hand on mine and said, quietly, "After the ships burned we saw you and a giant sailing on *'Heart of the Dragon'*."

I smiled, "That would be Leif's son, Haraldr. He is huge and a good warrior."

"Was the drekar fully crewed?"

They looked at each other and Kara said, "No, father. It was not."

"The Norns wish me to sail on this raid."

"So it would seem."

"Yet many of those I lead will not return."

"That would be my conclusion." Aiden was no warrior but he had a sharp mind.

"I have five moons to make my decision." I laughed, "For an old man like me that means I can change my mind twenty times twixt then and now." I finished the ale and held out the horn for another. The dark beer was the best. "And what other news?"

"Æthelred is now King of Northumbria. There is still peace there and he keeps the Danes from Eoforwic. He has taken up residence there. We had news from Agnete that most of the Danes have headed south for there appear to be better pickings in the land of the East Angles. Even the Mercians are becoming bolder now that Egbert is dead."

"I hear a but in your words or caution, at the very least."

Kara laughed, "That white hair is deceptive. You are as sharp as ever. They also told us of a young Saxon called Rædwulf. I say young for he has yet to see thirty summers and yet he has attracted a following amongst the Northumbrians. He lives in the land north of the wall. He has taken Din Guardi, that which they now call Bebbanburgh as his home."

I looked up from the bread and cheese, "That is a stronghold indeed. Does the King not fear him?"

"He should for Carr has told Ketil that Rædwulf has ambitions to be king. He has entered into an alliance with the tribes of the Pictii. The story he tells is that it is to secure his northern border and to protect his churches from the heathens from the north."

I laughed, "There is nothing left in their churches. We have stolen it all." I smeared the bread with butter, "Then we have nothing to fear for this Rædwulf is a threat to the Northumbrians and not to us."

They looked at each other. "Rædwulf needs to make a name for himself. We have not dreamed it but when we heard the news and we spoke the three of us came to the conclusion that the easiest way for him to make himself both a hero to the Saxons and a true rival to the King was to defeat Vikings in battle."

I put the bread and cheese down uneaten. I had been complacent. The death of my wife and the need for revenge against Æthelwulf had meant I had not looked north. Now I saw that had been a mistake. "Then I must journey to visit Ketil."

"Grandfather, you have just returned."

"It is not a long journey and I have not seen my old friend since before the great raid."

"Do not go alone."

"Daughter the day that I cannot travel the Land of the Wolf alone is the day I hand over power to another. Have you dreamed my death?"

They shook their heads.

"Then I will travel to see Ketil. I will leave in four days. I have others I must see first."

Atticus was pleased that we would be going on a journey. He was keen to cross the high divide. He wished to see the Roman wall. What concerned him was the wildness of the land. "What about wolves, lord?"

"There are few of them left these days and they are only a danger in winter when there is little food. They take the odd lamb but you and I are too scrawny to make a meal for them. We will leave Uhtric here."

"That is wise lord. He is not a well man. The other servants can tend to him. He deserves it."

Leaving Atticus to attend to my domestic arrangements I visited Bagsecg. "It is good to see you, jarl. The whole of the clan talks about your great raid."

"And I have a boon to beg. Haraldr Leifsson gave great service. He will be coming to you for mail and a helmet. He only has coin from one raid. Whatever he offers take it and I will make up the shortfall."

"I will not rob him."

"I know but he is a giant and he is proud."

"Of course. Why do you do this?"

"I too grew up without a father. Haraldr lives high in Lang's dale with a grandfather. His story is too similar to mine for it to be an accident. His father was one of the most loyal men who ever served me. The Norns have woven our webs together. I would have him safe and besides," I shrugged, "I like the lad!"

"And that is a good enough reason. When he comes I will make it myself. I make few byrnies these days. It will do me good to enter the workshop once more."

I visited Olaf, Rolf and Rollo and told them what I had learned. I contemplated visiting Aðils Shape Shifter but Rollo told me that Aðils had become a father again. He would be busy with his children. I needed not him. We took a pack horse with gifts for Ketil's wife. Brigid had had some fine pots. I would no longer need them and they were too good to gather dust. It would be a long day's ride. Atticus took a wax tablet and stylus with him as well as the maps Aiden had made. He intended to improve the accuracy of them. We called in at Windar's Mere first. I told Asbjorn the news of the raid and the possible threat from the east. It did no harm to be vigilant.

Then, instead of riding up the western side of Ulla's Water, I took Atticus up the high Roman road we called High Street. It afforded a fine view on both sides and, although exposed, was a pleasure when the sun shone. Atticus was used to Roman roads. He was a Greek but even he could not get over the fact that they had made such a road in what was such an exposed place.

"You know, lord, we know less now than in the time of the Caesars. Even in the east they have lost some of the skills the Romans had. Will we get to see their wall? I should like to."

"It is another twenty miles but I suppose we could. We can visit the Stad on the Eden. It will mean a longer journey south but I have not visited my men here for some time. It is good."

Over the years Ketil had moved his home further west towards the higher ground. There had been an old settlement there. Pasgen ap Pasgen had known it. The place was call Pennryhd. The people there had long gone; wiped out in raids by either the Picts or the Saxons. They had left their earthworks. When Ketil's clan had outgrown the Roman fort, he had moved there. People still lived in the fort and, if trouble came, it was close enough for the clan to shelter behind the stone walls. His new home was bigger and better laid out. It was a direct copy of Stad on the Eden. We rode beneath the gate and fighting platform. Sven Thorirson waved to us as we passed under. We would have been spotted miles before we arrived for that was another reason Ketil had moved. He had a better view of the land around and could watch out for foes approaching.

Seara was with her husband. "Jarl Dragonheart you have kept away too long. Does my cooking frighten you?"

I smiled, "Seara, your food would please the Allfather himself. This is Atticus of Syracuse. We have brought gifts for you."

Atticus waved over two of Ketil's bemused warriors and had them lift the chests from the horse. When Atticus opened it Seara squealed. "These are finer than anything I have!" She threw her arms around Atticus and kissed him.

It was his turn to look bemused. He turned to the two men, "Fetch the chests and I will help my lady organize them."

The two men looked at Ketil who nodded. When they had gone he smiled, "He is a strange one."

"And yet the Norns sent him to us for a purpose. His skills enabled us to take the crown of Wessex from the Queen's head."

"Then let us go and drink. I can see this is a good tale."

It was the edge of our world up here, close to the high divide. Ketil had come as a young warrior from Windar's Mere and he had tamed it and made it his own. He had been an ally of the young Northumbrian prince who had tried to take on the Danes. After he had lost not only the battle but his life Northumbria had become our enemy. Hitherto Ketil had kept the raiders at bay but an army was a different matter.

When I had finished speaking with him he nodded. "When I sent the message about this Rædwulf I wondered if the threat might grow. It has. Carr travels far to the east and he has seen them fortifying their burghs. Dunelm has become a mighty fortress. Æthelred has most of his forces by Eoforwic and south of the Dunum. If he thought his northern borders were guarded then he was wrong. His raiding parties have probed further and further south."

"If he comes, can you hold him?"

"Until you get here?" I nodded, "Possibly. How long would it take you?"

I realised that the best of our forces and the bulk of our warriors were now closer to Whale Island than Windar's Mere. Windar's Mere was a day away. "If you let Asbjorn and Ulf know then men could be with you in one day. I would be a day later."

Atticus had joined us, having organized the pots and charmed his way into Seara's affections. He was laying out his maps and his styli when Ketil had asked me the question. "You could be quicker, lord."

"Quicker? How?"

"As we were travelling north I noticed that you keep herds of horses."

"They are ponies, mainly."

"Even so they could still bring you here faster than on foot and fresher too. If you had horses waiting at, say, Windar's Mere, then you could change them there and be here even quicker. And, if I might suggest, Lord Ketil, if you have horses waiting for your riders then, when you send the message south, you could reach Jarl Dragonheart at the speed of the fastest of horses. Half a day would be possible."

Ketil grinned, "You have brought a magician with you! He puts a smile into that most difficult of places, my wife's mouth, and now he provides the solution to our problem."

"Atticus does have his moments but you would also need to keep scouts out north of you to give you warning of their advance."

"They are in place now."

Seara had the food ready and she served it on the new platters I had brought. She looked so pleased that I wondered why I had not done this earlier. As we ate we finalised the details of our plan and then I asked Ketil about Rædwulf. I discovered that he was a Saxon thegn. He was distantly related to the King. Many Northumbrians felt bitter about their defeat and subjugation by both the Danes and Egbert. They sought a stronger leader. From what Ketil said, this was just such a leader. As the ale flowed so we became less worried. We talked ourselves into a scene which would see Rædwulf heading due south from Dunelm and taking Eoforwic and the kingdom.

Atticus and I left the next day for the wall. We rode due north. I had seen it many times. I had fought upon it, beyond it and behind it. It had always been a friend for we knew how to use it. Atticus, too, was impressed. He got down on his hands and knees. "In Syracuse I saw things as old as this but here in the far north of what was the Roman Empire." He shook his head in disbelief. "To build a wall from sea to sea.... And now that I see it with my own eyes I realise just how substantial it is."

"And yet they were driven away from here."

As we mounted our horses he said, "Yes lord but it was not the men on the wall who lost it. It was those who sought power. It was those who tried to gain crowns. I admire you, lord, for you could be king and yet you choose not to be. Those in Rome who came before Caesar would have applauded you."

The Stad on the Eden was just a half day ride from the Roman fort we had viewed. The jarl was now Jarl Ráðulfr Ulfsson. He was young but he was dynamic. He had improved the already impressive defences and he was active in taking his men and his drekar to raid those who lived north and west of him.

He was pleased to see me. I was almost tiring of repeating the stories. However, when I told him about the Saxons of Northumbria he nodded, "I was going to send you a message, Jarl Dragonheart but I felt foolish. We had heard of Saxons raiding villages north of the Eden. They took slaves. I thought nothing of it but, from what you have told me, that is part of a greater plan."

"How so?"

"The settlements they raided lie on the valleys and roads which lead to the gates in the walls. I could not work out the plan. It seemed unlike the Saxons. Now it seems clear. What would you have me do?"

"The same as Ketil. Keep scouts north of here and be ready to send riders on the fastest horses to tell me of the danger. You hold. You stay behind your walls and let them bleed upon them. I will bring a Viking warband and we will defeat them by forcing them against your walls."

He pointed south, "We have had heavy rains. The waters are receding. It is but fourteen nights since the road to the south was barred by water. The ground there is treacherous. If you have to come to our aid then use the higher ground to the east."

We left before dawn the next day for I was anxious to send word to Ragnar and Gruffyd. They needed to be alert and ready to move. Atticus came up with another of his ideas. "Lord it strikes me that your long ships could make the journey from Whale Island to the Stad on the Eden faster than men on either horses or foot. They would be fresher too. You and the men from Cyninges-tūn could reach both settlements in less than half a day."

We rode hard to reach my home before dark set in. I had much to put into place. My son and grandson planned to go raiding. That might have to wait. I would need their warriors and their drekar.

Viking Warband

Hand-drawn map showing:

The Land of the Wolf

- STRATHCLYDE
- NORTHUMBRIA
  - Stad on the Eden
  - Caer Ufra
  - Ketil's Stad
  - Myrdyan's Cave
  - Ulfarberg
  - Dunhelm
  - Windar's Mere
  - Dunum
  - Hvitebi
  - Cyninges-tun
  - Ulfarrston
  - Mag (island)
  - Sigtrygg's Stad
  - Whale Island
  - Eoforwic
  - Fulford
  - Stamford
- MERCIA

N ↑

Chapter 5

Atticus and Aiden worked well together. They got on with the plans to have horses gathered to use for our men. My daughter and her husband had concurred with our plans. Ylva was not in their hall. She had gone to Whale Island for Bronnen was with child and experiencing difficulties. Although not a mother, Ylva had great skills and had helped many other young mothers. I sent word to my warriors that we might be needed in the next few weeks. I might not be able to call on as many as I might have liked. Some would be busy with their farms. I would be able to count on my Ulfheonar and warriors like Beorn the Scout and Aðils Shape Shifter would be available to fight. Cnut Cnutson would also be ready to carry my standard for we would be riding to war.

That night, as I sat in my hall, I wondered if this would be the last battle of the old Ulfheonar. We had lasted longer than most warbands. More were dead than now lived. Aðils was the youngest and he was now twice a father and content to live in his remote dale. As I drank my ale I heard Atticus singing away at the table. I looked over. He was poring over a map and making marks on a wax tablet.

"What makes you so happy, Greek? I did not think you were warlike."

"Nor am I, lord. I am a man of peace but I like the precision of the planning. If Aiden and I calculate aright then we will save the lives of your clan. That is a good thing." He looked worried, "Promise me, lord, that I will never have to wield a sword. I do not think I could hurt anyone."

"Never fear Atticus. You will not be called on to do so. We value your other talents far more."

I rode with him, the next day to speak with my son and grandson. Raibeart ap Pasgen was also needed. I asked him to keep his ship ready to sail if danger came. We needed our men to reach the Eden within a day of any attack. Einar Fair Face would not be joining my son. His wife needed him. That was not his decision but Ylva's. My granddaughter could be quite forceful. We managed the journey, there and back, in one day. I was sore and I was tired at the end of it. This was the Allfather's way of telling me to let someone else make those journeys.

Haraldr came to speak with me a day later. He had been to see Bagsecg to have a helmet made. It would not be ready for the raid but when we went to Bruggas again it would. "Are the Saxons of Northumbria rich, jarl?"

"As rich as the men of Wessex? No. But some wear mail. Is that what you are thinking? You need coin for your byrnie?"

"Aðils Shape Shifter told me how we use the shield wall. If I am to be of any use then I need to take blows. Mail will help me."

I shook my head, "Take the blows on your shield and be patient. Often a battle will be won by those who have the most strength. Have you horses in the Dale?"

He nodded, "Aðils has a small herd. He likes horses."

I pointed to the beacon which stood on the rocky crag. "When the enemy come we will light that. If you and your people see it then do not come here. Ride for the Stad on the Eden. It will save time. I would not ask you to go alone but Aðils knows his business. You will be in good hands."

"I know. He is like the father I never knew."

When he left I felt a chill from the Water. Leif's spirit was there. I now knew that he had sent Aðils to Lang's Dale. *Wyrd*.

The rider arrived at my hall just before noon, two days after I had spoken with Haraldr. He threw himself from his lathered pony. "Jarl, Jarl Ráðulfr Ulfsson sent me. Saxons have been heading south and west. They were thirty miles from the Eden when he sent me."

"Karl One Leg, light the beacon. Erik, sound the horn. Folkmar, take a horse and ride to Whale Island. Tell them to sail with all haste." None wasted time with words. They just acted. "You have done well. Rest."

The young warrior shook his head. "If you have a horse I will ride back. The Eden Valley is my home."

With warriors like that, how could we lose? When I reached my hall Uhtric and Atticus had my mail and padded kyrtle ready. Atticus fussed like an old woman. "You will be careful, lord. I would hate to have to train a new lord. I find this life comfortable."

Uhtric grunted, "Fear not. He will return. He is the Dragonheart and has the sword which was touched by the gods. These are merely Saxons!"

I clutched the wolf around my neck. It did not do to make such statements. The Norns were spinning. I put those thoughts from me as I hung my helmet from my saddle. With my shield on my back I was ready to ride north. Even as I waited for my warriors to reach me I wondered about Ketil. If they took the Stad on the Eden then Ketil would be cut off.

The alternative was that he was under attack too. I almost cursed myself. "Atticus, find a spare horse and send a rider to Windar's Mere. I want Asbjorn to ride to the aid of Ketil."

Karl One Leg heard me, "Jarl Dragonheart, I will go."

"Are you certain?"

"Your home is well guarded and it is time this old warrior did something more useful than merely walking your walls."

I nodded and looked around. I had twenty men with me. "Tell the rest to follow! We head north by Elter's Water and the Grassy Mere." Haaken One Eye and the men who lived south of my home would take longer to reach me. I had four Ulfheonar with me. We would pick up other warriors as we headed north. The beacon would alert all my warriors that their jarl needed them and my messages would have told them where to find me. I dug my heels in. Ubba responded and we headed north. We would take the most direct route. We would ride close by Elter's Water and the Grassy Mere. We would pass Úlfarr's grave and ride along the Dale of Mungo. It was forty miles and that was a long way. There would be spare horses waiting for us at Threlkeld. Atticus had shown great skill in managing to gather so many horses in such a short space of time. There would not be enough for all of my men. I could not ensure that all of my warriors would arrive at once. The first there would have the hardest fight and that would be me, my Ulfheonar and the men of Cyninges-tūn. It would have to be enough.

As we neared Elter's Water I saw Aðils, Beorn the Scout and Haraldr waiting for us. Olaf burst out laughing. Olaf was a big man and, when on the back of a horse, his feet almost touched the ground. We had both wondered how Haraldr would manage. He had a horse which was at least a head taller than any other horse I had ever seen. "By the Allfather is there something about Lang's Dale that they breed giants?"

We did not slow, they joined with us. "It is good to see you Aðils Shape Shifter. Olaf wonders at the horse which Haraldr rides."

"When I first went to live in the Dale I explored it. There are many hidden dells and sheltered areas. I found a mare and a foal. The mare was bigger than most of the horses I had seen but this is the foal. He is full grown. It took me some time to make him take a saddle. I was going to ride him but Haraldr suits him. When we return I will find a big mare. I think that we could use such large horses to pull a plough."

Rolf Horse Killer said, "Or carry giants."

An idea began to form in my head. "Aðils, could you and Beorn ride ahead and scout out the stad? You take first choice of horses at the Dale of Mungo. You have more speed and fresher horses."

"Aye jarl."

Haraldr said, "Could I go with them, jarl? We live in the same dale and…" His voice tailed off as he realised that he had no argument.

Aðils answered for me. "We could do with someone to guard our horses and Jötnar is a strong horse. He will be able to carry Haraldr."

"Then ride."

Olaf Leather Neck shook his head, "Aðils is a deep one. He finds a wonderous horse and calls it giant!"

We looked behind as we heard the sound of hooves on the turf. It was Haaken One Eye and the warriors who lived at the southern end of the Water. I hoped they had not pushed their horses too much. There were eighteen of them and they were spread out in a long line. We slowed slightly so that they could join us. I had also spied riders joining us from Skelwith. That would be Ulf Thirlsson and his sons.

Haaken seemed happy. "I had been so bored that we waited each day for your signal, Jarl Dragonheart. Our beasts are well fed. It bodes well for this battle!"

"We have less than forty men, here, Haaken One Eye. If the Saxon, Rædwulf, comes to make war he will bring an army and we have a warband."

"A Viking warband!"

My men all laughed and cheered. I did not like this over confidence. I blamed myself. We had yet to taste defeat. Every Saxon army we had met we had beaten. In my heart I knew that, one day, we would be defeated. The dream of my daughter had shown me that the Saxons were capable of defeating us. Would this be that day?

The path we took rose and fell. It twisted and turned as we snaked our way north. The Saddleback to the east told me that we were close to the horses waiting for us. We were more than half way there. I was saddle sore and my back ached but it was an hour or so past the sun's zenith and most of the men I had led were still with me. One or two had lamed horses and walked. They would catch us but not for some time.

Lars Lame Foot had fought with me when he was a young man. The tendons of his right ankle were severed when we had fought Guthrum the Skull and his Danes, he had married and he mined close by Tarn Crag. His injury did not stop him from mining and, along with the food he grew, he and his four sons made a good living. When Atticus had sought horses, I had sent word to Lars for he and his sons bred ponies. They used them to haul ore to the Stad on the Eden and down to Bagsecg. It was as though the Norns had caused the wound so that he could be of service to the clan. They were hardy and sturdy. *Wyrd*.

Three of his sons would come with us and, as we approached I saw that his wife had food prepared, I could see the smoke from their fire, and the ponies awaited us. I turned in the saddle. "We do not tarry. Change saddles and eat while you ride!"

Olaf snorted, "And make water, Jarl Dragonheart!"

I dismounted and Lars Larsson ran to change my saddle over to the largest of the ponies. Lars Lame Leg limped over. He pointed north. "Aðils and the others left some time ago. There were four men from Calth's Waite who rode in while they were here. There are seven of them now."

I nodded and took the oat bread from his young daughter. I clambered back into the saddle. "We will return your ponies and, I hope, your sons."

He nodded, "They are good lads, jarl. They have swords and shields. Mayhap they will return with Saxon helmets and treasure."

I dragged myself, wearily into the saddle. I did not know how Hrolf the Horseman could enjoy riding so much. To me it was something to endure for as short a time as possible. Twelve of the men we had brought would have to walk. There were not enough ponies. I did not have enough men to fight a Saxon army. I had a small warband. Until the rest of my men arrived from Whale Island it would have to do. Ragnar, Raibeart and Gruffyd would be bringing three drekar crews. They would have to sail up the coast of the Land of the Wolf. They would be dependent on the winds. When they reached us there would be more than one hundred and fifty to join our band. Beorn met us just five miles from the Stad on the Eden. He had grown bulkier in the last three years. I saw that his cheeks were red and he was out of breath. Now I knew why he had declined to raid Wessex with the rest of the Ulfheonar.

"Jarl, the Saxons are attacking the walls. There are more than two hundred of them."

I nodded, "Aðils and Haraldr?"

"They rode to the west. Aðils said that with the wind from the south he might be able to meet the drekar and guide them in. The Eden can be treacherous at this time of year. The land to the south and west is flooded. There have been heavy rains. The Saxons have to move slowly.

They have brought timber to make bridges. All that they have done thus far is to surround the walls. Jarl Ráðulfr Ulfsson's archers are making them wary."

I turned to Olaf Leather Neck, "If you were the Saxons would you attack at night?"

"With archers on the walls? Aye."

"Then we must make them fear an attack. Beorn, I want you to lead the ones who are not Ulfheonar. There is some high ground a couple of miles east of the stad. Hold them there and when you hear the howl of the wolf then have your men bang their shields and chant. If the Saxons come then withdraw. You have done this before I think."

He grinned, "Aye, Jarl Dragonheart. I have missed this."

"Lars Larsson wait here for the stragglers. Gather them together and march towards the sound of the chanting."

"Aye jarl."

Haaken nodded, "And we will howl and attack them."

"No, Haaken, there are too few of us these days. We howl and draw them to us. The Ulfheonar have a reputation. Let us use it. I just want to delay the Saxon attack until we have more men."

While Beorn led the bulk of my warband to the east we urged our horses due north. All of us knew this land well. The warrior who had built it, Thorkell, had been an Ulfheonar. We knew where every dell and tree lay. We stopped at the small copse which was close to the boggy area which had been recently flooded. It would guard our horses. We left our shields on our saddles and took off our helmets. We needed stealth and we needed silence until we were close. We drew our swords. Olaf carried his mighty axe over his shoulder.

The Northumbrians were noisy. They had no need for silence. They had surrounded the stad. They outnumbered the defenders and whoever led them would assume that no help was forthcoming. The nearest Vikings were at Pennryhd and Cyninges-tūn. We spread out in a line with Cnut Cnutson behind us. He had a lame leg. He would not be able to move as quickly as the rest of us. We crept close to their camp. They had fires and we could hear them speaking. It soon became obvious that they were planning a night attack. It made sense. Our archers could not see as far in the dark. The Saxons would attack well away from their fires. I had chosen the perfect place to appear. Their camp was half a mile from the walls and ditches. If we drew them out then we might forestall an attack until morning.

We were hidden by the undergrowth. It was uneven ground. I looked around to see my escape route. The others did the same. I stood behind a low elderberry branch which jutted and twisted out from the base of a tree. A warrior racing to get at me would not see it. I raised my sword. My men, in turn, raised their swords. As the last sword rose I lowered mine and howled like a wolf. The other five emulated me and the howl seemed to roll to the east. Looking into the Saxon camp I saw white faces turn to the woods. The younger ones looked up to the sky. After a few heartbeats, we stopped and there was an eerie silence.

Then a Saxon voice shouted, "It is a trick.! I have seen this before! They are men dressed as wolves. There is nothing to fear."

I howled again and this time my men joined in almost immediately. I saw men recoil. The Saxon voice shouted, "Get them!"

Just as they started to move I heard banging from the east and a chant. It was Beorn.

Ulfheonar, warriors strong
Ulfheonar, warriors brave
Ulfheonar, fierce as the wolf
Ulfheonar, hides in plain sight
Ulfheonar, Dragon Heart's wolves
Ulfheonar, serving the sword
Ulfheonar, Dragon Heart's wolves
Ulfheonar, serving the sword
Ulfheonar, warriors strong
Ulfheonar, warriors brave
Ulfheonar, fierce as the wolf
Ulfheonar, hides in plain sight
Ulfheonar, Dragon Heart's wolves
Ulfheonar, serving the sword
Ulfheonar, Dragon Heart's wolves
Ulfheonar, serving the sword

That really made them stop. The cries were from their front and yet the chanting came from further away to the north and east. All thoughts of an attack faded. We could have left then but that was not our way. We had drawn swords and they needed to taste blood. As the chanting rolled on we howled again.

The Saxons grabbed swords and spears. They raised shields. I could not hear their words but I saw two thegns, recognisable by their byrnies and fine full-face helmets, organize two bands of Saxons. It was not the whole army. I estimated there to be no more than forty in each group but it meant they could not attack the walls. Just then I heard another chant. This time it came from within the Stad on the Eden.

> **The Dragonheart and Haaken Brave**
> **A Viking warrior and a Saxon slave**
> **The Dragonheart and Haaken Brave**
> **A Viking warrior and a Saxon slave**
> **The Dragonheart and Haaken Brave**
> **A Viking warrior and a Saxon slave**
> **The Dragonheart and Haaken Brave**
> **A Viking warrior and a Saxon slave**

It was Jarl Ráðulfr Ulfsson. The remaining Saxons formed a shield wall. They were expecting an attack. I heard a priest began to chant. I saw him by the firelight. He was holding a large cross. The Saxons began to move towards us. We were standing in the dark and we could not be seen. I knew that so long as we remained still we were invisible. We stopped howling. I held my sword behind me. A Northumbrian moved towards me. The elder branch was a man's body length from me. The Saxon did not see it for he was peering into the foliage to try to see me. He fell forward and the two men behind laughed. As he scrambled to his feet my hand darted forward and Ragnar's Spirit entered his throat. I stepped back. One of the Saxons said, "Egbert! Are shadows tripping you?"

I was back into the foliage when they stepped on his body. The Saxon sounded surprised when he found his comrade's bloody body. "He is dead!"

Just then there was a strangled scream from my right as another died. Then the Saxon leader shouted, "Kill them!"

They could not see us but it made no difference. They ran into the woods. I stood behind a tree and as the first Saxon passed me I swung my sword and ripped into his stomach. The man behind looked down and did not see the blade which split his skull. I turned and ran. My wolf cloak hid me. I trusted my men to do the same. When we had run thirty paces I stopped. Ahead of me I saw Cnut Cnutson. He pointed to a piece of rope he had laid between trees. I nodded to him and stepped back into the bole of a large elm tree. Cnut nodded.

Behind me, I heard the Saxons as they clattered and crashed through the undergrowth. Some fell and tripped over obstacles. It would just make them angrier. I could hear the sound of men charging all through the woods. This suited the Ulfheonar. They were at home in the dark and the night. Cnut put his hands together and howled. It had the desired effect. The Saxons ran to him. He had his sword and seax drawn and that was all that they saw. As they tumbled over the rope and lay sprawling on the ground I stepped out. Using the sword with two hands I hacked into the back of one Saxon before ripping it up into the chest of another. I whirled and brought my sword into the neck of a third. Cnut had butchered the four men who had fallen over the rope and the other three fled. A Saxon horn sounded three times. I heard the Northumbrians running back towards the safety of the camp. I howled. Cnut howled. I heard four more howls. My Ulfheonar were safe.

Cnut began searching the bodies whilst I kept watch. It soon became obvious that the Saxons had decided that they had lost enough men. Cnut had swords and purses. I pointed to the horses. "Go back to the horses. Send any warriors here to remove the helmets and mail from the dead. The Ulfheonar will watch."

"Jarl, I am Ulfheonar."

"Then you know better than to disobey me."

He nodded and headed back. Cnut Cnutson had done enough. When the dawn came and he guarded my standard he would do far more good than searching bodies. I took out my seax as well as my sword as I headed back to the Saxon camp. I needed to reassure myself that they were doing exactly what I thought they were doing. My caution was well placed as a sword flashed from the woods. Any mail other than that made by Bagsecg and I would have been wounded. The sword slid along the oiled links. As it was my body reacted without me knowing. The seax slashed across the Saxon's throat. His hands went to the wound as he tried to stem the flow of blood. His eyes glazed over and he sank at my feet.

I moved closer to the hubbub that was the Northumbrian camp. There were wounded men and there were injured men. They were being tended to. I saw the two thegns with their heads together. They barked out orders but they were too indistinct for me to make out. Their meaning became clear as a line of sentries with shields and spears faced the woods. There would be no attack on the stad until morning. By then I would have enough men to make an attack.

I stepped back into the woods a little and then shouted, in Saxon, "I am Jarl Dragonheart of the Land of the Wolf. I wield the sword that was touched by the gods. Leave now and you might live. If you stay then the wolves will come. We will slaughter you and devour your flesh. Your White Christ and his whey faced priests will not help you!" There was a brief moment of silence and then four howls sounded almost immediately behind me. I turned and headed back. My Ulfheonar ghosted from the woods. All of them were grinning.

As we walked back Haaken said, "I am sure that one of them shat himself before he fled. It was either that or one of Olaf's farts."

Olaf snorted, "If it had been one of mine you would have been blinded!"

They were in high spirits and we had achieved all that we could. We had delayed the attack. Victory depended upon my son and grandson arriving. Their voyage was in the hands of the gods and their precocious winds.

Chapter 6

We all managed some sleep but we were hardly rested. All of the men we had brought and the stragglers gathered close by the boggy ground. I was one of the first awake and I went around to see if we had lost men. We had not. Beorn told me that the Saxons had advanced towards them but he had kept the warband moving backwards away from them. The Saxon horns had drawn them back. I counted fifty-eight men. Of those I had seven who were Ulfheonar. A handful, perhaps eight, had never raided and never fought. I would not risk those in the front rank. They could guard the horses. I had sent Asbjorn to Ketil. The only help would come up the Eden and that would depend not only on the wind but the tide for the Eden was not the widest of rivers.

The Ulfheonar sat around me. We ate the last of our rations. Olaf emptied his ale skin into his horn, "You have a plan, Jarl Dragonheart?"

I nodded. "We make a wedge and we advance towards the Saxons."

Haaken One Eye nodded, "A bold plan and one which should ensure that we all have a glorious death."

"I did not say it was a good plan. You asked if I had one and I have."

Cnut Cnutson shook his head, "You do not plan to engage them, do you Jarl Dragonheart?"

"No, Cnut. I want them to face us and prepare a shield wall to stop us." I waved a hand to the north. "The boggy ground to the south protects us there and the river is north of us. Ragnar will bring our drekar along the river. From this little island of high ground, we can see the river. When the Saxons see us halt they will take it for weakness and they will advance. We meet them spear to spear and hope that three drekar appear in the river. When they do then we will have the Saxons surrounded. They will have fallen into my trap."

They were all silent until Beorn said, "And if your son and grandson do not arrive on time? We know that the sea, the tides and the winds follow few rules."

"Before I came away I asked Aiden and Kara a question." I was aware that all of the warriors, not just the Ulfheonar, were listening. "I asked if they had dreamed my death and they said they had not. Of course, that does not mean I might not fall in this battle and become a prisoner but I have faith in Kara and Aiden."

I saw that all of them, Ulfheonar included were clutching their dragon, wolf or hammer of Thor.

Haaken One Eye laughed, "Then I am satisfied. The few hairs I have now are white and that was the result of meeting with a witch. Kara is a witch that I trust. I will stay as close as I can to the Dragonheart!"

I then gave instructions for the formation of the wedge. With the Ulfheonar forming the first three ranks, the fourth would be those others who had mail. The rest had, at best, leather. The final ranks were the ones without helmets. When we were ready and the horse holders assigned we formed the wedge. We would not be travelling through the woods. We would march due north to the Roman Road and then along it until we were in sight of the stad and the camp. The road passed through the small piece of high ground. Once there we would taunt the Saxons until they attacked us. They could not afford to have a warband in their rear. Whoever led them would know that he had to rid himself of our threat.

We were hidden from the camp and the fort by the slightly domed section of road. It was Roman and had a good surface. While we walked along the road we would not be a true wedge. As the first seven rows would be able to march in a wedge formation then I was not worried. When I saw the smoke spiralling from the camp I said, "Haaken, let us have a chant to help us and to tell the Stad that we are coming?"

"Of course!" He sang the song of the death of Eystein the Rock. It was appropriate because it sang of the arrival of ships. It would give hope to those inside the stad.

Through the stormy Saxon Seas
The Ulfheonar they sailed
Fresh from killing faithless Danes
Their glory was assured
Heart of Dragon
Gift of a king
Two fine drekar
Flying o'er foreign seas
Then Saxons came out of the night
An ambush by their Isle of Wight
Vikings fight they do not run
The Jarl turned away from the rising sun
Heart of Dragon
Gift of a king

Two fine drekar
Flying o'er foreign seas
The galdramenn burned Dragon Fire
And the seas they burned bright red
Aboard 'The Gift' Asbjorn the Strong
And the rock Eystein
Rallied their men to board their foes
And face them beard to beard
Heart of Dragon
Gift of a king
Two fine drekar
Flying o'er foreign seas
Against great odds and back to back
The heroes fought as one
Their swords were red with Saxon blood
And the decks with bodies slain
Surrounded on all sides was he
But Eystein faltered not
He slew first one and then another
But the last one did for him
Even though he fought as a walking dead
He killed right to the end
Heart of Dragon
Gift of a king
Two fine drekar
Flying o'er foreign seas

    As I crested the rise and saw the camp the fifty odd voices were in full song. Our singing had alerted the Saxons and they were facing us although they were not in any kind of order. I stopped just a little way over the top of the rise. From where the Saxons were camped they would have no idea how many men were behind me. They would see the tip of a wedge. When it was unfurled they would see my wolf banner and know that the Dragonheart was here. The voices had suggested more than I actually had. I held up my sword and we all stopped. Every voice stopped at the same moment. Haaken often spoke of the power of voices singing and chanting together. This was the power of silence.
    Olaf Leather Neck said, loudly, "Now we will see what these Saxons have in them."

There were five thegns now. The other three must have been in a different part of the camp. The fact that they gathered together to speak told me that Rædwulf was not with them. I felt a chill down my neck. He would be at Pennryhd. I put that thought from my mind. Before me were over one hundred and eighty Saxons. We had slain more than fifteen the night before but now they could see us. We had no surprises left. The ground fell away from the sides of the road below us. It was not a steep ascent but if they tried to come in one long line then those on the sides would have rocks, bushes and trees to contend with. They made the decision to come in a column. With ten men wide and ten men deep, they hoped that they would overwhelm our wedge. It was then I saw that I had underestimated their numbers. More men came from the western side of the Stad on the Eden. That meant they had abandoned their plans to take it until they had beaten us. Now was the time for our drekar to sail up the Eden. Then I saw that it was low tide. There would be no ships for a while. We had to hang on and take whatever they threw at us.

"Cnut, let them see that the banner flies!"

The wolf banner was unfurled and raised and my men cheered. From inside the stad I heard another cheer. The banner was worth twenty men. If the banner flew then I lived and we had hope. The Saxons were not well practised in this and it took longer to form up. They had a wall of shields at the front and then the others were held over their heads. They feared our arrows. We had none but they did not know that. They had spears. A horn sounded and they began to make their way up the road. The front rank had at least four men with mail. The front third all had helmets. The priests, I saw that there were five of them, followed the column with their cross. Two carried a box. I had no doubt that it contained bones. As they were from Northumbria I guessed they would be St. Cuthbert's. I had seen at least four feet and hands of St. Cuthbert for sale. I wondered if the priests just dug up any bones that they could find.

When they were fifty paces from us Olaf Leather Neck, standing on my right shouted, "Shields!" Unlike the Saxons we did not put our shields over our heads. There was no point. The Saxons had no archers. And, as they would be below us when they struck, we needed to be able to swing overhand.

The thegn who led them roared, "Charge!" when they were ten paces from us. They were not in step and so they lost some of their cohesion.

I was the target for their spears along with Haaken One Eye and Olaf Leather Neck. We were in the centre. I had my shield before me. My eyes peered over the top. I was more than happy for them to thrust their spears at me. A spear was unsteady when held in one hand. The head wavered. These men had marched four hundred paces holding the spears out. I watched the spearheads rising and falling with every step.

Olaf shouted, "Brace!" I felt the weight in my back increase and knew that they all had their right leg slightly back and were leaning into their shields. Then the Saxons struck. Four of the ten spears came for me. Haaken One Eye and Olaf had three each to contend with. I moved my shield slightly as they thrust them at me. One spear struck my shield. One glanced off the side of my helmet and the other two were forced up by the metal edge of my shield. At the same time, I stabbed upwards. The Saxons were too concerned with their spear thrusts and I found a gap. Ragnar's Spirit hit metal.

Olaf yelled, "Push!" We had the advantage that we had the slope with us. The men at the back had nothing else to do and they pushed. The Saxons before us could not move and my sword was forced through the mail links of a poorly made byrnie and into the chest of the warrior before me. It was not the thegn. He was slightly to my left. I saw Rolf Horse Killer reach over with his long axe and hook the thegn's shield. He pulled back and Haaken One Eye rammed his sword under the neck of the thegn. It came out of the back and spattered blood over the Saxons who had yet to come into action.

Two men were dead in their front rank. That became four as Olaf swung his axe. It hacked through the arm of one Saxon. He pulled away and tried to stop the fountaining blood. The axe carried on and bit into the thigh of a second. Olaf was strong and the leg was completely severed. Our men were still pushing and, with four dead men, our wedge drove into their second and third ranks. Rollo and Rolf could now bring their weapons to bear.

I lunged forward. The man before me still had his shield up to protect the thegn whose body was being trampled. My sword went through his chest. I twisted and the life left his eyes. We had momentum as the weight of our men bore down on the Saxons. Rolf Horse Killer and Olaf had long Danish axes. Spears could not get past their shields and they could not penetrate our mail. They were made of soft iron and not the steel of our swords and axes. They should have stabbed at our legs. There he had no mail. Instead, they jabbed and poked at shields and mail. I remembered Haraldr's mail when Olaf had begun to split it. We were having the same effect on the Saxons. As we forced our way down the road so the sides had to try to walk on the rough ground. They stumbled and fell. They were butchered.

The horn we had heard sound in the night sounded again and the Saxons did not just fall back. They fled. I was not stupid enough to charge after them. I had fifty odd men. There were still two hundred Saxons. I shouted, "Hold!" I was followed by Ulfheonar and they stopped the men behind. I saw that the remaining thegns had formed their men into a treble line. Spears had been planted before them.

Olaf Leather Neck shouted, "Reform!" Then he said quietly, "We have done what you wished. It is not glorious but we should wait here. There is no point in wasting lives. They are going nowhere."

I was about to agree when I looked slightly to my right. I saw the masts of my drekar and I saw a giant leap from one of them. It was Haraldr Leifsson and I saw Aðils, Ragnar and Gruffyd. My men had come. The Saxons were about to be attacked in the rear. Even as I raised my sword to order the charge, I saw the gates of the stad open as Jarl Ráðulfr Ulfsson led his men from the stad to fall upon the unprotected rear of the Saxon line.

Olaf Leather Neck laughed, "Of course, I could be wrong!"

I raised my sword, "March!" Haaken started the chant and we marched down to end the battle of the Eden.

The Dragonheart and Haaken Brave
A Viking warrior and a Saxon slave
The Dragonheart and Haaken Brave
A Viking warrior and a Saxon slave
The Dragonheart and Haaken Brave
A Viking warrior and a Saxon slave
The Dragonheart and Haaken Brave
A Viking warrior and a Saxon slave

The Northumbrians had nowhere to go. Their only escape was over the boggy, flooded ground. The few who tried that were slain by slingers and archers from the Stad. We came at them from three directions and although my warband was the smallest, we were the ones they feared the most for we had slain so many already. We brushed aside the planted spears and we began to reap Saxons. Few who faced us had mail. Our swords and axes found flesh with every blow. Their numbers did not help them for our shields were better and their weapons could not pierce mail. Soon the seven Ulfheonar were overtaken by warriors who were keen for glory, for honour and for treasure. By the time I met with Jarl Ráðulfr Ulfsson and Ragnar the battle was almost over. The last few warriors were being slain.

The Jarl beamed. His face was bloody. He had carved his way through the Saxons. "You promised that you would come and you did." He pointed to the road. "When I saw how few men you brought I was humbled that you achieved so much."

"I knew that my son and grandson were coming by sea. We had to hold them until they came."

Ragnar said, "Aðils and that giant of yours are the ones who should be thanked. We might have had to wait until high tide if it were not for them. They had scouted out the waters and brought us in. Haraldr was the first off the drekar. He has no helmet!"

I laughed, "Bagsecg is making him one." I pointed east. Their leader, Rædwulf, was not with them. Either he sits at home or he is further east attacking Ketil. I sent Asbjorn the Strong there but I have a feeling that this attack was a diversion to draw us here and that Rædwulf attacks with a much bigger army."

"Our men have had the most rest. We will march."

I nodded. "The Ulfheonar will come with you. Jarl Ráðulfr Ulfsson we leave you to deal with the dead and guard our ships. I will send our horses back with the men we brought. You will divide the spoils?"

"You trust me with that honour, Jarl Dragonheart?"

"I trusted your father. He never let me down. I look in your eyes and I see the father." I saw Gruffyd striding over to me. "A man is judged by the actions of his children and grandchildren. Just as mine never failed me nor will you fail the memory of your father." I turned and cupped my hands, "Ulfheonar! We march!"

It took longer than I would have liked to give orders and to recover our men. Ragnar insisted that the Ulfheonar ride. "Of all the men who fought this day you eight deserve the honour and you have done the most."

As we headed along the Roman Road east I saw Lars Larsson leading the men who had fought with me south. I heard them singing as they rode. For some, this would be their only battle. They would return to their farms, or, like the Larsson brothers, to their mines and they would recall the day they followed the wolf banner. They would tell their children of how they fought behind the sword which was touched by the gods and carved their way through a Saxon horde. They had been part of a Viking warband. Many years hence, when they died and were laid to rest, their families would ensure that they held the swords they had used that day. Whatever they had been, now they were warriors who had fought with the wolf.

My seven Ulfheonar were with me at the fore. Jarl Ráðulfr Ulfsson had sent two of his men on ponies to act as scouts and to ensure that we were not ambushed. I rode with Haaken One Eye and Aðils Shape Shifter. We both wished to hear the tale of the giant and the Ulfheonar. Beorn the Scout and Cnut Cnutson rode behind; they listened. Olaf, Rolf and Rollo brought up the rear. I knew that their talk would be of their axes and the battle. The three lived for war.

"When we sent Beorn back we saw that they had encircled the defences save by the boggy area and the river. I did not wish to risk coming back through their lines. Haraldr is a stout warrior but shape shifting is not one of his strengths." We laughed. "We headed towards the sea and left our horses there. We heard the howling and the songs. We were not there but I could see it in my mind. When dawn came I left Haraldr with the horses while I returned to the river. I scouted it out and saw that there was a passage through it but it was not an easy one. I took off my mail and breeks and I swam the river. When I neared the Saxons I swam to the bank and spied their lines. I was close enough to hear them. They spoke of the wolves in the night and ghosts who had appeared and disappeared at will. They talked fearfully. When I returned to Haraldr and dressed we continued, on foot towards the sea. When I spied, *'Heart of the Dragon'* we waved and boarded."

"Your timing was perfect. We had defeated one Saxon column and they were about to send another."

Aðils concurred, "We saw the flight and Haraldr was ready to leap into the water long before we reached the shore. He is keen to be as his father was."

"Ulfheonar?"

"No, Jarl Dragonheart. He knows he has not the skills but his father held your banner and defended your back."

Cnut Cnutson said, "And he could do that for I am no longer Ulfheonar."

"You would give the banner to someone else?"

"Jarl Dragonheart I would die protecting you and the standard, you know that but when we marched with those men behind us I saw that I could lead them. They are the men of Cyninges-tūn. They follow you and the Ulfheonar but they need a leader. Karl One Leg leads them in Cyninges-tūn. My leg just slows me up. I am not as old as Karl. I could lead them when we raid or go to war. If you think I have the skills."

"Of course you have the skills. What think you Ulfheonar, should we have Haraldr Leifsson carry my wolf banner?"

Haaken said, "Jarl Dragonheart, do you remember when Leif first carried your banner?" I shook my head. There had been so many battles. "It was just north of here when we fought the barbarians from the north. We were close to the Roman wall. Then he was not Ulfheonar but the Norns spun and he was there with your banner. It seems to me that this is nothing to do with us. The Norns have picked him. The gods seem to approve. This is *wyrd*."

I could see that Haaken One Eye was right and I remembered Leif and the standard. His son would be the one who guarded my back.

Beorn the Scout said, "And I have seen that I, too, must seek another way to serve you jarl. I am slower than I was. I still have the skills as a scout but I am not an Ulfheonar. I thought that the Allfather would have taken me in battle before now. I have sons and I would see them grow. Last night, when I led those men I knew I could make the right decisions to keep them safe. When we fought this morning I was behind Olaf, Rollo and Rolf. They kept me safe. I watched them. That was what I was like when I was younger."

"Beorn the Scout, Haaken One Eye and myself, we are older than you."

Olaf must have been listening for he said, "Jarl Dragonheart from what I have heard the Norns and the gods conspired when the two of you stood on the fighting platform in Norway defending old Ragnar. They chose you and marked you. There is a bond between you. The tomb under Wyddfa, the witch's cave in Syllingar… you will never be too old. I am happy just to stand behind the two of you but I confess I am envious of the blood that ties you together."

We rode in silence. The words of Beorn, Cnut and Olaf were true and they set each of us thinking. This was the end of the Ulfheonar. They would still come with me and fight at my side. Once there had been enough of us to determine the outcome of a battle. Now that was not true. I watched the sky ahead begin to darken as night fell. We would not reach Ketil before dark. The setting of the sun behind us seemed to be the setting of the sun on the wolf warriors.

Chapter 7

We had passed a Roman mile marker and so we knew we were just under two miles from Pennryhd when the scouts rode in on lathered ponies. "Jarl! Pennryhd is surrounded as is the old Roman fort. We saw many fires."

"Is there fighting?"

"No, Jarl Dragonheart but there has been. We heard the carrion feasting."

I held up my hand. We would camp and rest. This was not the time to charge in recklessly. My men had fought a battle. We had little sleep. Ketil would have prepared his defences. We would plan our attack. We would have a cold camp and march to battle on the morrow. With sentries set we ate cold rations and drank from the waters of the Eamont river. I sat with my son and grandson.

"Sámr wished to come you know."

I laughed, "He is a feisty cockerel. He was disappointed when you told him no?"

"He was. Then he remembered that he would be sailing with you, soon, back to Bruggas. Then Ulla War Cry and Mordaf began to clamour to serve as ship's boys with him."

Gruffyd shook his head, "Ebrel was not happy, father."

"If you two wish me to refuse to take them then I will. I do not mind being the villain to keep harmony in your homes. I was married to a Christian and know the problems that creates."

"You gave your word and you are never foresworn."

"I also said that both you and your wives had to be happy about it."

Gruffyd said, "We are both men. We will make the decisions in our own halls." He gave a rueful smile. "At least when I upset Ebrel I will have silence."

Ragnar laughed, "Why is it that women think a silence in our homes hurts us? For me it is welcome!"

Haaken and Olaf Leather Neck came over, "Jarl Dragonheart, what are your plans for the battle?"

Gruffyd said, "We meet and beat the Saxons!"

Shaking my head, I said, "It is not so simple. Pennryhd is on a hill. It is a small hill but it means that we have to march uphill to reach them. If their leader is with them then they may well have Saxon hearthweru, the housecarls. They wear mail. We have one hundred and forty men. We know not the enemy numbers. We need to use that which makes us superior. How many archers are in your crews?"

Ragnar said, "We brought thirty bows."

"Then we use those to punch a hole in their shield wall. We make a boar's snout."

"Boar's snout?"

Ragnar had fought alongside me more than Gruffyd. He explained to my son. "It is two wedges. What the Dragonheart intends, I think, is for the archers to weaken the centre while we attack the weaker warriors on either side of their mailed men."

I smiled. My grandson was more like me than his father had been. He could think and he could plan. "You are right, Ragnar. Once we penetrate their first ranks then Ketil will lead his men from the ramparts and fall upon the rear of the Northumbrians. My only fear is that those who surround the Roman fort may join them." I shrugged. "We shall see." We had to take one battle at a time.

We rose early. I was up before dawn. Beorn and Aðils had been up even earlier and had scouted out the enemy lines. Despite Beorn's protestations he was still a better scout than most men but Aðils had lost none of his skills. In fact, having lived in the remote dale, he had become even better. I was eating some two-day old bread when they arrived back.

"This is a larger army, Jarl Dragonheart, and Rædwulf is there with them. We heard his men talking of him although we did not see him. He calls himself prince. We could not count them accurately. They were sleeping but by the number of fires I would think that there are more than two hundred of them. There are more at the old Roman fort."

"And the ground between here and there?"

"There is farmland. Animals have been grazing. It rises slightly but it should not stop a well-drilled wedge."

"Then let us wake the young who seem to need more sleep than we old."

We went around the camp and woke everyone without horns. The Saxons would see us soon enough but I wished them to think that their diversion had worked. We marched in two columns. I led one and Ragnar the other. When we were within range of them we would deploy into a line with two wedges. Gruffyd and his men would follow Ragnar and Raibeart, me and the Ulfheonar. Haraldr was given the standard. He and Cnut were the middle two in the fourth rank. The men did not take much rousing. They ate on the move. We left our horses where we had camped. They would be there when we returned.

Smoke rose in the sky from the Saxon camp. I wondered how long they had been besieging Pennryhd. I did not think they would have begun that attack before the one on the Stad on the Eden. Ketil had been prepared but he was vastly outnumbered. His archers would keep the Saxons at bay but eventually their stock of arrows would diminish and there would be an attack on the ramparts. I wondered why the Roman fort was still occupied. That concerned me. Although the road was Roman, since the legions had left trees and shrubs had grown. No one had thought to keep them in check and so the view of both the road and the land around was somewhat obscured. We were within a five hundred paces of the Saxon camp when we finally saw it.

As soon as we did we went into our formations. The two wedges were seven ranks deep and the rest of the warriors formed three lines behind the two of us. The thirty archers were in the middle. We had begun to form lines when the Saxons saw us. Their attention had been on the ramparts. There was fighting already. I saw ladders across the ditches. The scattered bodies told me that the Saxons had already begun to lose men. As those inside Pennryhd saw us so a cheer went up.

A shout from Beorn the Scout who stood with the archers told me that we were ready. Our archers would be hidden. They would be behind three ranks of spears. They would not release until we were engaged with their warriors. We began to chant. It helped us to keep the rhythm. We used one that Haaken had devised to help us row quickly.

Push your arms
Row the boat
Use your back
The Wolf will fly

Ulfheonar
Are real men
Teeth like iron
Arms like trees

Push your arms
Row the boat
Use your back

The Wolf will fly

Ragnar's Spirit
Guides us still
Dragon Heart
Wields it well

Push your arms
Row the boat
Use your back
The Wolf will fly

    We did not move straightaway. We marched on the spot. I raised my sword and Ragnar did the same. When I lowered it, I began to walk as did Ragnar. Ragnar's wedge had spears. Mine did not. As we marched I saw the Saxons reacting to our move. There was a mailed warrior on a horse. He had a full-face helmet with a red plume. That told me he was no warrior. His horse was white and he wore a red cloak. This was Rædwulf. He used a sword to marshal his men into position. As I had expected he put his mailed men before him and then his priests with their crosses and boxes. I guessed they had been robbing more graves.

    The Saxons like to use the fyrd. These were the freemen who worked the land. They owed service to their thegns. It was not a bad system. It was in their interests to fight for their lord. If he died then a new one might be worse than the one they had lost. The problem came when their lord was killed for the fyrd of the thegn had no reason to stay and they would flee. My men knew that. We sought out the thegns. We fought those with mail. There was more honour and greater rewards. You cracked the thegns and their walls of warriors crumbled. The chant gave us a faster pace than normal. It was a risk but it was worth the gamble for the Northumbrians were struggling to get into line. As we neared them I saw consternation amongst their leaders. Rædwulf and his lieutenants, all of whom were mounted, were engaged in a heated debate. I saw one of the older greybeards pointing to the two wedges. He could see what Rædwulf, apparently, could not. My wedge would strike the thegn whose banner was a crow, while Ragnar's would strike the thegn who had the crossed swords. Neither thegn had any mailed men near them. They had their hearthweru. They were like Haraldr. They wore leather armour and had helmets but they were undressed compared with the Vikings who would strike them. The old greybeard had fought us before. Rædwulf had not. He was about to get a lesson in Viking tactics.

They had some warriors armed with javelins and a few slingers. The slingers were a greater danger. I heard Cnut say, "Haraldr, watch your head! You have no helmet. Hold your shield above your head."

"Yes, Cnut."

Most of the javelins landed well short. One stuck in my shield. I left it there. It would be returned to the Saxons with interest when we struck their line. A slingshot clanged off my helmet. I had a leather protector and padded hood beneath it but, even so, I knew I had been hit. Most stones hit our shields. It sounded like hailstone on stone. The fact that they were using javelins told me that we were close. We had stopped chanting. We had no need. Our bodies were as one. We all stepped off on the same foot. When we swung our weapons, it would be as one. The Saxons who waited us fought as individuals. Those who had fought before knew to wait and judge the strike. The ones who had never fought often panicked. So it was with the crow band we faced. The thegn and the two men next to him did not thrust their spears at us but the others rippled along the line as they stabbed at nothing. It was a wasted effort and, as they drew their spears back for a second strike, we closed with them.

The thegn lunged at my body. His two bodyguards did the same. It was a waste of effort. They hit my shield and that was all. Rolf and Olaf swung their long Danish axes as I brought my sword in a sweep at head height. My sword caught the top of the thegn's helmet as his shield managed to deflect my sword. His two bodyguards had no such luck. Olaf's axe hacked through the leg of one while Rolf's smashed the shield of his Saxon to kindling and broke his arm. I punched with the boss of my shield. My blow to the thegn's helmet had jerked his head back. The shield exaggerated the movement and he began to fall. I stuck forward with my sword. The gods looked kindly on me for my blade went under his byrnie and into his groin. It was a feral scream which marked his death as he was disembowelled by Ragnar's Spirit. With three men dead in the centre my wedge began to scythe through the ones at the side. The fyrd fell. Even those warriors of mine without a byrnie were better protected that the Saxons they fought.

A spear rammed against my helmet and a wood axe struck the edge of my shield. A sword clanged off Ragnar's Spirit. All were trying to get at me and, in doing so, they signed their own death warrant. The Ulfheonar were around me and while blows were striking me they were not striking them. We broke through their front rank. I heard a Saxon horn sound three times. I looked to my left and saw that my archers had managed to slay all of the priests. Two of those on horses had been slain along with their mounts. The horns sounded again, twice and the mailed men in the centre began to move back as one. As I had worked out, they were the best. They were now isolated for Ragnar's wedge had advanced too. Rædwulf might not be a warrior but he understood strategy. He was moving his better troops back. Those on the side also fell back. Their move was not by choice. They were trying to get away from the deadly weapons wielded by my men. They were forming a circle. It would take time but we would slowly whittle down their numbers and slaughter them.

The Weird Sisters weave complicated webs. They are intricate. They trick and they trap. I had wondered at the two signals. Suddenly Haraldr Leifsson shouted, "Jarl Dragonheart! Saxons are coming down the road from the east."

Behind me Olaf Leather Neck said, "They are the ones who were attacking the fort."

Raibeart and his men were behind us. If they were attacked on their right, with no shields to protect them then they would be slaughtered, with or without mail. I made a quick decision. "Wedge! Turn right, Make a shield wall!"

I heard Cnut instructing Haraldr. At the front we did nothing but Raibeart and his men stopped facing Pennryhd and turned to present a solid wall of shields to this new foe which was marching down the road towards us. Haraldr's height had saved us. He had seen them when they left the fort. Now they were in the dip and would suddenly appear. Had we not turned then it might have gone badly for us. As it was this would be a real battle, a bloody battle, warrior to warrior.

To my left Haaken said, "Jarl Dragonheart, they are shifting those housecarls to face us." They were able to do so for my men who advanced upon them had no mail. They could not press home an attack. The archers managed to hit one or two as they moved but, when we killed the fyrd who were before us and blunted our weapons, we would face Saxons who had yet to fight. They would be Northumbrians who would be fresh and the best warriors that Rædwulf had under his command.

"Then we show them that we are Ulfheonar! We are the Clan of the Wolf and this is our land. If they want it they must kill us!"

My men all began to bang their shields and to chant.

Clan of the Wolf never forget
Clan of the Wolf never forgive
Clan of the Wolf fight to the death
Clan of the Wolf never forget
Clan of the Wolf never forgive
Clan of the Wolf fight to the death

Our archers did what I hoped they would. They shifted from the mailed warriors to the ones without mail. I did not think we had many arrows left and we needed to make them all count. The various movements had meant that Haaken and Olaf were no longer behind me, they were next to me. Rolf was next to Haaken and Rollo next to Olaf. Cnut and Haraldr stood behind me. Haraldr was a reassuring presence. While we waited for the inevitable assault I took the opportunity of slipping my dagger, Wolf's Blood, into my shield hand.

I heard Rædwulf shout, "Charge! These are heathens! They have slain God's servants! Slaughter them all!"

Olaf Leather Neck shouted, in Saxon, "Easier said than done, Saxon!"

The mailed warriors came at us. They each bore a spear. They were three ranks deep and they had spears sticking out over the shoulders of the front two ranks. I found myself fearing for Haraldr who did not have a helmet. I think that made me fight harder. Haraldr had never known a father. The Ulfheonar fought that day as though we were his father. I did not wait for them to strike at me. I stepped forward and swung my shield up. Even a veteran spearman finds it hard to hold his spear and stab using just one hand. The spearheads screeched along my shield and helmet but no harm was done. I stabbed at the gap between two shields. I felt it grate along metal. I ripped it sideways and was rewarded by a grunt from the warrior to my right.

Olaf Leather Neck shouted, "Watch out behind." He brought his Danish axe over, one handed and it smashed down on to the helmet and skull of the Saxon in the second rank. My sword was still ahead of me and I ripped it sideways. It tore into the neck of the Saxon who faced Olaf.

Rolf Horse Killer, encouraged by Olaf's success, yelled, "Watch out behind." As he swung, the warriors in the second rank moved back. Only a fool would wait for an axe to split his skull. We were pushing and the warrior in the front rank was forced back by the press of men and it was his skull which was split.

We were not having it all our own way. We had five Ulfheonar who were able to battle the mailed warriors on an equal footing. The ones to our left were not as skilled and I saw that Rolf was going to have to turn or risk an attack from the side.

My son and grandson had found that their enemies had either moved or melted away. I heard Ragnar shout, "Men of Whale Island, Jarl Dragonheart needs blood! Make it Saxon blood. Let us spill it!"

I forced myself to ignore what was happening to my left. We had a battle ahead of us. The death of four of their men created a gap. I took advantage and, stepping forward, smashed my shield into the face of the nearest Saxon. He was held in the press by the men behind and a spear is a hard weapon to use in close combat. I still held my dagger in, my left hand and I swept my shield towards the warrior to my left. The man I had just hit with my shield was still groggy and he never saw my dagger as it tore across his throat. A spear from the third rank jabbed forward and slid off my mail. I suspected it had damaged my byrnie but I could not afford to stop and examine it. We were driving the Saxons inexorably backwards. There was a roar as Ketil led his men and Asbjorn brought his warband to attack the rear of the enemy ranks.

For one brief moment I thought that we had not only won, we had destroyed the threat that was Rædwulf. I was wrong. The Weird Sisters were spinning. When Ragnar and Gruffyd had brought our left flank to fall upon the mailed warriors it had alleviated the pressure on the Saxon right. Horns sounded and the horsemen and fyrd suddenly fled. They headed north. The mailed warriors, the thirty who were left, could not disengage. I did not think that they would have chosen to. They fought on. The close proximity of our best warriors to theirs meant that none saw the flight of Rædwulf and a third of his army until it was too late. Even Haraldr was too busy to use his height to see. Some of the Saxons had seen the opportunity to seize my banner. He and Cnut Cnutson were fighting for their lives and my banner.

It was Beorn the Scout who saw the flight, "Jarl Dragonheart! Rædwulf escapes!"

It was one thing to know that and another to do anything about it. A warrior fights one battle at a time and this battle was to the death. Neither side would give quarter. We were hard pressed but Gruffyd and Ragnar brought fresh blades and youthful arms to hack and slice into the right flank of the mailed Saxons. Ketil and Asbjorn had lost many men and they sought revenge. When they entered the fray, it became butchery. We had all seen too many friends die to give quarter. The last stand of the Saxons was a brave one but they were surrounded. My sword became so blunt that it was almost an iron bar. I sheathed it and used my dagger. I slashed, ripped and gutted warriors who had so many wounds that their mail ran red. My shoulders burned from the effort. And then it was over and we had won.

    The last man fell and an eerie silence descended on the battlefield. There were none to give the warrior's death for they had fought on with terrible wounds and dying. As I looked over the corpse covered battle field I hoped that the Saxon threat from Northumbria was extinguished, at least for the moment. I still had work to do but my northern borders were temporarily safe. Rædwulf had fled. I would need to find him and end this. I looked around and saw that my son and grandson lived. They were bloody and they had wounds but they stood. My Ulfheonar lived. Ketil, Asbjorn and Raibeart had wounds but their raised swords told me that they would fight again.

Chapter 8

We could have pursued their fyrd but it would have availed us little. They were beaten men. Their thegns, who survived, were dead or they had fled with Rædwulf. They had tried to take on the Vikings and they had lost. There would be no appetite for another such incursion. I was counting on that. We were exhausted. Rædwulf would escape, with his thegns. I had not yet finished with him. I saw that Gruffyd had a wound to his leg. My grandson and Einar Fair Face supported him. Ragnar had a scar across his face. Ketil and Asbjorn both had serious wounds. Raibeart was the one who had escaped relatively unscathed and so I put him in charge. "Give any wounded who cannot be healed a warrior's death. Fetch in our wounded and then have our men strip the dead. We will make a bone fire yonder. We will let it mark the place where Northumbrian dreams were shattered. Take the heads from ten of the mailed warriors who died bravely and have them put in sacks."

"Aye jarl."

We had healers with us. Unlike the priests of the White Christ ours were warrior healers. Any who could not be healed were given a sword and sent to Valhalla. We saved more than we slew. I walked over to Ketil and Asbjorn. Asbjorn had lapsed into unconsciousness. He had suffered a blow to the head. "What happened?"

Ketil said, "When they came we sent riders. The Saxons were cunning. None made it to bring us aid. When Asbjorn came they tried to ambush him. He barely made it to the Roman fort. We were separated and did not know if you knew of this. We lost many men, Jarl Dragonheart. We cannot let this wrong go unpunished."

"And we will not. Are you able to ride?"

"I am."

"Then tomorrow we take the Ulfheonar and twenty men who can ride. We go to Dunelm and we make our demands on this Saxon who seeks the throne of Northumbria."

Ragnar said, "And what of us?"

"You have done your duty. You return to Whale Island. I leave you to divide the spoils."

"But should we not go with you?"

"It was me they came for and it is me who will beard the beast in his den."

"Twenty men?"

I laughed, "Twenty men and the Ulfheonar! That will be enough!"

Haraldr wished to come with us but his large horse was still at the Stad on the Eden. The horse we found was the biggest which Ketil owned but Haraldr's feet almost trailed along the ground. We left early the morning after the battle. Smoke still rose from the pyre of the dead Saxons. Farmers would spread the ash on their fields and the enemy would feed our people. *Wyrd.*

Ketil's wound was to his leg. The healers had used fire to seal the wound. Wrapped in honey, vinegar and herbs I could see that it pained him as we rode north and east towards the island citadel that was Dunelm. With a river sweeping around three sides it needed no ditches. The Saxons had a church there made sacred by the one they called Cuthbert. Rædwulf would go there. It was in the heart of the land he controlled. It was a fortress the equal of Din Guardi. The rivers in this part of the world dominated the land. The Dunum, the river from which I had been taken, marked the northern edge of the land which Æthelred controlled. Dunelm was the stronghold he would choose.

We would not make the journey in one day. It was sixty miles. We headed first for the home of Carr. He was a scout and knew the land east of us well. On the way to his home we found dead Saxons lying by the road. They had succumbed to their wounds and been abandoned. My men shook their heads and clutched their amulets as we passed them. They had not been given the warrior's death by their comrades. They had been abandoned. We would not even contemplate such an action. We were shield brothers. Carr took us by ways which the Saxon army had not used. They, too, would take longer than one day to reach Dunelm. If the dead we had seen was a measure of the Saxons we pursued then we might even beat some of the stragglers back to the safety of their stronghold. They would travel by the Roman Roads. Carr's route took us further north. It was a wild country. There were few people and it appeared to be one huge forest. It teemed with game. The paths he used were also used by the animals and we saw sign of wild pigs, deer and, inevitably, wolves.

The high divide had to be crossed but here it was less desolate than further south. When the Romans had built their road, they had chosen the highest and most exposed route. I could see why. If Rædwulf had had men there we might have been easily ambushed. As it was the only people we saw were those who eked out a living close to the edges of the forest. We camped at an abandoned hut. It looked ancient. One of the wattle and daub walls remained and it afforded some shelter. There was a stream nearby which explained the position of the hut.

Ketil asked the question that was on the minds of the others, "What will you say when you meet this would-be king? We do not have enough men to fight him."

I nodded towards the hessian sacks we had brought. "We killed most of his best warriors. I want him to know that they are all dead. I want his men to see that their leader abandoned them. I do not think they will try to attack us. Then I will demand reparations for their attack."

"Reparations?"

"Ketil, we do not want the land of the Northumbrians. We are happy with the Land of the Wolf. Nor do we want to have to fight against these Saxons. They are like fleas on a dog. No matter how many you kill more will breed. I want him to pay us not to attack him. If he wishes to be king then he has to defeat or usurp Æthelred. He had thought to enlarge the land he controlled first. Now that he can no longer do that then he might be willing to accept a peace which allows him to gain the throne."

Haaken nodded, "And that is why you, Jarl Dragonheart, lead this clan. With due respect to your grandson, Ragnar, he would not have the mind to come up with such a plan."

"He is young and he will learn. When I was his age this would not have occurred to me. I would have brought the whole of my clan over to fight and defeat them rather than a warband. There are times to risk young men's lives and times to use old men's heads. This is a time for old men's heads."

The next day was a harder one. The wounds and the riding were taking their toll. Ketil looked in pain and the Ulfheonar were no longer young men. However, we showed what we were made of as we joined the Roman road. We could see the citadel of Dunelm. Ahead of us, just a mile away was the last remnant of the army which had escaped us. The banners of the Saxons drooped and the fyrd who remained trudged wearily. There were at least ninety of them. There had been more who had fled. Some would have gone directly to their homes. Others would have died. I guessed that those who remained with Rædwulf lived north of Dunelm.

Our appearance startled them. Perhaps they thought I had brought my whole army. I smiled to myself as that idea was born. Rædwulf and his mounted men abandoned the foot and galloped for the bridge over the Wear.

I laughed, "Come, let us see if we can make these Saxons fill their breeks!"

The men I led were the best that I had. They saw this as an opportunity for glory and honour. We had yet to be defeated and what we saw before us was unlikely to do so. We dug our heels in our mounts. The exception was Haraldr who just slapped the rump of his horse with his mighty ham-like hands. The panic amongst the Saxons was clearly visible. None wished to be caught by Vikings. The press at the bridge was such that I saw men falling into the waters of the Wear. The gates of the citadel lay open. If I had had an army with me then I might have been able to capture it. They slammed them shut leaving thirty of the fyrd cowering outside.

We reined in close to the bridge. Saxons did not have many archers but if we had gone any closer might have risked an arrow from the few that they had. I took off my helmet and drank some ale. "Give the horses water. Haaken, Olaf, fetch those sacks."

It was almost laughable. The fyrd who cowered were on their knees praying to their god to save them. My men were laughing and attending to our horses. We reached the far side of the bridge. We were just two hundred paces from the walls. They were only wooden but they were still a barrier. I saw Rædwulf on the fighting platform.

I cupped my hands and shouted, in Saxon, "Rædwulf, you came to my land to make war on my people. You are not a king but you would be one." I waved my arms and Haaken and Olaf opened the sacks and emptied the bloody skulls on the ground before us. I saw the priests on the walls make the sign of the cross. "These were the brave warriors you sacrificed. My men thank you for their mail and their swords. They make us stronger and the deaths of these make you weaker."

I waited. I was in no hurry. The longer his men stared at the heads without Rædwulf speaking made his position more desperate.

"What is it you want, Viking?"

I pointed behind me, vaguely to the west. "I have an army which has enjoyed a great victory over Saxons who came treacherously to make war. They are keen to continue that war. They wish to make Northumbria a wasteland."

When he spoke, I could hear the fear in his voice, "What do I need to do to make peace with you?"

I spread my arms, "We Vikings have something called weregeld. Your people, when they were warriors, had the same thing. We wish payment for the dead and as a punishment for your raid. We want thirty horses and five hundred gold pieces. You have until the sun begins to set." I took out my sword and pointed it at the walls, "Those of your men who escaped the slaughter on the Eden will tell you of the wolves who came in the night. If night falls and no payment is forthcoming then," I swept my sword to the west, "the wolves will come and we will enter your walls. None will be spared. Your church will be destroyed. Your warriors will be butchered. Your priests will be crucified and your women and children enslaved. It is your choice. It is your decision. Our blades have not yet tasted enough blood."

I saw the priests and thegns close by speaking with him. Haaken said, "Clever Jarl Dragonheart. He thinks our men are beyond the hill in the forest."

"I am not foresworn. I did not say so."

He laughed, "As I said, this is why you lead this clan!"

Rædwulf held up his hands, "You give your word that you will leave when we pay you?"

"I do but if you ever come again then the next time there will be no payment! There will be fire and there will be blood. The great divide marks the edge of your land. Any Saxon warrior found on our side will be given the blood eagle. What say you?"

"I say that I will not allow my men west of the high divide."

"Good. We will wait beyond the bridge." My men cheered as we returned to them. "Take off the saddles and rest the horses. Rest yourselves. We will leave after dark. I do not think that they will try anything but it is better to be careful. We have achieved that which I wished. Your lands, Ketil Windarsson, are safe."

As we made our way to the horses Ketil said, "And I have learned a lesson, Jarl Dragonheart. I thought I had been vigilant. I was not. We will not be content to wait for enemies to sneak into our land, we will guard our borders."

Rædwulf kept his word but I noticed that he did not come himself with the horses and bags of coins. He sent ten of the fyrd and four priests. The priests kept hold of their crosses. One had a strange looking staff. I discovered from Atticus that it was called a crozier. They scowled at us but did not say a word. We saddled the new horses and loaded the bags onto the spares. We headed west into the setting sun. With fresh horses and using the Roman Road, we were able to make fifteen miles before we needed to camp. It meant we reached Pennryhd before dark, the next day. I gave half of the ransom to Jarl Ketil Windarsson and Jarl Ráðulfr Ulfsson. I also left them half of the horses. Haraldr and Aðils' horses were waiting for us at Pennryhd. Jarl Ráðulfr Ulfsson had realised that Haraldr needed his mighty beast to carry him. We celebrated our victory at the Stad on the Eden. I did not begrudge the young warriors the drunken night. They had earned it. I saw and drank sparingly.

My small band of Ulfheonar and Haraldr Leifsson left for my home the next day. I was weary. I was getting too old for such travelling. I needed my steam hut and I needed to bathe. I wanted to sleep in my own hall.

We bade farewell to Beorn, Aðils and Haraldr north of Cyninges-tūn. I knew that Beorn would never fight as Ulfheonar again. He would lead men but the wolf cloak would remain in his chest. Aðils, too, was keen to stay on his farm in the dale. It was almost as though this was the end of something. I would now have but four Ulfheonar who would go to war with me. I was aware that Rolf and Rollo now had families. When would the call of their loved ones outweigh the lure of the raid?

Ragnar had sent my share of the treasure to my hall. I distributed half of it amongst my people. The ones who had lost warriors were given more. The money would not compensate for the loss; it would never do that. It was there to make sure that they lived as well as possible.

Atticus fussed over me. He saw the nicks and damage to my mail and shook his head. He knew that such damage could have led to a wound, "You are the leader, lord! Others should fight."

"And they do but I lead."

"You are strange people. In the land of the Empire when a warrior becomes successful and older he commands others. He sits on a horse and waved his sword to direct them where he wants them to go."

"I am content."

And I was. Atticus had, while I had been in Frisia and in the north, made my home more comfortable. I wondered what old Ragnar would have thought. His mountain top hut had been just one small room with a bed for him and a shelf for me. He also expressed a desire to come to Bruggas with me. Atticus had had wall hangings made which kept the hall warmer and brightened it up. He had had women make cushions so that my chair was now almost as comfortable as my bed. He was a thoughtful servant.

"There are things there, lord, which we need. You have almost run out of spices. A man cannot live without pepper, cloves, nutmeg and the other spices. You have coin!" He acted as a moneyer for me. He knew to the groat how much I had. He had even suggested that we mint our own coins with a wolf on them. "I am certain that the Saxon moneyers cheat us. I have examined the coins we were paid and not all are true metal. Some have other metals in them!"

We all knew it went on. Others would nick a piece from a coin. It was hardly noticeable unless someone else nicked a piece. I thought he was right but it seemed like a lot of hard work and we did not need it. He had my mail repaired for me and new seal skin boots made. My travels and the sea had worn them out. He had a full-sized seal skin cloak made for me. He did not wish me to suffer in the winter storms. We would be travelling to Bruggas at the end of Þorri. He was fussy but he was right.

The next moons flew by. Ragnar and Gruffyd raided the Welsh and brought back sheep and wheat. We had Samhain and then Yule. I visited my family at Whale Island and Kara and Aiden dreamed for me. They still warned me of the slaughter of the Vikings. I wondered how I would get out of joining Hvitserk Ragnarsson. Part of me hoped he would not get enough ships and I would be saved the embarrassment of refusing to lead them. When I visited Ragnar and Gruffyd, at Yule, I saw Erik Short Toe and had him prepare my drekar for the voyage. I would not need warriors. I needed rowers and so, apart from Olaf and Haaken, who insisted on accompanying me, I sailed with those who had goods to trade. Raibeart Ap Pasgen wished to come too.

As winter was upon us Atticus and I travelled down two days before we were due to sail. That meant I had time with my son, grandson and great-grandsons. As we were just trading and there would be no raid I wondered if the boys would still wish to travel with me. They did. I saw both Astrid and Ebrel as the boys affirmed their decision. I said, "I am willing to take you but only if your mothers agree. It is winter and the seas can be dangerous. And of course, you will be able to have lessons from Atticus as he will be sailing with us." I wondered if the threat of studies might have put them off but it did not.

The three of them pleaded with their mothers who had, of course, little choice in the matter. Travelling in the harsh seas of winter meant a different sort of preparation. They needed seal skins boots and capes. We would be sleeping on deck and so they would need good blankets too. They were all excited but I knew that Sámr had some idea of the hardships we would face. He counselled the other two and I saw the first signs of the man he would become. As there was no rush to reach Bruggas for the ransom would be waiting for us no matter what, Erik waited until we had winds from the north. That meant that the Land of the Wolf would be covered in a blanket of snow. The winds came from the far north and always brought snow. For all but our crew that would mean staying in the halls and occupying themselves with all the tasks that waited for winter; carving fish hooks from bones, sewing, making handles for axes and swords, adding adornments to helmets and mail, repairing shields and, of course, making more Vikings!

As we were using our sails Mordaf and Ulla War Cry were thrown into the art of sailing immediately. Sámr came into his own. Along with Lars Long Nose, they offered advice and help. They warned of dangers. By the time the sails were set to the satisfaction of Erik Short Toe, half a morning had gone and we were passing Man. If the gods were kind then they would not be needed again until we came close to the coast of Ynys Môn. Sámr made them don their new seal skin capes and ordered them to take shelter beneath the awning which had been rigged over the mast fish.

Ulla War Cry did not take kindly to being ordered around, "Who are you, Sámr Ragnarsson to tell me what to do?"

Sámr stood over his little brother, "I am, along with Lars, the senior ship's boy and what are you, Ulla War Cry? Until you learn how to climb the mast in a storm then you are a piece of cordage without a purpose."

Ulla looked at me and I shook my head, "Do not look at me. I am jarl on this voyage and besides Sámr is right. You begged to come on this voyage and that means, until you learn to be useful then everyone can tell you what to do. Sámr had to endure this on his first voyage. No one made you come. Now that we are set on our course there is no turning back. You have made this decision and you have to live with it. That is how you become a man. Those who fail and cannot live with the choices they make are nithings."

Atticus, shivering beneath two cloaks and a blanket, shook his head, "You breed hard men, lord."

"If a boy survives a couple of voyages then he is almost ready to become a warrior. If he fails, or, as sometimes happens, dies, then that is the Allfather's way of saying he was not a Viking."

"And I thought my life as a slave was hard. It was nothing compared with this." He pointed to the mast. "I would not go up there on a sunny day, on dry land, with the aid of a ladder! Yet they shin up with the ship pitching over that black and unforgiving sea."

I smiled, "Aye, and you are Greek. Your seas are benign. Your storms are like the showers of Einmánuður in the Land of the Wolf. If we are to survive in these seas then that is what we must do. The Allfather made us Vikings by putting us in the harshest land that there is. That is why we go to Valhalla and you do not."

We stayed at the Puffin Island. The boys enjoyed collecting their eggs. We ate well. Atticus was more interested in the monastery perched high above the sea. "These are not like the monks I saw in Cent."

"No, these are simple men who honour their god by their devotion and prayers. We leave them alone for they are not greedy. They do not seek power. I admire them for they live where life must be hard. They are the closest men to Vikings that I have seen in the world of the White Christ."

We sailed south and crossed the mouth of the Sabrina. We skirted the rocky coast of Om Walum. The wind was in our favour and all was going well. Perhaps we were complacent. It was winter but the winds were aiding us. We grew confident. We talked of our destination and we forgot our journey. It was as we were about to begin rowing that the winds died and, worse, fog began to rise from the sea like smoke. Ulla War Cry, Sámr and Mordaf had to earn their berth for Erik could see nothing. With the rowers just keeping our way, we picked our way east. We only had one man to an oar. We were not going to war and the ship had a half empty feel.

It was Ulla War Cry who made the mistake. He shouted, "White water!" He was clinging to the forestay. A wave or perhaps a Norn made the drekar pitch. Ulla might have been excited to have reported the white water or he may just have been unlucky, but he slipped from the stay and into the sea. I was frozen but his brother was not. Sámr threw off his sea boots and dived into the sea. Both boys could swim but Ulla had on his sea boots which threatened to drag him down.

As he disappeared I yelled, "Back oars!"

Lars Long Nose grabbed a length of rope and secured one end around the mast. Holding the other end, he peered over the side. The white water meant rocks. The sea currents were making us bob up and down and, in the murk of the fog it was hard to see anything. Suddenly he shouted, "I see Ulla War Cry! Catch the rope!"

He hurled the rope and I peered into the grey, white flecked swirling sea. I saw my great-grandson. He looked tiny. I clutched the dragon around my neck. In my head I intoned, *'Erika, save your great-grandsons. They are beyond my reach. Save them.'* I opened my eyes as there was a cheer. I saw that Ulla had grabbed the end of the rope and was being hauled on board. His boots were gone. I looked for Sámr and, of him, there was no sign. As Ulla was dragged on board Atticus came and threw a blanket around him. I picked up the blanket draped boy. He looked so tiny. He was too young to be at sea.

He was coughing and spluttering. He had swallowed sea water. I shouted, "Look for Sámr! He will be close by!"

Atticus said, "Put him on the deck lord and on his side. I will get the water from within him."

I did as Atticus said. I saw that his eyes were closed and he was no longer moving. Atticus put him on his side and began to massage his back whilst pulling at his middle. Suddenly Ulla convulsed and, coughing, brought up sea water. He retched and vomited and then began to cry. I picked him up and held him close to me. It was as though he was a bairn once more. I rubbed his back and began to speak into his ear, "You are safe. Njoror did not want you. You are safe."

His sobs gradually subsided and he said, "Where is Sámr? He saved me. He dived beneath me to take off my boots."

I said, quietly, "We are still seeking him. He is a good swimmer. He will surprise us yet."

Gradually the fog dissipated. The grey murk of mist was replaced by the bright blue sky of a chilly Einmánuður afternoon. The water was as still as the icy Water of my home in the depths of winter. The crew lined the side. Ulla shouted, forlornly, "Sámr! Sámr! Sámr!" I put my arm around him.

Erik Short Toe came down the ship, "Jarl Dragonheart, I do not like to be the one to say it but he is gone. He is in the Otherworld."

I closed my eyes and tried to picture him. If he was gone then Erika would appear. She would be with the spirit of Sámr. They would put my mind at rest. Neither would allow me to be tormented. Nothing came into my head. "No Erik, we search until dark."

He nodded, "And that will not take long, Jarl Dragonheart. The afternoon is fading fast."

I walked to the other side of the drekar. I could see, in the distance, the small islands and large rocks which made up this land. We were close to Syllingar! Suddenly there was a cry, almost a scream, from the bow. I ran, fearing that someone had seen Sámr's beaten body. Instead, I saw a terrified Lars Long Nose. He was pointing ahead, "Jarl Dragonheart I swear I saw a rock rise from the ocean and look there is an island. See the smoke which comes from it. This is magic."

Atticus had joined us, "No, Lars. There was some fog lingering there. The afternoon sun has burned it away. Islands cannot rise from the sea."

I did not contradict Atticus. In a way he was right. The island had been hidden but it had been hidden by the power of the witch who lived there. I knew where Sámr was. Haaken, Olaf, Raibeart and Erik joined me. I saw, even on the face of Olaf Leather Neck, the most fearless warrior I knew, horror etched in every line.

Haaken stroked his white hair, "Dragonheart if he is there...."

"Then the witch wants her revenge. We should have made a blót. Kara should have made a spell of protection but all that is in the past. It is too late. I must go to the island and face her." I turned, "When Sámr returns then you must leave."

"I will come with you this time Jarl Dragonheart. Haaken One Eye endured it once. It is my turn."

"No, Olaf. You are a brave warrior but the witch wants one thing, me. I must exchange my life for Sámr. I have lived long enough. I have done enough. Haaken, you command until you return to Whale Island."

He nodded. They all gave the silent agreement. They knew I was right. Ulla War Cry and Mordaf grabbed my legs, "You cannot leave!"

"I must. Sámr gave his life for you Ulla War Cry. I can do no less for him." I held up my hand, "Let us row to the island. Jarl Dragonheart will descend, once more to the bowels of the earth. It has been both an honour and a privilege to lead such a Viking warband. No jarl ever led better warriors."

They knew I was going to my death and they began banging the deck with the hilts of their daggers.

"To your oars!"

It was almost a funereal pace as we edged across the glassy sea to the smoking island. To protect me I had my sword and dagger. Around my neck I had the dragon and the wolf. The Allfather had had a purpose when he had sent me from the Dunum to Norway. He had made my sword the most powerful in the world. I had to trust that he would protect my great-grandson and, if I deserved it, me.

We reached the beach. Erik and Haaken had done this before. Lars leapt ashore. I felt that was an incredibly brave thing to do but he and Sámr were ship brothers. It was what you did. He wrapped the rope around a rock to keep her bow on. I took off my sea boots and jumped into the water. It was bone chillingly cold. I knew the path I must take. I walked on the virgin sand and headed behind the large rocks. It was as all the other times I had descended.

I entered the black maw that was the cave. This was not like Myrddyn's cave. That had a wide entrance and a high roof. This one felt like you were descending into a tiny grave. It was hard to put one foot in front of the other but I somehow managed it. There was a glow but it was not as bright as it normally was. The smoke I could smell was old and it was dead. I had to watch my footing for the stones were slick. As I turned the corner I saw that the fire had not been doused. It was a soft red glow. I took a breath as I stepped around and peered into the dark.

I heard a cackle, "I will say this for you, Dragonheart, you truly have the heart of a dragon. You know that you come to your enemy. You believe, in your heart, that you will never leave this cave alive and yet still you come."

"The last time you took my granddaughter, Ylva, and now you take my great-grandson. You are a barren old crone who cannot conceive herself. It is sad that you have to steal my children to gratify yourself." I could not see her but I felt her presence.

The cackling laughter came from closer to me, "Not only fearless but reckless. You risk my ire and insult me. If I did not know that your mother worshipped our cult I would swear that you had sprung from my womb!"

"Enough of this. I am here to exchange my life for Sámr. I know you have him. I can now almost smell your magic! Where is he?"

The laughter was gone and the voice was filled with contempt, "You are a mortal and cannot fathom the mind and the plans of a Norn! You know nothing of this! You stole that which we wanted and one day there will be vengeance. Some day you will suffer such terror that it will drive you mad and then we will be satisfied. For the moment you serve our purposes. You are here to do our bidding. Do not command me! I command you!"

The cave suddenly filled with red. It was a mixture of fire and smoke. I could see nothing save red. It was as though blood had become smoke. The heat was all around me. I was burning. It was the heat of a dragon! The witch had conjured a worm to end my life. I began to cough. My eyes watered. The heat became so intense that I felt as though I would melt. Then I struggled to breathe. It was as though the smoke or the dragon or the witch, I knew not which, were strangling me. I flailed my arms but there was nothing to grab. I tried to fight but I was fighting smoke and heat. I found myself falling and the light went. It became black.

I was falling. My arms flailed. I saw Sámr. He was bound to a stake and, at his feet a fire burned. All went black. I opened my eyes and drew my sword. I looked beneath my feet. It was not sand. It was blood covered bodies. They stretched as far as the eye could see. They were Vikings. Most of them were Danes and I did not recognise them. They were not my clan. There were shattered spears and broken shields. I walked across them. Some were still alive for they moaned as I passed. Their bodies were slippery. I looked up and saw a shield wall. It was a Saxon shield wall. There was a king. He had a crown and next to him was a queen. I saw him put the crown upon her head. It was Osburga's crown. This was King Æthelwulf and his Queen, Osburga. He turned and, seeing me, began to laugh. I found that I was sinking into the dead and dying bodies. They were like human quicksand. The more I struggled the quicker I sank. My waist was beneath them. As my head slipped down I found myself drowning in dead men's blood. I closed my mouth and then my body was beneath the dead. I could not breathe. All went black.

"Jarl Dragonheart! Great Grandfather! Wake! What is happening?"

I opened my eyes. I still held Ragnar's Spirit. I was in the cave. There was a dull glow from a dying fire and Sámr sat, cradling my head. I smiled, "You have been to the Otherworld and you have survived. After this there is nothing for you to fear. Come, help an old man to his feet. We will talk when we are outside."

"But how do we get out? We are trapped!"

"Trust Ragnar's Spirit. It will find a way." I held my magic blade before me and I held Sámr's hand with my other. There was a glow from the blade. Some would say it was a reflection from the glow of the fire but I knew that it was the Allfather. I saw a lighter patch of dark and we walked towards it. The light became lighter and then we stepped out of the tomb-like cave. It was morning. As we walked into the sand I saw **'Heart of the Dragon'**. She was bobbing at anchor. The crew saw us and gave a cheer. They chanted, 'Dragonheart'. We had survived. The Norns would punish me but only when I had done their bidding.

Chapter 9

A breeze sprang from the north west and Erik wasted no time in hoisting the sail and getting us away from the enchanted isle. Atticus brought a cloak for Sámr. His wide eyes were filled with terror. No one said a word. There were questions in men's eyes but none dared speak. After they had set the sail the ship's boys came to see Sámr. Lars gently touched him as though he might disappear. Haaken handed me a horn of ale and Olaf gave one to Sámr. We raised them to each other and we drank. The two of us were bound now.

Erik shouted, from the stern, "The island has gone! It has vanished beneath the waves."

Atticus dropped to his knees and clutched his cross. He began to chant in Greek. For the first time in his life he had experienced the supernatural. I smiled at Sámr. He held my hand still. "Now you can speak. Tell me what you saw."

He shook his head, "You would not believe me! I saw it and I do not believe it."

Ulla War Cry blurted out, "You were drowned!"

"I thought I was. I found myself being dragged down. I sank to the bottom of the sea. When I looked I saw that I was held by the weed which clings to the rocks but I could not free myself. I pulled and then I banged my head. I dreamed or perhaps I went to the Otherworld." He shook his head. "I know not."

I said, quietly, "Just tell me what you saw, what you smelled, what you heard and what you said."

He looked at me, startled. "How do you know?"

"Just speak."

"I was in a hall. There were three women. They were not pretty like my mother or Ebrel. They were not kind looking like my grandmother or Great Aunt Kara. They had eyes which burned. They had talons for fingers and they had no flesh on their bones. Their hair was made up of writhing snakes. When they spoke, their words felt like ice. Their lips did not move but I heard their words. They chanted and told me that the Dragonheart must lead the Danes."

I leaned forward, "Tell me exactly what were the words they chanted. It is important."

He closed his eyes and when he began to chant it was as though the words were being spoken by someone else for it was not his voice.

> **The Dragonheart has a mighty sword**
> **He is known to keep his word**
> **When the Danes ask to lead their spears**
> **He must put aside his Danish fears**
> **His sword will make the Saxons shake**
> **He will live but the Danes will break**
> **Viking deaths are not the worst**
> **If he fails to lead then the clan is cursed**

He looked up at me. "I remembered every word! How did I do that?"

"You did not. You were bewitched." He looked afraid. "Fear not, when we are home Kara and Aiden will cure you."

Haaken asked, "And your dream, Jarl Dragonheart?"

I shook my head, "I will wait until I tell Kara but it confirms what Sámr said. I have no choice now. I must lead the Danish ships. There is no alternative. It may mean my doom but I cannot have my family and clan cursed."

Sámr nodded, "The old witch," he shivered, "she stroked my hair with her talon and said that you dared not spoil their web again. She said I would die in a pit of snakes." He threw his arms around me. "Please!"

"Fear not. I know now what I have to do. This is not of my making. It is not my choice but I cannot allow innocents to suffer because of me. I cannot fathom their plan. Perhaps it is just mischief but I will go along with them for the good of the clan."

The crew left me alone as we headed east to Bruggas. I could do nothing about the Norns. Whoever I took with me to Lundenwic would have to know that they would, in all likelihood, die. Who would choose to follow me? One thing was certain. My grandsons and great-grandsons would not be in the crew. I ran through my ships to choose the one which had the smallest crew. The Norns had given me an impossible task. I did not mind Danes dying but how could I allow men of my clan to die for them?

When we neared Bruggas I saw that they had built beacons to mark the entrance to the port. It made Erik's task easier. It was late by the time we had navigated the tidal estuary and so we slept aboard. We had time enough to visit Isaac and await the Danes. We were the only drekar in port. It was winter and journeys were harder. I set a good watch but I did not sleep well. When I spoke with the son of Ragnar Lodbrok would I be foresworn? I knew that the raid we planned would end in the deaths of many Danes. I could not walk away. The Danes expected me to lead them and the Norns had willed it. Whatever I did would not end well.

When I woke I made sure that my offspring remained on the drekar. I had come close to losing two of them. Haraldr, Haaken and Olaf would accompany me to Isaac's, Raibeart would go to the market. I wore my mail. I think I feared a killer. I knew not why. Olaf and Haaken always wore their mail. There was a calm reassurance about Haraldr. He was the least experienced of us and yet he seemed so calm that it inspired confidence. *Wyrd*. As we passed 'The Saddle', Sven was throwing out a drunk. Freya was behind him. She saw me and rushed out. Throwing her arms around me she kissed me. "Jarl Dragonheart! At last, we have a real man in this town!"

I hugged her and smiled, "You are kind to an old man!"

"Kindness does not enter into it. We hear how you dealt with those raiders to your land. You are a true leader and Viking. Is it true that you will raid Lundenwic?"

I felt a chill on my neck. If an alewife in Bruggas knew of the attack how much more would the Saxons know?

"We will be here for a few days. I would brew more ale. The Danes are coming."

She nodded. "We had been warned. That means you raid with the sons of Ragnar Lodbrok." She lowered her voice. "Be careful Jarl Dragonheart they are like their father. They are treacherous."

I put my arm around her shoulder and squeezed. "I am not a young innocent warrior. I know what they are like. I go into this with both eyes open."

She had old eyes. They were older than her body. She saw all of life in her ale house. There was wisdom there. I doubted that she could read. Making marks on a wax tablet was not the same as reading but she had something better. She had knowledge. Her eyes bored into mine. "I will have food ready when you have completed your business with old Isaac."

I laughed, "Do you know all and see all?"

"In Bruggas? Yes. This is my town."

It was a damp day. The drizzle had flecks of sleet in it. I was grateful for my seal skin cape. We did not have as long to wait when we knocked on the door of Isaac the Jew. The same warriors admitted the four of us. Isaac was in his cushioned seat poring over a parchment. A warming fire made the room cosy. He smiled when he saw me. "You came to the day. I like precision. Most of the Vikings I deal with spend so long drunk that time means nothing to them. You are different. You know that time is as valuable as gold and must not be wasted."

"Was the trade successful?"

His face became serious, "It was and we received a good price but I should warn you, Dragonheart of the Land of the Wolf, Æthelwulf has put a price on your head." He rolled his eyes, "Literally, your head. Five hundred talents are promised to whoever brings him your head." He waved a hand at my three men. "You are wise to surround yourself with such men. And the books brought a good price. We sold those to a Count of the Franks. He had a monastery he was going to endow. These Christians have a strange religion. Their leader was a poor carpenter and yet they think they can buy their way to heaven." He shrugged. "It makes money for us both. Oddvakr, fetch the chest with the coin."

One of the warriors left the room. "Tell me, Isaac of Bruggas, what do you hear of a Danish raid on Lundenwic."

He gave me a cunning smile, "Do not try to use guile Dragonheart it is not in your nature. You mean the raid you are to lead?" I nodded. "The Danes have been using your name all along the western coasts. There are many who wish to follow your magical sword. If you are asking me do the Saxons know then the answer is yes. I am no warrior but even if I was a warrior as great as you I would not undertake this venture."

Oddvakr returned with the chest. "I am afraid that I have no choice in this matter."

"All men have choices, Jarl Dragonheart."

I opened the box and put my hands to the bottom. I brought out golden coins. Satisfied I closed the lid. I waved my hand at the house in which he lived, "And you chose to live here in this damp and dangerous part of Frisia instead of a warm, lemon-fragranced garden by the Blue Sea?"

His eyes became sad, "I was driven out by the ones who follow Islam. It is not the same."

"It is, Isaac of Bruggas. Both of our Fates are determined by others and we follow the course that was set out for us. All that we can do is the best with what is given us. We both survive and we both do well. That is all that a man can do."

He stood, "I can see why you have lived so long, Jarl Dragonheart. May God watch over you. I hope that you survive and that we can do business again. We trust each other, I think."

I clasped his outstretched arm, "We trust each other."

Haraldr carried the chest. We had seen other warriors in the streets on our way to Isaac's but now that we knew there was a price on my head there was an air of danger. We went directly to the drekar. We secured the chest in the hold. Raibeart and the other merchants had not returned and so we waited with Erik and the crew. Sámr, Ulla, Mordaf and Lars sat together. They seemed almost afraid to be out of each other's sight.

"Haraldr, I would have you watch those four. We will send you food and ale from the 'Saddle'."

He bowed his head, "It would be an honour Jarl Dragonheart. Young Sámr is made of good stock. To have survived the sea and," he clutched the amulet around his neck, "and the witch." He shook his head, "How can any man fight the spirits?"

Haaken One Eye rubbed his thinning, white hair, "It is not easy, Haraldr but the Allfather favours the Dragonheart. When he fights them, he is not alone."

Raibeart returned and he and the others had serious expressions on their faces. "Was it poor trading, Raibeart ap Pasgen?"

"The trading was good but the news was not. Æthelwulf has put a price on your head. He was outraged that you almost took his wife. The rumour is that she is now guarded by ten housecarls. She and the King's sons never leave his burgh in Wintan-Caestre. It is good that you wear your mail. The price would tempt many poor men to end your life."

Olaf Leather Neck growled, "And they would have to get past me to do so!"

I did not want men to die for me. I had to find a way out of this dilemma. "Come, half of us will go to the 'Saddle' now. I am hungry and ready for a drink." I looked at the four ship's boys. "Do you wish to come? If you do not then Haraldr can watch over you."

They looked at each other. Sámr said, "If you do not mind, Jarl Dragonheart, we are content here. My mind is too full of thoughts and the noise of the alehouse would be too confusing." He looked up at Haraldr. "Besides Haraldr has good stories to tell of life in Lang's Dale

"Perhaps that is what you need. Do not dwell on the cave."

"I have to. I need to understand what it means and what I must do. Be careful."

"Thank you, son of Ragnar, it is good that you think of an old man."

When we entered the alehouse, Freya had cleared a table for us. "Here to celebrate, Jarl? Old Isaac gave you much gold I hear."

"And no doubt your prices will reflect our success."

"Of course. We are a small town and we help each other." She leaned closer and spoke into my ear, "And we listen out for those who would be a knife in the night. When I hear of anything then I will let you know."

The food was good; it was hot and hearty. It was perfect for such a damp day and the ale, warmed with a poker, flowed freely. None of us drank as much as we wished. Until I was safe in Cyninges-tūn I would be on my guard. The days were short still and we left the ale house in the dark. Sven checked the street before we left. We did not ask him to do so. He nodded, "The ones on the street I know. They might be beggars and thieves but they are not killers. Freya has put the word out. We will hear of those who might wish you harm."

The Danes did not arrive for three days. They came in two drekar. We watched them negotiate the tricky passage to the quay and tie up. I recognised Hvitserk Ragnarsson. There were two other warriors dressed as finely as he. They would be the other jarls. He waved as they tied up. A young warrior left the drekar and came down to speak to us, "The jarl would speak with you. Will you come aboard?"

Mindful of the threat from those wishing to take the bounty, I shook my head, "Tell him we will meet him in the 'Saddle'. Our business can be conducted over food and ale."

The young warrior did not seem offended, "Of course, Jarl Dragonheart."

The three of us headed down to the alehouse. I wanted the majority of my crew on board my drekar. We were three Ulfheonar. We could handle whatever danger came our way. As we entered I said, "Sven, we have some Danes coming to speak with us."

He nodded, "We will watch your back, jarl. Freya is fond of you."

I took off my cape and shook the water into the street. It had been a short journey from the ships but if we had not had our capes then we would have been soaked. Cloaked and caped men walking towards us had been a threat on our walk and I was glad to be in the cosy warmth of the alehouse. Freya brought over the beer. She was about to say something when Hvitserk Ragnarsson entered. The two Danes with him had tattooed faces and pieces of bone in their hair. They looked like savages.

Hvitserk Ragnarsson smiled, "You came! That is good, Jarl Dragonheart. These are two of my brothers, Sigurd Snake in the Eyes and Halfdan Ragnarsson." The two men grunted and sat down. I could see that Hvitserk Ragnarsson was the one who was closest to normal. Freya brought ale. She held out her hand for coins. Hvitserk counted it out and Freya shook her head. He paid more. I hid my smile. She was charging him for our ale.

Sigurd Snake in the Eyes snapped, "Get on with it little brother. The more time we spend here in Bruggas the less time we have for raiding,"

Hvitserk Ragnarsson nodded, "I have good news jarl, I have the promise of over three hundred and ten dragon ships. I told you that your name would draw men."

"So you did."

Halfdan asked, as I drank some of my beer, "Well? Will you lead us?"

"I told you that I would think about it. Your plan to raid Lundenwic does not need three hundred ships. You could take the burgh with ten ships and good men."

Olaf Leather Neck wiped his mouth with the back of his hand, "Or forty ships filled with Danes."

Haaken laughed and Halfdan and Sigurd's hands went to their knives. I kept my voice steady, "Peace. If you cannot take banter then we will bid you farewell. If you have three hundred ships then you do not need me." The brothers looked at one another. "So there is something else apart from the raid on the Temese. Speak. Like your brother I am anxious to be gone. We have waited here three days for you. The port fees are an expense I like not."

"You are right, Jarl Dragonheart. Lundewic is the start. We leave our ships in the river and we take our men to Wintan-Caestre. If Lundenwic is rich then how much richer will King Egbert's old capital be?"

"And why do you need me?"

"You have fought the Saxons in battle before. We have raided but you have defeated King Egbert himself. No other warrior has managed that. And we thought to have a kingdom here."

"With me as king?" The three of them nodded. "Then you have the wrong man. I seek no throne." I thought back to my dream. I thought of Sámr's dream. The Danes were doomed and I would be the one who would lead them to that doom. If I did not do so then my land and my clan would be cursed. I could live with a curse on me but not those I loved. "However, I bear no love for Æthelwulf. I have no doubt you heard he put a price on my head."

Sigurd Snake in the Eyes smiled, it was not a pleasant smile. "It is a small fortune."

Olaf leaned forward, "Do not think to claim it Dane." Sigurd looked down and saw that Olaf's seax was touching his groin.

I smiled, "There will be no treachery, Olaf Leather Neck. It is in our new friends' interest to keep me alive. I will lead you. So long as you obey my orders then I will ride at your head. If there is dissent or disobedience then I will leave. Is that fair?"

Only Hvitserk Ragnarsson assented. That worried me. "We will gather the fleet at the Isle of the Sheep at Harpa. This is a great day!"

I drained my ale and nodded, "Until Harpa." I waved over to Freya. She came to my side. I gave her one of the coins we had from Isaac. "Thank you for your hospitality. It will be some time before I return."

"Take care. A man only has so much luck. Do not waste yours on feckless Danes."

She was right. I had had more than my fair share of good luck. Was I about to risk all? It was the Norns.

Part Two
The Great Viking Raid

Chapter 10

I spent the voyage north closeted with Atticus and my Ulfheonar. Atticus had not been idle. When we had been in Bruggas he had uncovered information. He had used his wax tablet to help him to remember. We knew that there were another three brothers who were back in Denmark. They had ravaged the land of the East Angles. There was little left there to take. Atticus also learned that King Æthelwulf had sent his thegns to pay Isaac. They had not hurried back to Wessex. They had asked many questions about me and the Land of the Wolf. King Egbert's son was as cunning as his father.

The four of us worked out what we ought to do. "I will not risk my family on this venture. It seems I am doomed to die. I will take *'Red Snake'*."

"*'Red Snake'*! She has not sailed for four years. She is rotten!" Haaken was disappointed.

"And she is just a threttanessa!" Olaf Leather Neck was outraged.

"The Danes did not say I had to bring a large ship or a large crew! I will not risk a ship I care about. Bolli and Erik can make her seaworthy. She has served us well. If this is her end then let us make it a glorious one." They nodded. Atticus looked confused. He did not understand our love of ships. "And I take only volunteers who know that we are not coming back."

Atticus said, "You do not know that, lord. The Danes may succeed besides the rhyme Sámr told was that you would live."

"The Norns are devious. They play with words. If I was leading three hundred ships with jarls I had chosen then we might succeed. I am leading Danes. I am no fool, Atticus. When we have conquered Wessex then they will kill me, take my sword and fight amongst themselves until just one remains alive. He will be king!" I shook my head. "They will fail. My dream told me that. I will do nothing to make that happen. I will not be foresworn, even to Danes. I said I would lead them to victory until they disobeyed me and I will do so. That is why, Atticus, I will take only volunteers. I will take no married men."

"Save Ulfheonar."

I looked at Haaken One Eye, "You wish to die?"

"I have stood back to back with you since the fighting platform in Norway. Our threads are twisted together so much that we cannot separate them. This married man will be with you and there is naught you can do about it, Jarl Dragonheart."

We passed Man and approached Whale Island. I was not looking forward to telling my grandson and his wife of the disaster which almost befell their family. I was a man and that was what men did. They faced up to those things they did not want to do but knew they had to. As we approached my land I gathered the three boys around me. "What happened at Syllingar was a most frightening and, in many ways, wondrous thing. You, Sámr, thought not of yourself but your brother and risked your life to save him. It was also terrifying. I will the one to tell your parents. Do you understand?"

They nodded.

"Sámr I will send for Kara, Aiden and Ylva. You need their help."

"I am well."

Haaken was behind me, "No you are not. I remember that I was haunted by the nightmares of the witch for many months. Sometimes I wake up, even now, and I am sweating and shaking. Your father, Mordaf, also met the witch and he took some time to recover. You will do as the Dragonheart says for you owe him a life, Sámr. He risked his own life to bring you back. He was willing to exchange his for you. No man can ask more."

"Then I will do as you say for I am always your warrior. Before I am your great-grandson I am a member of the Clan of the Wolf."

The three of them were kept busy as we tacked into the narrow harbour. "Haaken and Olaf, bring the chest ashore as soon as you can. I must speak to Ragnar and Gruffyd as soon as we land. I know that the crew will be eager to tell their tale. I would prefer the truth came out before the legends begin."

It was not wet but it was cold. The wind was from the east. It penetrated cloaks and kyrtles. My family, waiting to greet us, were well wrapped up. I stepped off the drekar first. The three boys waved at them and then carried on with their duties. I put my arms around Astrid and Ebrel. "Come, take this old man inside where there is a fire. I am chilled to the bone."

Ebrel said, "But Mordaf..."

"Mordaf is a ship's boy. He has duties to attend to. He will come when Erik releases him."

Ragnar said, "Let us go inside so that Dragonheart can tell us what happened."

"You are galdramenn now?"

He laughed, "No but you have never in your life worried about being cold. You wish us to go inside and then you will tell us."

Ebrel said, "The boys are well?"

"The boys are well. Come inside and let me tell all."

When they were seated and my cloak removed we sat. Atticus came in and stood behind me. I told them of the fog, the rocks. I told them of the cave and the dreams. I told them of my promise to the Danes.

"But you said the boys were well."

"And so they are."

Atticus said, "Mistress, I have spoken with them. If that had happened to me I would still be shivering and shaking but Sámr and Ulla War Cry are Vikings. My lord has not lied. The boys are healthy." He looked at me and I nodded.

"But I will send for Kara, Aiden and Ylva. If there is a spell on him then they can remove it." I looked at my son. "Remember?"

He smiled and put his arm around Ebrel. "I met the witch. I survived. Sámr is strong." He looked at me. "But I do not like this raid on Wessex. From what you say it is doomed to failure."

"Perhaps although it is hard to tell where the Norns are concerned." I saw Ragnar look at Gruffyd. "And before you say anything else you will not be raiding with me. I take only volunteers and only single men. If it is doomed to failure then the fewer I lose from the clan the better."

The door opened. A chill wind came with it and Sámr, Ulla War Cry and Mordaf stood there. It was as though a dam had burst. Astrid ran to her sons and hugged them. Ebrel picked up Mordaf and began to examine him as though he was possessed. When Sámr broke away from his mother he said, "I am not married, Jarl Dragonheart. I will come raiding with you."

I shook my head, "No, you will not. There is no argument. I sail with just twenty-eight warriors and no ship's boys. I will be my own helmsman. That is my decision."

I knew there would be arguments but I had made up my mind. I divided the coins from the crown and the books and left the next morning with Atticus and Olaf Leather Neck. The snows had melted leaving behind a muddy morass. The journey was less than pleasant. As we headed north Atticus questioned me closely. "Why are you so certain that you have to do as this Norn creature wishes?"

Olaf Leather Neck answered for me, "I am a warrior and I fear no man. These Norns are not men and they are not human. You cannot kill them."

"They are not real."

I turned to him. "Then where did Sámr go? You saw me disappear beneath the earth and return after a night had passed. Where did I go? What happened to the island?" I pointed to the leather tube he carried. In it were maps. "You marked the position of the island on your charts?" he nodded. "Then you could find it again easily."

"Of course, lord."

"No, you could not... We have tried. Aiden and Erik know exactly where the island lies and yet we have never found it unless the Norns wished us to. It appears when the Norns command. That is why I must do as the Norns have instructed me. The fate of my family, my clan and my land depend upon it."

"You are a strange people, jarl."

When we reached my home, I did not go to my hall I went to speak with Aiden and Kara. I could see that they were disturbed as soon as I began to speak. I finished telling them and Kara nodded, "We sensed that there was danger. The spirits came to us but the Norns hid themselves from us. You have to lead them."

"And we will lose." I said it as a statement and not a question. They both nodded. "How can you be so sure?"

"The Norns are punishing the Danes. I know not why. Perhaps they did not show them enough respect or they have offended the gods. There may be some other purpose. It does not do to delve too deeply into the minds of the Weird Sisters."

"And you will help Sámr."

"We will leave tomorrow. Ulla War Cry will have been affected too. He was sent into the sea by the Norns. He is part of their plans."

Before I went to my hall I walked around the Water to the place where I had had my first hall and the grave of my first wife, Erika. "Soon I may be with you wife. Thank you for interceding and saving Sámr. I need you to watch over all of them for I fear that I may not be here for much longer. If I do not die with a sword in my hand then remember me."

Perhaps it was my imagination but the Water suddenly flecked white and a breeze came from nowhere. In the skies above some migrating geese called. It was Erika. She had answered me.

I had my land to put in order. I left Atticus in charge of the hall. My first choice would have been Uhtric. Now he was getting too old. I spoke with Bagsecg. I gave him the coin to make three byrnies when the boys were old enough and a sword for each of them. I had more money than I would ever spend and I wanted it to be used for my offspring. I also took one of his helmets. Then I spread the word that I was looking for twenty-six warriors to go on a raid and that there was little likelihood of coming back alive. That done I left for Whale Island. I had a moon to prepare an old drekar for sea. *'Red Snake'* had been the drekar of Magnus the Foresworn. When we had slain him and his warband we had taken his ship as weregeld. We did not change the name; that was bad luck but the ship had served us well. Her hull was still sound. A coat of pine tar and new rigging and a sail and she would fly once more.

I went directly to the dock for Erik and Bolli were already working on her. They stopped when I arrived, "I can steer her Jarl Dragonheart. I am not afraid."

"I know Erik but I told you, single men only. Do you think I cannot steer?"

"Of course not it is just that you have yet to go to sea without me there. I sailed with you as ship's boy and then captain. This does not feel right."

"Is she sound?"

"She is sound. As she has been out of the water there is no weed. The pine tar is drying. She will need six days in the water for her timbers to swell. The mast is a good one. We have the sail and rigging ready to fit. All that we really need to do is to replace the steerboard withy."

"Good."

My reception in Ragnar's hall was a little frosty. I could see that he was still annoyed that I would not take him. I sought help from Aiden. "Tell my grandson that I think of him. He must stay here and lead the clan."

"Of course he must but Sámr must go with you." I looked at Kara. She had said it so calmly that it was almost like someone asking for a horn of ale.

"I told him no!"

"And you were wrong."

Astrid shook her head, "I cannot lose him!"

Kara said, "You will not." She held Astrid's hands in hers. "After we spoke with Sámr and we had put a spell on him we dreamed. We were lucky that Ylva was here visiting Bronnen for it was her power which allowed us to speak with Skuld."

I turned, "The Norn who predicts the future?"

"Yes, father. We saw, through a fog, the same fog which almost cost Sámr his life, Sámr grown a man with a wife and child. We saw not the faces of the wife and child but we saw Sámr. He will not die on this raid and he must go for his fate is tied to yours. We have not seen you in the future but in my heart, I know that if Sámr does not come with you then you will perish. If he comes with you then he will survive. As for you?" She shrugged.

Astrid said, "I do not believe in your witches!"

"And I do not believe in your god and his son who was killed and reborn but tell me this, sister, how else do you explain Sámr's story?"

Silence filled the hall. Astrid was beaten. I, too, was defeated and Sámr had a grin as broad as a sunrise on his face.

I walked, the day before I left, with Gruffyd and Ragnar. Haaken and Olaf Leather Neck were on the drekar assigning benches. With only one man to an oar, the balance was crucial. As we had Haraldr too we had to find another who was almost as big. Haraldr was also the only one without a full mail byrnie. We had so many volunteers that we had been able to choose young warriors with mail. We might have a small warband but we would be the best. Every warrior had a bow. All were good archers. I had the Saami bow and Aðils Shape Shifter had loaned his to Haraldr.

"You have a plan, grandfather?"

"Of course."

"I mean a plan to escape. It is obvious to all of us that the Norns intend for the Saxons to defeat you. I cannot see how they will do it for you have never been bested by a Saxon yet. So I ask again, how will you escape?"

I smiled. Ragnar knew me well. "We will take Lundenwic. With the numbers of men, they speak of we cannot do anything else. Then we march to Wintan-Caestre. I intend to have four of our men to sail *'Red Snake'* to the Isle of the Sheep. The land around there is boggy. It is full of inlets and tidal marshes. If things go badly for us then I will head there with whoever survives. If we can reach our ship then we will sail home."

"It is a long way from Wintan-Caestre to the Isle of the Sheep."

"Atticus has calculated it and it is one hundred miles. That is three or four days of hard marching or two days flogging a horse to death."

Gruffyd asked, "Why there and why not Lundewic? There will be ships at Lundenwic."

"And that is where every Dane who survives will flee. It is where the men of Wessex will go and it will be a trap! I have little enough hope but I am gambling on the Saxons following the largest army and not a small Viking warband."

"You forget that there is a price on your head. They will seek you first."

"This time I will not be wearing my wolf cloak and I have an open helmet. I hope to remain unrecognised by the Saxons."

Ragnar laughed, "There is little likelihood of that but you have a plan, at least." I nodded. "You will watch out for Sámr."

"He will be one of the four who sail the drekar down the Temese. I will keep him, if I can, from danger but we must believe Kara. She does not lie. If she says she saw him a man grown then he survives."

In the end there had been thirty of us who sailed. Twenty-six oarsmen, myself, Sámr and three replacement oarsmen. They would also act as crew when we sailed south. Atticus, Aiden and Erik all concurred. It might take twenty days to reach the Temese. I would allow a month for us to reach the Isle of the Sheep. I wanted to reach it first for it was a crucial part of my plan. It was a tearful farewell. I ended it by shouting, "We have the wind, farewell! Sámr, cast off!" Astrid had to jump off the drekar or risk coming with us.

It was some time since I had steered and the entrance was a tricky one. With the exception of Haraldr, the crew were all experienced. Although all were single not all were young. At least twelve had wives who had died. It meant that, under the guidance of Olaf and Haaken, we made the sea faster than I might have expected. Once there I let the wind take her. I needed to get the feel of her. I had Sámr and the two warriors who were assisting me to adjust the sails in the waters east of Man. We sailed quickly between man and Mercia. When I was confident I decided to risk the straits close to Ynys Môn. She was a lithe drekar and the winds were right. I felt the tension on the drekar as we rushed towards the incredibly narrow gap between the island and the mainland. Wyddfa towered over us and I sensed the presence of the spirit of Myrddyn and the Warlord. That made it easier and we skimmed through to the other side. We had saved half a day and I was happy.

Haaken One Eye came to the steering board, "The gods were with you then! I thought, for one moment, that we were going to end up on the rocks. Why take the risk?"

"There was no risk. The Norns have a task for me. Until I have completed it then I will be safe. After...? We will wait until that unlikely event occurs."

Haaken pointed to the masthead. I just had a white pennant flying. There was no wolf on the sail. "Why no banner?"

"They want the Dragonheart and his sword. This is not the Clan of the Wolf going to war. We are swords for hire. I can live with myself if I believe that. I will do my best to help the Danes achieve a victory. I would love to slaughter the King of Wessex and all of his men but I do not think it will happen."

He nodded, "It feels strange to be sailing without the rest of the Ulfheonar. I know the faces of some of these warriors but that is all."

"And is that not sad, Haaken One Eye? Times past we would have known them all. We would have supped with them and sung our songs together and now we struggle to remember their names."

We reached Syllingar a day later. It was getting close to sunset. I had Sámr close by the steering board for I saw the fear on his face. He was trying to hide it but I knew my great-grandson. Ragnar had given him Wolf Killer's wolf amulet which he wore around his neck. I leaned over to him. "Close your eyes and you will see the face of the grandfather you never knew."

"How will I know him?"

"You will know him. Now close your eyes and trust me."

He did so and I saw him look up in surprise a moment or two later. "I saw him and he smiled. He spoke in my head. He told me the Norns will not harm us."

"We are nearly through these waters and they will not bother us this voyage. On the way home, it may be a different matter. We will face that terror if we need to."

We did not sail far once we had passed the islands. I pulled in along the southern coast of Om Walum at a beach with a high cliff guarding it. We beached the ship and lit a fire. It was a risk but one I thought worth taking. There were no burghs close by and it would take an eagle to reach us. It meant we had hot food and slept ashore. When we left the next morning, the effects were obvious. The men were able to row with renewed vigour. We had to row towards the wind in order to take advantage of it and head east. We sang.

> *From mountain high in the land of snow*
> *Garth the slave began to grow*
> *He changed with Ragnar when they lived alone*
> *Warrior skills did Ragnar hone*
> *The Dragonheart was born of cold*
> *Fighting wolves a warrior bold*
> *The Dragonheart and Haaken Brave*
> *A Viking warrior and a Saxon slave*
> *When Vikings came he held the wall*
> *He feared no foe however tall*
> *Back to back with brave*
> *A Viking warrior and a Saxon slave*
> *When the battle was done*
> *They stood alone*
> *With their vanquished foes*
> *Lying at their toes*
> *The Dragonheart and Haaken Brave*
> *A Viking warrior and a Saxon slave*
> *The Dragonheart and Haaken Brave*
> *A Viking warrior and a Saxon slave*

It was the right song. It was the song of Haaken and me. With the wind from our quarter *'Red Snake'* flew across the seas. We would not need to row again. When we turned west into the estuary of the Temese this wind would still help us. We sailed without stopping. Haaken and Olaf took a turn each at the steering board while the crew slept and we rounded the headland just as dawn was breaking behind us. We heard the bell of the church at Cantwareburh. They were safe from us but they were a marker. The bell, calling the Christians to church told me that we were close. We were almost at the Isle of the Sheep. The first part of our journey was over. Now I had to plan so that we would have a return journey home! I took out the map Atticus and Aiden had made. I knew that the map and what we learned over the next days might be the difference between life and death. This was not about gold or glory; this was about survival. We would be in the land of the Saxons where every man wanted my head with Danes who were untrustworthy and serving Norns who wanted nothing less than my death.

Map showing Mersea Island, Foulness Island, Lundenwic, Temese, Canvey, Isle of Grain, and Isle of the Sheep.

Chapter 11

The only people who lived on the Isle of the Sheep were the shepherds. They had huts. The shepherds did not spend all their time on the island. They came across by boat and stayed for a short time until relieved. They would tell the men of Wessex that Vikings were around. We would have to eliminate them. The crew had rested and so, when we found a small muddy inlet we anchored and I sent four men to make sure that there were none close by. There was a stream of sorts and it enabled us to hide the drekar. I had the men pull the drekar up into the shelter of some low bushes which had survived the winds which whipped across this land. We stepped the mast. We would be rowing up the river. The mast and the sail would just signal our presence. When the Danes arrived that would not matter but when we were alone it would put us in danger.

While the mast was being placed on the mast fish I left the ship with Haaken One Eye. We walked inland. The only paths had been made by sheep. They wove between patches of water and bog. The land appeared to be equally divided between land and bog. I could see why the Saxons used it for sheep. The grass was lush. When we had walked half a mile we turned and looked back. We knew where the drekar lay but she was hard to see. I spied, between us and the ship just a dozen or so sheep. It was unlikely that a shepherd would disturb us. We returned to the ship.

Our boots were muddy from the short walk and so we washed them before we clambered back on board. Olaf asked, "Well, Jarl Dragonheart, are we hidden?"

"We are. Today we rest and then tomorrow I want us to make ourselves familiar with this island. We need to know it as well as we know the Land of the Wolf."

"But why, Jarl Dragonheart?"

I turned to Sámr, "You and four others will sail this ship here after we take Lundenwic. You will need to hide from Saxon eyes. If the raid to Wessex goes well and we are successful then we will sail here and pick you up. If, as I think more likely, we are unsuccessful then we will have to make our way here across the land of Cent. I know not where we will land when we do. That is why all of us need to know this island."

Ráðgeir Ráðgeirson arrived back with the other three scouts Erik Red Beard, Siggi Einarsson and Sven Svensson. Ráðgeir lived up by Elterwater and his family kept sheep. He knew the ways of sheep and shepherds. He pointed south. "The majority of the sheep are to the south of the island and the four shepherds who watch them have a hut there. That side of the island is sheltered a little from the northern winds. They have built a wind brake of woven reeds and willow. I think they would only venture north when it is lambing season. The lambs are born already."

Olaf Leather Neck nodded, "It seems, more by good luck than anything, we have found the perfect place to hide."

Haaken shook his head slowly, "Olaf, can you not see the hand of the witches in this? The webs and threads are there to guide us and protect us."

I nodded, "Aye, Haaken, and when they have done with us they are there to bind us."

Over the next seven days we explored the island. We found the fresh water. We found the places where wild food grew. We even came close to the shepherds. If we had to land on the south of the island then it would be important that we knew where they frequented. We saw their boat drawn up on the beach. Lying in the undergrowth above the small river which emptied into the southern channel we saw a small huddle of huts on the far side. There were fishing boats there but no burgh.

On the seventh day we spied the first of the Danish drekar as they sailed from the north. There were six of them and they were all big. They sailed beyond us to anchor in the Medway between us and the Isle of Grain. It made sense. It could accommodate all of the ships which Hvitserk had promised. The next day another twelve arrived. That night we removed the bushes we had used to disguise us and we pushed off to row and join the Danish fleet. We were well rested but it was a hard pull up the Tamese. When we turned into the Medway it became easier for that river was sluggish and the estuary wide.

The Danes kept a good watch and we were hailed, "What ship?"

Erik Red Beard cupped his hands, "**'Red Snake'**, Jarl Dragonheart from the Land of the Wolf!"

"We are **'Dragon Smoke'**, Jarl Halfdan Ragnarsson is the captain. Anchor to our steerboard."

I saw, as we dropped anchor, that half of the ships at anchor had also removed their masts. It marked those captains who knew what they were doing. The Tamese twisted and turned. It was almost impossible to use sails. Whichever direction the wind blew you would have to sail against it at some point. Even with a sail furled so long as a mast and yard stood there was resistance to the wind. A drekar had sleek lines and was meant to be rowed. We set a watch and the crew slept. I leaned against the steerboard and peered into the darkness. My mind would not let me sleep and I ran over all the events which had led to this. I tried to work out what I could have done to avoid it. There was nothing. We had fought the Skulltaker and his witches. That had incurred the wrath of the Weird Sisters for Snorri had killed a witch. He had paid the price for that. It had been the theft of Ylva which had set these events into motion and I could not have abandoned my granddaughter. Knowing that I could have done nothing about it did not make me feel any better.

I watched the sun come up from the east. I saw the fifty ships which hove into view. I had never seen so many ships. They were outlined against the rising sun. We were not the smallest drekar but, as I looked at the ones nearby and the approaching fleet I could see that we would be dwarfed.

A figure appeared at the stern of **'Dragon Smoke'**. I recognised him as Halfdan Ragnarsson. He shouted across to me, "Jarl Dragonheart, I thought you would have come in your larger drekar."

I shrugged, "I did not think I would need a large ship and the waters of the Tamese are easier to negotiate with a smaller ship."

He nodded, seemingly satisfied and pointed east, "Here are my brothers. When they arrive, we will meet on the deck of '***Cold Drake'***, my brother's ship. She is the largest drekar. She has more than fifty oars!"

"Let me know when you want me."

Our interchange had woken the rest of my crew and we ate. Olaf was impressed with the size of the Danish fleet and the quality of their ships. "Perhaps this venture will succeed, Jarl Dragonheart. If each ship only has as many men as we do then there will be over thirteen thousand men. The Saxons cannot muster more than a thousand. They cannot stand against us!"

"Perhaps." I was not convinced. We would have more men than the Saxons and if we were just raiding Lundenwic, Essex, and Cent then I would be more confident. The one hundred miles to Wintan-Caestre was a long way for such a huge warband. When we left for the meeting I did not wear my mail but I took Ragnar's Spirit. I left Olaf on board for I knew that he had a short temper and I did not want to risk a blood feud. Haaken was a better choice of advisor. He had a sharp mind and knew how to read men's motives. He had one eye only but he used it well.

The *'Cold Drake'* tied up on the other side of us. We were dwarfed by the two largest ships in the Danish fleet. Their crew used ropes to pull us next to her so that Haaken and I could clamber over the side. Halfdan and Sigurd Snake in the Eyes came by rowing in a small boat. Hvitserk greeted me when I boarded. "Just one tiny drekar, Jarl Dragonheart? I expected all of your ships."

"My men raided here and they believe that we took the most valuable items the burgh possessed and we had just raided Wihtwara. I brought the warriors who wished for glory." I was not foresworn. The men who sailed with me came for the glory of protecting their jarl. "Besides we just fought a war against the Northumbrians. I needed my northern borders protected."

My answer seemed to satisfy him, "You will not be able to take much treasure back with you."

I smiled, "When last we came we took Saxon ships. They have large holds. You brought me here for my expertise as well as my name, did you not?"

"We did."

Just then his two brothers clambered aboard. I was about to ask where the rest of the fleet was when the lookout shouted, "Sails to the east!" I looked aft and saw the horizon filled with Danish and Norse drekar. Hvitserk had kept his word. They had a fleet. Lundenwic would not know what had hit it.

We left two days later. My tiny drekar led followed by the huge drekar of the three brothers. We did not sail at night. For one thing it was too dangerous and for another there was little point. The Saxons knew we were coming. When we had met Hvitserk had shown that he had a clever mind. He had acceded to my suggestion that some of the Danes should land on the south bank of the river. We had more than enough men to take the burgh on the north bank. If he planned on taking us south then we would need to hold the south bank. He assigned Guthrum Saxon Slayer for that task.

As we headed down the river with the crew rowing Sámr stood next to me at the steering board. I was teaching him how to steer. "But why do they need you, Jarl Dragonheart? They have many ships and many men. Even I can see that they will win."

"Two things, Sámr: my sword and my reputation. I have never lost against the Saxons. These Danes are no fools. They know that the Allfather favours me and they hope to benefit from it."

Sámr thought about that for a while. "Then when they have Wessex, what then?"

I turned to him and said, sombrely, "Then they will have no further use for me and I will be killed."

"But..."

I held up my hand, "What they plan and what they actually do are two entirely different things. You do not worry about that. You will be safe aboard this drekar and I will be able to concentrate on escaping!"

As we neared Stybbanhype I put the steering board over slightly. Sámr said, "What is wrong Jarl Dragonheart?"

I winked, "Nothing. Just take the steering board."

"Should I head back into the middle of the river?"

"No, I wish you to nudge the ship moored ahead. I will shout at you soon. I will not mean it. I am trying to deceive the Danes." I walked forward and said, "Be ready to withdraw the steerboard oars when I nod my head."

Olaf and Haaken knew of my plan already. I did not want my drekar to be trapped next to the quay by this huge fleet. I wanted to be able to sail back down the river.

As we neared the ship I nodded my head and the thirteen rowers slid their oars in as one. We bumped and stuck. I turned to Sámr, "Were you asleep?"

As *'Cold Drake'* drew alongside I shouted, "My helmsman made a mistake. I think my ship has been damaged. We will march and attack the east gate of Lundenburgh. We can be there before you!"

Hvitserk waved his arm in acknowledgement and the huge fleet sailed down the river. I patted Sámr on the back. "Well done!" I waved my men ashore across the Saxon ship. The four men who would guard my great-grandson and my drekar presented themselves. "See what you can find in this Saxon ship. Tie up to her so that she is a barrier. I doubt that the Saxons will bother you. When they see the fleet, they will flee north. You did well, Sámr."

"Take care, Great Grandfather."

Hrolf Eriksson laughed, "The Dragonheart is protected by the Allfather. He will return!"

I slipped my shield over my back and donned my new helmet. I clambered up the side of the Saxon ship and then dropped down to the river bank. My men were waiting. Olaf said, "The Saxons who lived here have fled."

"Good. Then let us run, Clan of the Wolf! We have a burgh to take!"

We had fought a battle here and knew the marshy ground. It was daylight and we were able to pick our way across it using the islands of dry earth as a path. Ahead of us we saw people fleeing towards the safety of the walls. There were not as many fleeing as I would have expected. There were none of the better off Saxons. The ones who ran were swine herds and shell fish gatherers; they were the poor.

I saw banners flying from the walls of the burgh. Haraldr had attached himself to me. His father had carried my banner and he seemed to see himself as my protector. We began to overtake the drekar. The last bend of the river caused them all to slow up. I knew that once they reached Lundenwic the fleet would fill the river completely. It would be like a giant bridge. I was not certain what would happen when the tide went out. That would be the Dane's problem. My drekar was safe.

We began to catch the stragglers trying to get inside the walls before the Danish ships. When they heard the jingle of our mail they turned in terror. Most ran north but a few tried to get out of our way on the riverside. I saw at least eight fall into deep, muddy holes. We ignored them and kept running. Two men pulling a cart with their families realised they would not be able to out run us with the cart and they grabbed their families and ran. They were the last ones to make the safety of the gate. As we neared it archers sent arrows at us. They were not very good. A poorly aimed arrow hit one of the Saxon women. Had he actually aimed the arrow at her then the archer might have been praised for it struck her in the middle of the head. We pulled our shields up and a few arrows smacked into them. We halted.

"Shield wall!" We had been prepared for this. As the men formed a wall four men by six I glanced to the river and saw that the first of the drekar was tying up. Soon there would be a huge Danish bridge filling the Temese. It would the largest longphort ever and the people of Lundenwic would be doomed. They would attack the sea gate and the west gate. They would flood Lundenwic with fierce warriors. I heard the clatter of arrows as the Saxons switched their bows to the threat from the river. I held my shield before me as shields were raised above us.

"March!"

We chanted as we marched.

Push your arms
Row the boat
Use your back

The Wolf will fly

Ulfheonar
Are real men
Teeth like iron
Arms like trees

Push your arms
Row the boat
Use your back
The Wolf will fly

Ragnar's Spirit
Guides us still
Dragon Heart
Wields it well

Push your arms
Row the boat
Use your back
The Wolf will fly

As soon as we began to move towards the gate stones rattled off our shields. With the exception of Haraldr, all of us were mailed. With our shields to protect us it would take a lucky stone to hurt us.

Olaf was on the right of the shield wall. He had his axe. When we reached the gate, it would be his responsibility to break through the gate. The last time we had been here we had destroyed the gates. This would be new wood. I doubted that they would have had seasoned wood to use. They had also done us a favour. By allowing the last few refugees in they had left the bridge in place. Once we reached the gate then they began to use larger stones. Haaken and I lifted our shields to protect Olaf. The stones crashed onto our shields but they overlapped and there was no damage. Olaf sang as he swung. I had my hand on the gate and I felt it shake. Galmr Hrolfsson also had an axe. I shouted, "Switch with Olaf, Galmr!"

"I do not need relief!"

"I am saving your axe so that you may hew Saxon heads and not wood!"

Galmr was fresh and his axe had not been dulled. Chips and splinters of wood flew from the door. The fall of stones had abated somewhat. I guessed that our small warband was not as big a threat as the hundreds who were hammering at the other gates and charging through the houses, warehouses and stores of Lundenwic. When a particularly large chip flew from the door I shouted, "Hold! Let us try brute force. Two steps back." Once we had moved the two steps I held my shield before me and shouted, "Charge!" Twenty-four mailed men with heavy shields are a mighty force. The gate had been weakened enough so that it burst open and we almost sprawled into the middle of the burgh.

There were more than a hundred men waiting for us! This was a trap. King Æthelwulf had known of our attack and he had packed the burgh with armed men. Of course, he could not have known the numbers that would be attacking. Perhaps he thought it would be the same number of ships I had brought last time.

"Reform!" They were waiting for us but our sudden entry had taken them by surprise. We had to reform. Already others were racing through the other gates. More Saxons were descending from the walls.

We formed three ranks. We would not wait. As the Saxons hurtled towards us we marched with swords and axes held above our shields. The thegn who led the Saxons came directly for me. My shield told him who I was. He had a spear. The Saxons believed, erroneously, that the longer reach of the spear gave them an advantage. I was not wearing a full-face helmet and the thegn jabbed his spear at my unprotected mouth. I had a new helmet and I trusted my blacksmith. I turned my head to the side as the spear came at me. At the same time, I thrust blindly towards him. I struck something that was soft. His spearhead glanced off the polished metal and over my shoulder. I turned my head and saw that my sword had sliced across his nose and his right eye. I raised my shield and punched. His head jerked back and I brought my sword diagonally across his neck and chest. His damaged eye meant he could not see and my blade tore through his mail and across his chest.

I could hear the sound of battle now. It filled the burgh. Since last we had been here they had added more buildings. We were fighting in the only clear space. It suited my line for they could not outflank us. There were buildings next to Galmr on one side and Ráðgeir Ráðgeirson on the other. Behind me Haraldr's long reach with his sword was proving more effective than the spears of the Saxons. Even as the thegn began to slip to the ground, pulled by the weight of his mail, the two men behind suffered wounds from the slash of Haraldr's sword. I stepped forward and thrust at the one to my right. My sword ripped into his chest. They had weight of numbers but we were all mailed and more skilled. It was butchery. We blocked their blows with our shields and sought gaps with our own weapons. In a perfect world we would have changed places with those in the third rank but to move would have been disastrous. I knew we were winning when we began to move forward over the dead who lay there. The new buildings were not high but they still obscured our vision. Our world was limited by the Saxons before us. I could smell burning. The Danes had fired something.

We were so close to each other now that I could not swing my sword. I put it in my left hand and drew my seax from my belt. It was a nasty slashing weapon. The Saxon before me was trying to get at me. His sword beat against my helmet. I raised my hand and drew my seax across his throat. As he fell I darted my blade sideways and it plunged into the ear of the warrior fighting Olaf. Olaf's axe could not be used effectively. He was punching with it. When the man I had stabbed in the head fell Olaf roared and punched with his axe. The blade tore across the shoulder of the man he was fighting. It ripped through the mail and his kyrtle. Blood spurted and Olaf head butted him. As he fell backwards Olaf swung his seal skin boot. He connected with something and, when he stepped forward there was a sickening crunch as the Saxon's head was crushed.

There was a gap ahead of us and our combined weight suddenly pushed the Saxons into it. They fell and as we raced after them it allowed those in the second and third rank the opportunity to bring their fresh weapons to bear. I sheathed my seax and began to use Ragnar's Spirit once more. I blocked the Saxon sword with my shield and dropped to one knee. I brought my sword up under a Saxon's kyrtle and into his body. My tip was still sharp and I twisted it inside his body. He was dead before I pulled it out. We had broken the bodies and the spirit of the men who had been waiting for us but, as we hurried to the centre of the burgh, I saw that some of the Danes had not been as lucky or, perhaps, not as skilled. There were Saxons still fighting.

"Clan of the Wolf, wedge!" We had lost two men to wounds but we had no more enemies before us. As my men formed behind me I raised my sword and yelled, "Ragnar's Spirit!" I led them, at a fast walk, towards the rear of the nearest Saxon line. I saw that they had some

Norse warriors almost surrounded. The young jarl was fighting desperately but they were not making much headway.

I used the tip to rip into the back of the first Saxon. Olaf and Galmr were on the right of the wedge and their axes swung at the same time. Two Saxons were almost cut in two. Haaken was using back hand swings and the pressure on the Norse began to ease. When I slew the next Saxon then the will of the Saxons broke. They were being attacked in the rear and they ran. I looked up at the sky. The sun had passed its zenith some time ago. It was dipping in the west. We had fought for half a day.

Haaken raised his sword, "Clan of the Wolf!"

My men banged their shields. The Danes just stood, exhausted with bloody swords. The Norse, with their young jarl, raised their swords and banged their shields, "Clan of the Raven!"

I took off my helmet and walked over to him. His mail looked red; it was covered in blood and gore. I saw that he has lost oathsworn. They had the symbol of the raven painted on their shields. I sheathed my sword and held out my arm, "I am Jarl Dragonheart of the land of the Wolf! You fought well today!"

"I am Sven Halfdansson. I am the nephew of Halfdanr Svarti. He is the head of our people."

"You paid a heavy price this day."

He scowled at the Danes who were rifling the corpses. "It is my fault for following the Danes. It was your name which drew me here."

"For that I am sorry."

"Do not be. As we tied up I saw you and your small warband attacking the gate. It is all that I expected of such a warrior. And that is the sword?"

I took it out and handed it to him. He held it and closed his eyes. When he opened them there was amazement in them. "It is true! I can feel the power! You truly have been chosen by the Allfather." He handed it back to me. "Tell me jarl, why do you lead this band of cut throats?"

I sheathed Ragnar's Spirit, "The Norns. I will say no more."

The young warrior clutched his hammer, "Then I sympathise with you. Once you fall foul of those sisters then your life is not your own."

I nodded and turned, "Haaken One Eye, make sure these Danes do not take all! Young Sven Halfdansson and I will share the bounty!"

The Danes who were nearby glared at me but they would not risk my wrath. They slunk off looking for easier pickings.

"Thank you, Jarl. I have lost half of my crew. I hoped to make enough coin to buy a bigger drekar."

"I will give some advice for free. Take all that you can from Lundenwic and then sail back to Norway. This raid is doomed."

"Will you be leaving too?"

I shook my head, "Would that I could but the web constrains me. I must bear the company of the sons of Lodbrok until the Norns release me."

He shook his head, "I thought that to be the Dragonheart must be the greatest gift a man could be granted."

"No, my friend. At times like this, it is a curse."

Chapter 12

I waved over Galmr Hrolfsson, "Take ten men and empty the houses we passed on our way in."

We could see the river gate and Sven Halfdansson shook his head as the three brothers entered like conquering heroes. "They waited on the river while men bled! Look at their mail! It is unmarked! They have no honour!" The Danes banged their shields and shouted the names of the three brothers and their father. I had been the name to get men to come on the raid but they were the ones who would garner the glory.

Olaf took off his helmet and picked up a bucket of water he found outside one of the houses. He poured it over his head to wash away the blood. "Is this to be the way, Jarl?"

"Perhaps Olaf but you know that our involvement is not voluntary. Until I am released I must follow their banner."

Hvitserk Ragnarsson left his brothers and came over to us. We were bloodied and battered. My new helmet was dented and scratched. My mail was festooned with the guts of the men I had killed and the three brothers had yet to draw weapons. "A great day, Jarl Dragonheart! You and your warband drew the Saxons to the wrong gate! You made this victory easier."

I pointed to the dead men. "There was nothing easy about this Hvitserk! The Saxons knew we were coming. There were more men and better defences than when last we raided. If King Æthelwulf knows about this then he also knows of your plan to take Wintan-Caestre."

He nodded, "That is right but knowing it and being able to stop us are two entirely different matters. You have seen how many men we have. We have ten thousand warriors! There are not that number of warriors in the whole of this land! As I told you in Bruggas, there is a throne to be had. Not just the throne of one little kingdom but the whole of this island and it is yours for the taking."

"And I told you, Hvitserk Ragnarsson that I have but one purpose, destroy King Æthelwulf."

He nodded, "So you keep telling me. You can bring your drekar closer to the gates if you wish."

I shook my head. "The river is too crowded. We will load our ship and camp by Stybbanhype. When do we leave for Wintan-Caestre?"

"Tomorrow night we will hold a feast in your honour. When we have had a counsel of war we will decide. There is no hurry."

He left us. Sven said, "He seems the most reasonable of the brothers. At least he afforded you praise."

"Do not be taken in, young Sven. He praises me with his mouth only. He is clever and he thinks to use me. I am to be sacrificed when Æthelwulf is dead. If you would heed my advice you will take your ship and leave."

"And I will, if I can untangle her from the others."

I looked at Olaf. "Take some men and help them free their ship." I turned back to Sven, "If you will allow my wounded men to be carried aboard your ship we will help you to row to Stybbanhype."

"Of course. We are short-handed as it is."

My men began carrying the mail, swords and other plunder from the houses. As I had expected there was not as much as the last raid. They had evacuated the rich and taken that which was valuable. We had enough to justify a raid but Queen Osburga's crown and the books we had taken made what we had insignificant. Already I could smell burning. Some of the Danes had broached the ale barrels and set fire to the town. That was a mistake for there was a risk to some of the ships tied up close to Lundenwic. I saw Haraldr. He looked happy. He improved as a warrior in every battle we fought. I waved him over. "Did you search the purses of the dead Saxons?"

He grinned and held a fat purse out. "I am learning, jarl. The better the warrior I fight the more coins he has." He nodded towards the purse. Half of this came from warriors you slew, jarl Dragonheart. I should split it with you."

"I need no coin. You take it all."

I slung my shield on my back and walked down through the gate to the river. I saw that many warriors had died taking the gate. The Saxons had been there in numbers to defend it. Sven's ship was in the middle of the longphort. Luckily there was but one ship astern of him. Unlike us the Danes had not left any crew aboard. Olaf clambered aboard the Dane which lay astern and he hacked through the ropes which bound it to its neighbours. He climbed back aboard looking pleased with himself. The current from the river began to tug the Dane towards the sea. It would not reach the sea. The bends and the current would beach it on the other side of the river.

Sven shouted, "Get the drekar loaded. Do not worry where we put it. When we reach the Dragonheart's ship we will store it properly." That told me that Sven was a good seaman. A poorly laden drekar could sink in the blink of an eye. "Put the jarl's goods at the prow!"

No one else seemed bothered about loading their ships. I heard the screams of women who had been taken and were being used by drunken Danes. I spied some warriors, on the southern shore, playing a game with the heads of the Saxons they had slain. This was not the way my men went to war. As the sun began to set in the west I saw the flicker of flames as fires were started upstream and south of the river. Hvitserk might be right about the numbers he had brought. The Saxons might not have ten thousand warriors but they had enough people who would not want Danes rampaging through their land. The battle, when it came, would not be as easy as they thought.

"Ready!"

Sven acknowledged the cry from his oathsworn. "Cut us free!" Axes chopped through the ropes. At first, nothing happened and then, slowly as the current caught us, we began to move. "Ready with the oars!" It was not our drekar but my men grabbed oars and prepared to help warp us downstream. Sven used the current and the steering board to turn us the right way and, once we were clear of the other ships, the men began to row. It was becoming dark and so I went to the prow and leaned out to see obstacles. The river was wide but there was a turn we would have to make. I shouted and waved my arm when it was time. I saw Stybbanhype ahead of us. My men had lit a fire and I saw *'Red Snake'*. I waved my arm to direct Sven to the north shore. My men took the ropes and tied the two drekar together. Both crews began to move our plunder to our drekar and to lift the deck before storing the rest.

I went ashore with Haaken and Olaf. I found Sámr and Folki Siggison. They were cooking a pig on the open fire. The smell made me salivate. Sámr grinned, "We slaughtered the pig and we have found treasure inside the church!" He pointed to the wooden church which I had missed when we landed. "It was only linen, candles and candlesticks but we found great quantities of food. The Saxons eat well." He suddenly realised he had not asked about the raid. He looked guilty, "How did the raid go?"

"We captured the burgh and the town. We will spend the night here and then you can sail to the Isle of the Sheep."

"That is still the plan, Jarl Dragonheart?"

"Nothing I saw has changed my mind. Einar, Benni and Erik were wounded. They will join you and the crew. I hope there is plenty of food. We have guests this night."

It was pitch black by the time the two drekar were loaded and ready to sail. As we ate I told Sven of my plan to send my drekar down to the Isle of the Sheep. The Norseman was more than happy to accompany her. He told me of his land. It sounded like the land where Ragnar had lived. His uncle and his sons seemed to be ambitious. Sven spoke of plans to unite all of the clans into one tribe which would become a kingdom. "The Danes have one. Why not us?"

I said nothing but I knew that having a king did not guarantee loyalty. He asked about our land. Haaken took over. He loved talking. He told of how we had conquered it and how we defended it. He regaled the Norse warrior with tales of battles against foes like Eggle Skulltaker. I think Sven thought that some of the stories had to be made up. As men retired I took him to one side. "Should you ever wish to raid with warriors that you can trust then sail to Whale Island. I have warriors and crews who raid. They would gladly take you with them. Do not risk Danes. I have yet to meet one I trusted."

"You are right and it has cost me ten oathsworn to discover that. We have treasure but that cannot replace the men we lost."

The next morning the two ships slipped out as the sun made the sky lighter. My men would watch my ship and Sámr. It was a hard parting but I felt better as I saw the two drekar slip away. He would be safe no matter what treachery the Danes attempted. We marched down the road towards Lundenwic. All night we had watched the fires burning. I had no idea what actually remained or what treasures had been taken before the fires took hold. There were no sentries on the walls. In fact, we saw no one ready to defend the walls against us. If the Wessex king had had men close then the Danes could have been butchered for, as we entered the burgh we saw them lying where they had fallen dead drunk. The burgh would need rebuilding. Many of the halls and buildings were blackened piles. We walked through to Lundenwic. That was even worse. Nothing remained.

Olaf asked, "Where are these brothers? Perhaps they burned in their own fires."

Haaken One Eye shook his head, "Loki looks after his own. They will be alive but I fear that many of their men will be dead."

We looked north and saw men moving. We headed there. I knew, from Atticus that there was a hall there. It was at a place called Tottenheale. Eorledman Aelric lived there when Atticus was a slave. I recognised them as the hearthweru of Hvitserk. I turned to Ráðgeir Ráðgeirson. "Take the men and scout north. See what the Danes have left. If you can find horses then so much the better. Meet us by the river."

"Aye jarl." He looked with disgust at four Danes who were vomiting in the ditch next to the road. "These are not warriors!"

"They are, Ráðgeir Ráðgeirson, but they are not warriors of the Clan of the Wolf. I am honoured to lead such men as you."

The three of us approached the hall that the brothers had taken over. The hearthweru, who had bones plaited in their beard and moustache, held up a hand. "Our jarl sleeps! Come back later."

I walked up to him, "I am the leader of this raid or did your master forget to tell you that? I am Jarl Dragonheart of the Land of the Wolf. I wield the sword which was touched by the gods and if you do not move then you will die!"

I do not know if it was my title, my voice of the threatening nature of Olaf Leather Neck behind me but it had an effect. The four of them moved aside and we entered the hall. I almost vomited when I entered. There were four young Saxon women just inside the door. Their bodies showed that they had been violated. They had been slain at the door. Their throats were slashed. Their bodies lay in a pool of blood. One looked to be no older than twelve summers. Haaken had daughters and he walked to the door, grabbed the cloak from a hearthweru and draped the bodies with it. His face was as cold and hard as I had ever seen. If a Dane spoke out of turn then there would be blood.

I heard voices from the rear of the hall. I headed for them. In the dim light of a fading fire, I saw the three brothers. They had blood on their hands. I knew who had slain the girls. I hardened my heart. I had my family, my clan and my land to protect.

"Jarl Dragonheart! You should have joined us last night! Saxon girls are ripe. It is a pity we only found a few of them."

I shook my head, "Halfdan Ragnarsson, the Saxons sent away all they wished to protect. Did you not notice that there were no rich Saxons in the town? Where were the merchants and the ladies of the thegns? They are somewhere else. The girls you had were the poor. They were here to make sure we did not suspect a trap."

"A trap?"

"The mailed men who awaited us were not there by accident. They thought to surprise us but we had greater numbers than they expected. The empty halls were deliberate. How much treasure did we find?" Their silence gave me the answer. "And your men squat and vomit in the street while the men of Wessex prepare your downfall."

Sigurd Snake in the Eyes looked in his empty horn as though his gaze would magic a drink. "We have ten thousand men. How can we lose?"

"You had ten thousand men. Look outside and you will see many dead warriors. They were not killed in the battle. The longer you stay here the less chance you have of victory. You asked me to lead, well I am leading now. Let us move before the sun is at its height!"

Hvitserk came over to me, "We will leave on the morrow. We will leave at dawn. You may be right but our men will be in no condition to march today."

"Then find men who are sober and can scout. We need to know what lies twixt here and Wintan-Caestre."

Sigurd Snake in the Eyes pointed his empty horn at me, "I am not certain we need you. What is to stop us from taking your sword and slaying you?"

Olaf Leather Neck suddenly swung his axe. He brought it down on the table between Sigurd and his brothers. The blow smashed the table in two. The three brothers fell to the floor and the hearthweru rushed in. "Does that answer your question?"

The silence echoed in the hall. I said, quietly, "We will meet you at dawn, on the other side of the river at Suthriganaworc."

"We were going to have a feast!"

"Have one but my men and I will not be there. We have plans to make. I want the King of Wessex dead!"

As we left Haaken said, "Well Olaf, we made no friends there."

"What else could I do?" He added, seriously, "Taking their three heads might have been a start."

We made our way back to Lundenwic. Whoever ruled this land after we had left would have to rebuild both the burgh and the town. It was desolate. The smell of burning and the dead filled our nostrils. The bodies lay where they fell. Soon pestilence and disease would take more warriors than battle. Not all of those who had raided lay drunk or were off raiding. I saw some warriors, Norse by the looks of them, loading their drekar with plunder. Unlike Sven they would not be able to leave.

They were at the furthest point upstream. There were four of them. As there was no sign of Ráðgeir Ráðgeirson we stopped to speak with them.

The four captains left their men and came to speak with us. "I am Harald Iverson. It is an honour to meet such a famous warrior. This is Erik Cold Blade, Snorri Haraldsson and Fótr Firebeard."

I could see why Fótr was so named. He had the largest and reddest beard I had ever seen.

"It is good to meet warriors who still remember why we came here."

"Aye the pickings have been good but the slaves we might have had were butchered!"

"Not that there were many of them in any case!"

I pointed south, "Their king knew we were coming. Did you not notice that it was just the poor folk and warriors who were on the walls? When we raided here there were priests, churches filled with treasure and women who were worth selling at market. There were merchants and the warehouses were well filled. I am guessing you found them almost empty. How much did you get from the churches?"

Harald shook his head, "Nothing. We thought it strange."

Erik Cold Blade smiled, "They must have taken it somewhere south of here. When we head to Wintan-Caestre we will find it."

"You are right but the King of Wessex will be gathering an army to meet us."

"Good, for an open battle suits me! Besides we have so many men that we will outnumber the Saxons."

Haaken was an observant man. "I have seen many dead warriors. I know that we slew many Saxons but almost as many of our men died either in the fighting or in the fires."

Harald took that information in, "But we have you, Jarl Dragonheart. You have never tasted defeat."

"And I have never led Danes. My battles have been fought alongside warriors such as you four. Men from Norway, Dyflin or the Islands. If they follow commands and do as I say then we have a chance."

We turned as we heard the sound of horses. Ráðgeir Ráðgeirson led my men. They rode ten horses. They were riding double except for Haraldr Leifsson who jogged happily alongside them. "Well done, Ráðgeir Ráðgeirson. What saw you to the north?"

"There are bands of Danes who are raiding the houses and farms north of here. They did not appear to have collected much worth stealing.

Viking Warband

These horses we took from six farms. The farmers and their families lay dead but the horses had been left."

"We need more but it is a start." I turned to the four captains. "I am taking my men across the river. The three brothers seem to think we can just walk across Wessex and fight a battle at Wintan-Caestre. I do not think it will be as easy as that. I intend to scout out the land. When the battle comes I would be honoured if you would fight with my warband."

They nodded their agreement. I had five crews on whom I could depend. Fótr said, "And there are others here from the isles and the fjords. We will speak with them. True warriors should stick together."

Ráðgeir said, "We took food and found one farm where the Danes had not discovered the ale barrel. We filled skins with it. We have supplies for two days."

"It is four days to Wintan-Caestre. We will have to scavenge as we go."

As we headed towards the middle of the longphort Haaken said, "If there are but ten more crews who are reliable then we might succeed. Perhaps the Norns have a different plan to the one we think."

I touched my wolf. "This is the Norns, Haaken One Eye. Assume the worst and you will not be disappointed."

Someone had laid planks and pieces of wood across eight drekar to make a bridge to the south. Suthriganaworc was almost as big as Lundenwic and had a large church. I could see now that it too had been burned down. One thing was certain, the Saxons would remember this raid. We led the horses across the makeshift bridge. If this was the main way across the river then it would take a long time for the whole of the army to cross. Even if the brothers made it by dawn it would take all day for the horde of warriors to cross. From what Ráðgeir had said there were still hundreds of men north of Lundenwic. The Mercians who lived there would not take kindly to Viking warbands wandering at will.

I was glad when we led the horses off the bridge and onto dry land once more. A Danish chief and his hearthweru wandered over to me. Like the brothers he had bones hung in his hair, "I am Guthrum Saxon Slayer. Hvitserk Ragnarsson put me in charge of this side of the river!"

His voice challenged me. I felt Olaf bristle behind me. I decided to ignore the challenge for the moment. "Good, for if I am to lead this army to victory over the Saxons at Wintan-Caestre I will need warriors like you who have scouted out the land." He frowned. "You have sent out scouts have you not Guthrum Saxon Slayer?" His face showed that he had not even contemplated it. "We leave tomorrow. What if there is a Saxon army awaiting us?"

He laughed, "There are none! The few we found we butchered. If there are any left in this land then we will swat them like summer flies." His men began banging their shields with their swords. I began to see just how clever the Saxon king had been. Lundenwic had been Mercian longer than it had belonged to Wessex. He had sacrificed it and made us bleed so that he could gather his best men and meet us on ground of his choosing. The longer our journey across Wessex the more men we would lose to disease, hunger and desertion. The land could not support ten thousand men. The sooner we scouted, the better.

"Then we will scout out the land. Hvitserk and his brothers will lead the army across the bridge tomorrow. Unless you wish it to fall into the river I would make the bridge more secure." I shrugged, "I do not command you, Guthrum Saxon Slayer. Do what you will, for the lack of a solid bridge does not bother me. I have crossed. As you say, you have been put in charge of this river bank." I smiled and led my men down the road south.

We led the horses. Ideally, we would need to find more of them. What we did do was to load them with our shields and spears. I carried my Saami bow. A couple of miles down the road we reached Pecheham and saw that it had just been abandoned. Guthrum had not advanced as far south as this. The huts, halls and houses we had passed had either been torn open or burned. I saw a hall. We went inside and searched but everything of value had been taken. The road led west and we followed it. We could see some of the goods dropped as the Saxons had fled for safety. Where was safe? A comb lay discarded. I saw pieces of food along with small bundles of clothes lying where they had fallen. Fear of us had stopped them from being retrieved. They had left in a hurry. Perhaps the King of Wessex had not expected us to land on two banks at once.

Brixges Stane had also been abandoned. There was a water trough close to the hall and we let the horses drink while we searched the hall and the other buildings. "Erik Red Beard, take some men and look in the woods to the south. There may be escaped animals there. We need food for the journey."

"Aye jarl."

This time we had a little more success. Galmr discovered a small chest which had been forgotten. In it was a chain of office and some rings. It was the first real treasure we had found. Leif Gunnarsson ran in. "Jarl, there are Saxons scouts. Six of them and they are coming through the woods. They are on horses. Haraldr is leading our men to get behind them."

I grabbed my Saami bow. "I want a prisoner and I want those horses. Most importantly, none escape. I want the Saxons blind."

Unlike the Danes, the men I led were all hunters. They were used to the woods. We entered the woods on the opposite side of the road. We followed Leif. Haraldr, Erik Red Beard and my other men were ahead of us. All we had to do was to cut off their escape route. Leif led us deeper into the woods and then he stopped. We all did. Leif came from the land above the Water, Grize's Dale. He made his living as a hunter and he had good ears. They stopped us from stumbling upon the Saxons.

I heard a horse whinny. Perhaps it smelled our horses. One of the Saxons said, "Brixges Stane is untouched. The Vikings have not come this far yet."

"Eorledman Æthelstan said they had not ventured far south at all. They were too busy drinking to seek us out. The King should bring the army now and destroy them. They are frightening when they are sober but drunk they are as weak as a newborn!"

"Peace Aelric. The King knows what he is doing."

It was Galmr who stepped on the twig. He was a big man and perhaps he was uncomfortable and shifted his weight. Whatever the reason the twig snapped and the Saxons alerted. I nocked an arrow and ran towards the sound of the voices. I saw a horse and a rider. I did not wish to risk hitting the horse and I sent an arrow, at forty paces, into the Saxon's shoulder. The Norns were weaving. Instead of wounding him, it carried on up and into his throat. He fell dead. My men obeyed my orders and the Saxons were surrounded. As they tried to escape two were struck by arrows. Olaf swung his axe and hacked through the leg of a Saxon and the last two were knocked from their horses. Olaf's Saxon lay bleeding to death. Olaf Leather Neck reached him and began to question him. The Saxon spat curses at him and then died.

I reached the two who had fallen from their horses. Haraldr had used the flat of his sword to knock one from his horse while the other had run into a tree. One was dead and the other lay at an awkward angle. I saw the bones sticking out from his leg. He stared up at me. "I cannot feel my legs."

"One is broken and I fear that you have broken your back. Would you have a warrior's death?"

"And how do I get that? Do I betray my king? No Viking. I will die slowly and go to God knowing that I have not helped you heathens." He forced a smile. "You are all destined to die. The land is rising and the people will come for you. You are all doomed and you will all die."

I nodded and, taking out my seax, I plunged it into his throat. "You are a brave man. Go to your God."

We had more horses now. We also managed to catch and kill four fowl which had escaped the clutches of the Saxons when they had fled. They would augment our rations. We headed back to Suthriganaworc. Guthrum Saxon Slayer had heeded my advice and the bridge across the river was a better structure. Already more men were coming across. Had my words sunk into Hvitserk too? Rather than heading to the river which was already overcrowded, we found a deserted and unburned house at the edge of the settlement. It had food and there was a place where they had lit a fire. The smell of the river was becoming more unbearable as each moment passed. The stinking dead bodies and the human waste deposited by the Danes made it positively unhealthy. Already I had seen Danes with the first signs of the disease Atticus had called dysentery. We just called it 'the shits'. I had seen men die from it.

Galmr found a large pot. My men stripped the birds and gutted them. Ráðgeir chopped them up and put them in the pot. Haraldr went out to forage some wild greens. While searching the hurriedly abandoned house Haaken found treasure; it was a broken pot of dried beans.

While we waited for it to cook we drank the ale. We sat outside on some of the abandoned carts we had found. Haraldr was grooming the horses. Ráðgeir said, "We now have almost enough horses for us. Just three need to walk. We can take it in turns."

"No, Ráðgeir, the Ulfheonar will walk. I want the rest of you to be scouts ahead of us. Our tired feet are a price worth paying for vigilance. The presence of those Saxon scouts was warning enough. I would know where they were."

The fire had made the hut unbearably hot and so we ate outside. The stew was good and hearty. Bread would have made it a feast. The wooden bowls the Saxons had left had augmented our own supply. Haaken looked east, "I wonder how Sámr and his crew are faring."

"I am happier that we were able to leave the two wounded men with him. There are seven of them and that is a lucky number."

We had just finished the stew when we heard feet coming from Suthriganaworc. The voices told us that it was a band of Norse. I saw that it was Harald Iverson, Erik Cold Blade, Snorri Haraldsson and Fótr Firebeard. They had their crews with them. Harald Iverson laughed, "I could smell the food and the ale. I should have known. You are all old campaigners then?"

Olaf laughed, "Aye that we are. You are welcome to join us. There is still some of the stew left. If you add water, greens and the last of the beans it will feed some of you."

"We have salted ham. Thank you, we will take you up on the offer. We could not stand the smell of the river. We thought to have a hungry night rather than one where we risked disease and worse."

As they sat down I asked, "The Danes still drink?"

Erik Cold Blade shook his head, "I like a drink but there is a time and a place. Stuck in the middle of Saxon territory does not seem the place to be so lax. You know that twenty Danes were found with their heads removed?"

The Norns' dream came to mind: Danish heads on spears. "Where?"

"North of Lundenwic on the Roman Road."

"I warned the brothers that the Mercians would seize the opportunity of reclaiming their town."

"Sigurd Snake in the Eyes almost went berserk. He took his oathsworn and they headed north to find Saxons to punish."

"They lack order. All the while the army shrinks."

"Four drekar left this afternoon and we heard of another six who were thinking about it."

"But not you four?"

"No, Jarl Dragonheart. We have not made enough coin yet. Your men all wear mail. We have but four byrnies between us. When we have mail then we can take the land from our neighbours. Ours is poor land. It is hard and carved out of rock. You do not know how lucky you are to have the Land of the Wolf."

"Oh but we do. It is why we fight so hard to keep it. I brought one drekar crew because I wanted my home safe."

We heard the sound of hooves. A Dane reined in, "Jarl Dragonheart, Hvitserk Ragnarsson wishes to speak with you."

"Where is he? If he is north of the river I will stay here."

"He and Halfdan Ragnarsson have come south of the river. They are in Suthriganaworc."

I stood, "Haaken take charge. Keep a place for me by the fire."

"Will you be safe?"

"As safe as anywhere. Do not worry. I do not think they have finished with me yet. They still need me to be the figurehead at the head of this army." As I walked behind the Danish horseman I reflected that it was my name, reputation and sword which had brought me to this situation. As Guthrum Saxon Slayer had shown me most of the Danes did not like me. The five Norse leaders I had met had all chosen to follow me. The Danes had not elected to do so. When I reached the fire in the middle of what had been Suthriganaworc I saw a body had been thrown onto the fire. It was vaguely recognisable as a man but other than that I could tell nothing.

Hvitserk was the most pleasant of the brothers and the eldest. Halfdan was the youngest and, in my view the most dangerous. Sigurd was like a wild dog but at least you knew how he would react. Halfdan brooded. Hvitserk held out a hand, "You were right, Jarl Dragonheart. The Mercians have attacked our men. We should have heeded your advice."

"What will you do with the ships?"

"Leave them in the river. We will assign guards for them."

"If you want my advice you would sail them to Hamwic and march the army the short distance to the burgh of their king. You could take Wintan-Caestre."

"That would take time."

"The Saxons have scouts on the road. Their army is not at Wintan-Caestre. We could take their treasure and beat them when they march back. The fyrd do not like to travel too far from home."

Halfdan spoke. He had a threatening tone. Even when he was being pleasant his voice still sounded aggressive, "We have over six thousand men. We will march across Wessex and plunder as we go."

They had lost many hundreds of men already. This did not bode well. "If you take treasure when you cross Wessex you will lose men when you escort it back to Lundenwic and the ships."

Halfdan laughed, "We will take the treasure with us. There are carts and wagons we can use!"

"And you have horses to pull them?"

"We will harness Saxons to them!" Halfdan seemed to think that idea was extremely funny.

Hvitserk came closer to me, "We have thought this through, Jarl Dragonheart."

I sighed, "You have scouts to range ahead of the army?"

"Scouts? Why do we need scouts?"

I did not answer his question. If they could not see the need for scouts then this venture was, indeed, doomed. "Then I will use my men. The last thing we need is to walk into a trap." I stood, "Is that all?"

"Will you not sup with us?"

"Tomorrow will be a long day. I will send my scouts out before dawn. I will await you at the village of Brixges Stane."

As I headed back towards my men I heard Guthrum Saxon Slayer laugh. He said, loudly, to one of his men, "I know not why the jarl follows an old man like that. I would bet that the story of the sword was just that, a story!" His men laughed. I turned and before Guthrum knew anything about it I had Ragnar's Spirit at his throat. I pricked his neck so that he bled, "Know, faithless Dane, that I am never foresworn and as for being an old man. Perhaps the Allfather has granted me wisdom. If you ever utter such words about me again then I will kill you. Do you understand?"

He was less than half my age and he was much bigger but I saw fear in his eyes. He nodded and the movement made his neck bleed more. His men, too, looked more respectful. As I sheathed my sword and walked back down the road I knew I had made another enemy. The list was long and growing longer.

Chapter 13

I told the others what I had said. Haaken shook his head, "Taking the fleet to Hamwic makes perfect sense to me, Jarl Dragonheart."

"And we have lost almost half of the army. Some will guard the ships but what happened to the rest?" I turned to the four Norse leaders. "If I were you I would get your ships and sail home."

Erik shook his head, "We told you, we need the coin. We will trust that the Allfather watches over you."

Olaf Leather Neck stretched, "Then keep your men close to Jarl Dragonheart. I have fought behind him for many years. You have more chance of survival with him close by."

I left a small watch and we retired. Sven Svensson woke me before dawn as I had asked him. I went to my men as they saddled their horses. "We will have to use the Roman Road, the one they call Stane Street. Have some men on the road but I want the rest of you covering the land to the sides of the road."

"Fear not jarl. We will keep a good watch. When the battle begins then we will be there with you." Ráðgeir swung into the saddle and waved my men forward.

I made water and then went to the whetstone. My sword needed sharpening. Olaf and Haaken heard me and they rose. "They have gone?"

I nodded, "Part of me hopes that they will find nothing and that I am wrong about the Saxons."

Haaken sliced some salted ham, "But neither of us believes that. We would not have found those scouts yesterday if the King of Wessex was not close."

Our new allies were up early and they prepared for war too. Surprisingly the Danes arrived sooner than I had expected. There were just two brothers. Sigurd Snake in the Eyes was not with them. "Where is your brother?"

"He and his men fought Mercians yesterday. He has a slight wound. He will follow with the carts."

I nodded, "My men are scouting. We had better start."

Hvitserk smiled, "You are the leader. We will follow!"

I did not believe it but I nodded and we moved off down the road. Vikings are untidy warriors. They jostle and they do not keep good order, unless they are in a battle. It meant that the army spread out behind me.

Viking Warband

They spilt into the fields, when we passed fields and when the fields stopped, woods. We could have covered more than thirty miles had the Danes not been easily distracted. Every church we saw on the horizon was cause for warbands to race off and sack them. Every hut, and hovel potentially held women and girls. Each stray animal was chased.

At the front, my four groups of warriors kept good time but the army became strung out along the road and that was the danger. Gaps appeared. We needed cohesion. Reluctantly I was forced to call a halt at noon. We ate what little supplies we had. I did not like the looks Halfdan Ragnarsson was giving me. I wondered if he thought I had outlived my usefulness. Most of those who had deserted with their ships had been Norse or islanders. They had been the ones Hvitserk had needed to boost his numbers. They had been the ones who came to fight alongside the Dragonheart. With them gone and the prize already taken, what did they need me for?

When the carts caught up with us I started the column moving. I saw that the Danes were having to pull the carts and wagons. They had not thought to find horses. The men who pulled them would be in no condition to fight when we found the Saxons. Our army would be tired and the Saxons, whom I had no doubt were waiting for us would be rested and fed. The next six miles were mercifully free of churches and other distractions. I began to think we might begin to speed up. Haraldr galloped up and ended that dream.

"Jarl Dragonheart, the Saxons are gathered ten miles down the road. They are at a place called Aclea."

"Is it a burgh?"

"They have no wall and it is just twenty houses. It is a mean little place."

The two Danish brothers had joined me. "I nodded, "The Saxons are down the road. How many men, Haraldr?"

"The King is there we saw the banner. We counted the banners of thirty thegns. Each of them had mailed men with them. Ráðgeir thought there were five thousand."

Halfdan smacked one hand into the other, "Then we have them! Let us push on and fight them now!"

Hvitserk concurred, "Your scouts have served us well, Jarl Dragonheart. You were right to send them forth!"

I shook my head, "It would be a mistake to attack without finding out if the Saxons are just at Aclea. There may be other warbands close by."

Halfdan became angry, "I think you have an ill-deserved reputation! The gods have presented us with a great opportunity. We outnumber the Saxons. The majority of their men are the fyrd. We attack today!" He glared at his brother who spread his hands and nodded. "Come let us run! Ten miles is nothing to a real warrior!" He gave me a look of pity. "The old men can follow at their own pace."

The two brothers and their hearthweru charged down the road making the men who had marched with us have to take cover in the ditches. I waved over Haraldr, "Ride to Ráðgeir. Bring my men back here. I have a bad feeling about this Aclea. There must be burghs closer to Wintan-Caestre he could have used, why Aclea?"

The word had spread down the column and men were eager to follow the sons of Ragnar Lodbrok. A royal army was the stuff of dreams. There would be crowns and torcs; there would be religious artefacts which could be sold for great profit. It was impossible to move until the carts had passed us. I saw a triumphant Sigurd Snake in the Eyes. He was sitting on the top of one of the carts. He had a bandaged leg. Once they had passed we were able to move down the road. To my dismay, a mile down the road I saw my men. They were walking towards us. Thorkell and Ulf were missing.

"What happened to the horses and to our men?"

Ráðgeir shook his head, "Those bastard Danes! They demanded the horses from us. When Thorkell and Ulf told them no they were slain. I am sorry jarl. We would have fought but we would have been cut down and we feared for your safety."

"Do not worry, you did the right thing."

"Then we can go home!"

"What?" I turned to Haaken One Eye. I pointed to the four warbands with us. "These men came for treasure. I came to end the blood feud with the King of Wessex. We may be going to our death but we cannot turn back."

"You will fight with these snakes?"

I was not certain any more. Perhaps they were right. The four warbands would be able to take goods from the Danish ships. I was about to order us to return to Lundenwic when a Dane limped towards us. He came from the north. He had neither shield nor sword and he was wounded. I could see that his leg had been badly cut. He fell at my feet. Looking up at me he croaked, "Jarl Dragonheart I was with Sigeberht the Bold. We were ambushed. There is a Saxon army."

"I know, we are heading to meet them."

He shook his head, "No, Jarl." He gasped as pain coursed through his dying body. "There are four thousand men coming from the north. They came upon us when we were at Sutton. I think I am the only survivor and I am done for. Do not let me die without a sword in my hand!"

"Haaken, see to him!" I turned to Olaf, "This means we have no choice. We must fight with the Danes. We cannot get back to Lundewic."

Haaken came over, "It was no use, jarl. He bled to death even as I tried to see to his wounds."

"Well, that is one Dane that we owe a life to."

We began to run. Unlike the Danes, we ran in fours. We chanted to keep the rhythm and we did not go too fast. The Norns had woven a web so complex and convoluted that I do not see how even Aiden could have fathomed it. King Æthelwulf was as clever as his father. It had not been Mercians who had killed the Danes, it had been the men of Wessex. Now I saw why he had chosen Aclea. It was a long day's march from Lundenwic. We would be too far from our ships to return to them. He was luring the Danes to fight him thinking that they outnumbered the Saxons. The dead Dane had not told us the make-up of this second army but I knew that it would have more warriors in it. Had the Danes not taken my men's horses then we could have ridden to warn them. Their own treachery would come to hurt them. As we ran I tried to picture the map. The Isle of the Sheep lay to the north and east of us. If we tried to head there now we risked being caught by the men from the north. We had to help the Danes and hope that we killed enough of the enemy for us to make our escape.

I saw the wagons and carts ahead. They had been abandoned. The trees encroached closely on the road at that point. The forest had crept closer to the road. The fact that they had abandoned them meant that Aclea was not far away. We struggled to get through the carts. The men who had been pulling them had been weary from the journey. A plan formed in my mind. "Olaf, I want you to get these men to make those wagons into a barrier across the road. We make our own stronghold. Haaken, come with me and we will find these Danes and give them warning."

Haaken said, "I would let them die!"

"As would I but we need their swords. If we can warn them then we might hold them off until dark and then be able to slip away." I did not think it was likely but it was worth a try. "Our bows might be the difference, Olaf!"

We had to force our way through the press of men trying to get to the front of the warriors. There were too many in front of us to see Aclea but I heard the clash of metal on metal. It was worse than I feared. Instead of forming a shield wall and advancing, the two brothers had just allowed their men to attack as and when they chose. There was no way we could reach those at the front. I saw Sigurd Snake in the Eye. He was riding one of the horses we had found.

He saw me and snarled, "What? Do you now beg to fight with us?"

I shook my head, "No, I come to warn you that there is a second army coming from the north! You are trapped."

"You lie!"

I had my sword out and pressed against his wounded leg in a flash, "I do not lie! What reason would I have? Tell your brothers that we must form two fronts or we will be destroyed."

There was doubt on his face but I saw that he believed me. He shouted, "Guthrum Saxon Slayer. Send a messenger to my brothers. Tell them there is a second army coming from the north. We will be trapped."

"Aye, my lord!"

"Turn and make a shield wall." He looked down at me. "Where do you fight?"

"We have made a barricade of the wagons up the road. We will try to hold them up. If we cannot we will fall back and join you."

"It is our bad luck that we join you just as the Allfather abandons you!"

We turned and ran the five hundred paces to the wagons. Was he right? Had we been abandoned? When I reached my men, I saw that they had used the carts and wagons to make a wall which looked like an inverted boar's snout. There were trees to the side and the end wagons touched them. It would force the Saxons through the trees. They would have numbers but they would find it hard to make a shield wall. Olaf had been clever. It forced the Saxons to fight us in a way which suited us, man to man.

I waved over Harald Iverson, Erik Cold Blade, Snorri Haraldsson and Fótr Firebeard. "Are you happy for me to command you?"

Harald Iverson grinned, "Jarl Dragonheart, it is one of the reasons we joined this fight."

"Good. My plan is simple we use arrows to thin them when they come down the road. The mailed warriors will be at the sides. When they come at us through the woods we stop them at the Roman ditch. We will see who will weary of the bloodletting first, us or the Saxons."

Snorri said, "But jarl, they will have fifty for every one of us. Have we each to kill fifty of them?"

"If you have to but those fifty are not all mailed warriors. Indeed, I doubt that they will all be warriors. I am hoping that they realise there are just a few of us and leave us to fall upon the Danes. They are doomed but we can give some of them a chance to escape by holding on as long as we can."

"Then we will make it a glorious end."

I shook my head, "Fótr Firebeard, we are not berserkers. This will not be our end. Tonight, and tomorrow will be a hard battle. Tomorrow night all will be weary. While they sleep we slip away." I pointed to Olaf and Haaken, "These are Ulfheonar and my other men know how to use the woods. We carve a silent path through their sentries and we head for the Temese. I do not lie. I think that many of us will die. We cannot escape that. The Norns have spun. But we do not give up. I have a great-grandson sitting on my drekar waiting for me. I wish to see his face again and any Saxon or Dane for that matter, who gets in my way is a dead man walking."

Olaf said, "Enough talking, Jarl Dragonheart. Get to your places and may the Allfather be with us! Haaken, you take that side and I will take this. Harald Iverson, divide your men equally."

I took my Saami bow and my arrows. I had just twenty arrows. They would have to do. I clambered up the barricade. Haraldr was there and he put down a hand to help me up. To my amazement, he was grinning from ear to ear. "What makes you so happy, son of Leif the Banner?"

"If I am to die then think of the story of my death. How I stood next to Jarl Dragonheart and fought fifty times our number."

I shook my head. "You are too young to die. Stay close to me and listen to all that I say. I would have us both get home. I saw that I might have saved my great-grandson but I had another young warrior to save. I owed Leif the Banner that much. Aðils had found him for a purpose. *Wyrd.*

I looked up at the sky. There were still some hours of daylight. The Saxons did not like to fight at night. We had to hold them until night fell. This first night they would be alert. They would have more than half of their men waiting for us to escape. We would rest and we would sleep. The barricade would only accommodate twenty men and we were the ones with bows. There were ten others standing behind the barricade. They also had bows

I saw Galmr with them. He was instructing them. "When the jarl and the others release their arrows, we know that the Saxons are there. We do not need to see them to hit them. The road is straight and we release into the air and let our arrows fall amongst them."

Haraldr had sharp eyes, "Jarl I see banners. It is the Saxons!"

I turned, "Ready! They come!" I could not get the vision from my head. It was the dream from the cave. '*I found that I was sinking into the dead and dying bodies. They were like human quicksand. The more I struggled the quicker I sank. My waist was beneath them. As my head slipped down I found myself drowning in dead men's blood.*' Was that blood to be the blood of my own men?

I nocked an arrow and peered down the road. My bow would outrange them all save Haraldr's. He had Aðils' Shape Shifter's Saami bow and he was bigger than I was. He would send an arrow fifty or more paces beyond mine. "Haraldr, you and I can send arrows further. Let us do so. Choose a target as far away as you can."

He laughed, "Jarl, even my eyes cannot see that far!"

"Then aim at the cross or the banner which is beyond their front ranks."

The Saxon army began to take shape. I saw that they had two priests at the front. They were carrying some sort of religious banner. They would be the first to die. It would dishearten the others. Behind them came men on horses. They were accompanied by men with banners and behind them marched their better armed men, the mailed warriors. The priests were within range of Haraldr and me but we waited. I knew the range of the bows we had brought. One hundred and fifty paces was a killing range. The Saxons saw the barrier and halted. There was a heated debate and then the leader, I recognised him by his actions, shouted something and waved to the left and the right. They were trying to outflank us.

"Erik Cold Blade, Snorri, they come for the flanks."

"We are ready jarl. We have made the woods harder to pass."

I smiled. Haaken and Olaf would have told them that. They would have made the approach a tangle of branches and undergrowth. The wild blackberries which grew there would slow down an attack as the thorny tendrils grabbed and tugged at men trying to get through them. The dying

Saxon had said that the land would fight us. We would use the land to fight the Saxons.

The Saxon leader shouted something and a horn sounded. The two priests began to walk towards us singing and the Saxon army trundled down the road. The horsemen stayed where they were and the men on foot filtered through them. Saxons do not fight on horses unless they have no choice. Their leaders were afforded a good view from the backs of their mounts. They were about to get a shock.

"Haraldr, we can reach those leaders. Once our arrows fall amongst them they will move. Let us see how quickly we can send our rain of death towards them."

"Aye Jarl Dragonheart!"

The priests were less than one hundred and fifty paces away. "Draw!" I heard the creak of bows as my men pulled back. I felt the power of the Saami bow. "Release!"

Even as my first arrow was in the air I had a second nocked and released. My first arrow hit the man next to the thegn who led. Haraldr's hit the leader on the shoulder and he fell from his horse. There was pandemonium. As I sent my third arrow I saw the priests had been killed and twenty others lay on the ground. Some were dead and some were wounded. The arrows continued to fall. The men on horses tried to escape but there was a press of men behind them. Some horses bolted and, in their panic, reared and flailed their hooves. Saxons died by their own horses. Some of the horses bolted through the forest. The men advancing there would have to watch for danger from their rear. Haraldr and I found man or horse with every arrow. Three horses lay on the ground kicking their hooves in the air. They were dying. I felt my back burning with the effort. I had six arrows left and already we had halted the enemy attack. They had not made a shield wall and, until they did, then plunging arrows would make a mockery of mail.

A horn sounded again and the ones who survived hurried back beyond the mound of dead animals and warriors. I had not planned it but our arrows had made a second barrier. I did not think they would be able to advance down the road. First, they would have to clear their dead. That gave me an idea.

I sent my last arrows into the men who scrambled over dead and dying horses. "Haraldr, take charge here. Keep arrows for their next attack."

I handed him my bow and clambered down. I picked up my shield and hefted it. Olaf Leather Neck was on one side of our defence and Haaken the other. I joined Haaken. He looked at me expectantly, "They were surprised. Haraldr hit their leader. Their horses caused much damage. Foolishly they did not employ a shield wall and they paid a price."

Haaken pointed into the woods. I could see metal. "And here they come!"

I drew my sword, "Ragnar's Spirit! Death to the Saxons!"

The hundred or so men I led banged their shields with their swords and roared. It was a message of defiance.

We had spread our men out. We had no second rank and we had no reserves. We stepped across the Roman ditch and into the eaves of the forest. My men had laid the snares and traps just eight paces in. We had eight paces to fight. Then we could fall back to the ditch. I hoped, by then, that night would have fallen. The Saxons had to approach us as individuals. Karl Olafsson was the first to strike a blow. He was one of my warriors from Windar's Mere. His father had fought alongside me. He bore his father's shield with the wolf painted upon it. The first Saxon who broke through the brambles stood no chance as Karl brought his sword across his body. The mailed Saxon had his throat ripped open and he fell across the fallen branches. He hung there, another barrier for the Saxons to pass.

The first Saxon I slew had a leather vest, shield and spear. Caught in the brambles he jabbed at me with his spear. I fended it away with my shield and hacked across his body. He did not die instantly. He fell and slowly bled to death. Around me, other Saxons were suffering the same fate as they came against a Viking warband which had nothing to lose. We fought because there was nowhere to run. A wild Saxon saw me and ran towards me with a wood axe in his hand. He did not look where he was going. I took a step back. He tripped over the dying man I brought over my sword and laid his spine open. I now had three bodies before me. Others had just as many. We had a wall. It was a wall of Saxon dead.

Suddenly a horde of them ran at us. They had shields held before them. They were not a continuous line. The trees and the undergrowth slowed some up. The shields they held before them limited their vision. My shield was held to the side. When I needed to I could pull it up in an instant. One Saxon stumbled. He put his arms out to regain his balance. I drover Ragnar's Spirit into his chest. As I pulled it out another appeared and he tried to use this dead comrade to leap up at me. I slashed my sword across his middle. He lay writhing on his companion's body. He tried to shove his entrails back inside. I had no time to give him a warrior's death as others were coming for me. I knew why they came for me. It was not because I was Dragonheart. It was because I was a white beard. I was an easy kill. Four more Saxons found that they were wrong. As darkness descended a horn sounded three times and the Saxons filtered and fled back through the woods.

I turned to Haaken, "Watch here while I check on the others." I went around and found that we had lost but six men. The Saxon wall lay all around us. "Erik, have the bodies stripped and then use them to make a barrier around us. Make the Saxon spears and swords into traps for the next attack."

"Aye Jarl Dragonheart. A great victory!"

"It is a start only." I turned, "Olaf, Haaken, Galmr!"

My three men ran to my side, "What is amiss, Jarl Dragonheart?"

"Nothing Galmr. I just have a plan for this night. Choose the six best men with knives. Tonight, we go out. They will try to shift the horses and their dead. I would make life hard for them. So long as that road is blocked then they must come through the woods. It will be a long day tomorrow but if we can hold them we have a chance to escape."

Now that our battle was over we were able to hear the battle to the south. Some of those from the north were now engaged with Sigurd Snake in the Eyes. We were surrounded.

"Snorri. Have your band make a barrier to the south. The Saxons had wood axes. Use them to cut branches. Use Saxon bodies too."

"Yes, Jarl Dragonheart." He held up the byrnie he had taken from a dead Saxon. "Already four of us have mail! You have brought us good fortune."

"Perhaps!" We would have a small stronghold. Eighty paces from east to west and a hundred and fifty paces from north to south, it would not be the largest fort but it was all we had and we would defend it with our lives.

Chapter 14

The battle sounds died away as night fell. The woods were filled with the sounds of wounded men who had been forgotten in the battle. They moaned for friends to come and help them. We took off our mail. We used the charcoal from the fire to blacken our faces and hands. I took Wolf's Blood and a seax. I gathered the men I would lead around me. "We do not have enough warriors to waste any. Strike only when you know that you will not be seen. Our purpose is to slow down the removal of the dead and to spread terror. You can only do that if you are alive." I did not look at my Ulfheonar when I said that. They would need no guidance from me. "When I give the howl of the wolf then return. That is my command."

We slipped through the woods. My men had left a gap in the wall of warriors. As I stepped through them I saw that this was my dream. *'I found that I was sinking into the dead and dying bodies. They were like human quicksand.'* Did this mean we had interpreted the dream incorrectly? Was it Saxon bodies I saw? Could we win? I put those thoughts from my mind. I had to concentrate on killing.

My movements were so well practised that I did not think about them. I did not have my wolf cloak but, other than that, everything else was the same. I watched where I placed my feet. I sniffed the air. I looked ahead before moving. All of that took time but it was time well spent for it meant I approached the Saxons silently. I heard them as they laboured to move the bodies. With two men to a body they had begun with the dead warriors first. The horses would be more difficult to shift. I saw Haaken to my right. I gestured ahead with my seax. Two Saxons were carrying the body of a thegn. With the mail it was heavy and they were struggling. At one point they dropped it. A voice called out to ask what was amiss.

"Nothing! We tripped!"

Haaken nodded. We would take these two men. Haaken and I had fought together for so many years that we could almost read each other's thoughts. My hand was around the mouth of one and my seax slipping across his throat even as Haaken did the same with the other. The body of the thegn crashed to the ground. The other Saxons laughed and one shouted, "Clumsy oaf!"

It was tempting to take the mail but that would have been noisy and taken time. Haaken and I moved a little closer to the road and waited for the next two men to come by with bodies. I had to hope that my other men were enjoying the same success as we were. When we heard the next two lumbering through the undergrowth Haaken slipped around one side of the tree. As the first Saxon came next to me I rammed Wolf's Blood up under his ribs and into his heart. He and the body fell. The other Saxon grew another mouth as Haaken killed him.

Inevitably some of my men were spotted. I heard a cry, "Vikings!" It came from the far side of the woods.

I gave a howl and with two weapons ahead of me Haaken and I raced towards the road. There were ten Saxons there and they were labouring to remove a horse. They had had to resort to using axes to dismember the beast. The ten Saxons were looking to the far woods. Siggi Einarsson and Folki Siggison joined as and we burst amongst them while they were hacking the dead animals to pieces. This time there was no need for silence. I tore Wolf's Blood into the side of one while I ripped open the stomach of a second. Olaf Leather Neck appeared from the other side. He had picked one of the axes they were using to dismember the horse. His axe took first one head and then another. I hacked and slashed at shocked, stunned and surprised Saxons. It was one thing to know that Vikings were near but another to have to face them in the dark of night. There were none left alive.

"Back!"

We hurried down the road. There were noises from the Saxon camp as they realised that the men they had sent to clear the road had been attacked. I saw Haraldr and the ones we had left behind looking anxiously as we came through the gaps in the walls they had made.

Erik Cold Blade asked, "Did it work?"

"I am not certain but we have delayed it in any case. They will attack again tomorrow."

Haaken wiped his blade on his cloak, "With any luck they will attack the Danes instead of us."

"Haraldr, how many arrows do we have left?"

"In total, Jarl Dragonheart just under two hundred."

"Then give my Saami bow to one who can use it and pick the ten best archers to defend the road. When they are gone, they are gone."

Snorri Haraldsson said, "Jarl Dragonheart, get some rest. We will set the watch."

"I am not too old to stand a watch."

"No but without your mind we are doomed. We wish to live and you give us the hope that we might."

Before I slept I sharpened my weapons and used oil on my mail. I needed sleep but I needed to be protected in battle and my mail and sword would do that. As I curled up in my cloak I felt more hopeful than I had since we had discovered the second Saxon army. We had held them and, from the lack of noise further south, the brothers had too. We had another long day to endure. If we survived that we just had an eighty-mile march to the Isle of the Sheep. I fell asleep to the sound of blades being sharpened on whetstones.

Haaken shook me awake. It was still dark. "What is it?"

"We heard noises and movements from the Saxons. I think they were trying to be quiet but the sentries heard them."

"Rouse the camp."

"They are roused. You are the last." He handed me my sword. "Harald sharpened it for you last night. He is a good lad. His father would be proud."

I smiled, Ragnar's Spirit had been doubly sharpened. I grabbed my ale skin and took a deep drink. It was stale now. Three days in a skin did not improve the taste. It was wet. I took out a piece of cured venison and bit a chunk off. It would take some time to chew. The chewing would make me less hungry. It was the time to fight rather than eat. When I reached the men, I was greeted by smiles. There was an air of confidence amongst the men. We had been outnumbered and we had held off the enemy. More than that we had hurt them in the night. They had not completely cleared the road. They would have to either come through the woods or from the south. I wondered if the brothers had thought to fight their way back to us. Had I been in their position then I would have done so. To stay where they were just meant a longer journey back to the river. Then I realised, they thought they could still win. They still had the dream of conquering Wessex. That had been their plan the whole time and I had been the means to do so.

We stood in silence and I listened. I could hear, in the lightening morning air, the sound of men moving through the undergrowth. If they thought they were being stealthy then they were wrong. We stood in a long line. Without reserves any breach would be disastrous. We each held our shields and our sword and axes. Haraldr led the men on the barricade. Olaf the men to the east, Snorri the band to the south and I had the west. Snorri would be the one who would need to be reinforced. They had just a few hewn logs and branches to slow down an enemy. I was ready to go to his aid.

As the sky grew lighter so I made out white faces. Unlike us they had not tried to disguise themselves. Then I heard a shout form the road and Haraldr yelled, "Release!" The Saxons would have used the difficult light to get close to the archers. At the same time the Saxons ran towards us. They still had the bloody, stinking bodies, undergrowth and tree branches to negotiate. I saw that they had axemen who hacked through the branches. They could not try the same tactic with the bodies. They were slick and slippery with blood and gore. We stood behind them.

A horn sounded and we heard the clamour of men as they charged. The first Saxons who attempted to try to climb the bodies slipped backwards. Others, waiting behind, used them as steps to climb up on to the top of the bodies. Two men stood above me. They were tottering a little. The spears they held did not help their balance. I slashed Ragnar's Spirit and struck the legs of two men. My sword had been well sharpened and I cut one of the legs in two and hit something vital in the other. They fell back and their blood added to the barrier. The two spears fell at my feet. I rammed my sword into a body and grabbed a spear. Normally used as a thrusting weapon the Saxons were so close that I was able to throw it and at a distance of three paces I could not miss. It struck a warrior and threw him back. I picked up the second and rammed that up into the body of the Saxon who had clambered onto the wall of dead. Others, who had tried to avoid the wall of logs and undergrowth had run into hidden spears and swords. I picked up my sword as more Saxons came, bravely, towards the ever-growing pile of dead.

I had a brief respite from attack and I looked up and down the line. Haaken still stood as did most of the other men on my side. One of Snorri's men came running towards me, "Jarl Dragonheart, we are hard pressed."

"I will come. Haaken, take charge. Galmr, Siggi Long Face, come with me." I grabbed another spear from a fallen Saxon and ran the thirty or spaces to the southern barricade. Here the Saxons had begun to climb up the barricade. I saw that six of Snorri's men lay dead. Six would be replaced by three. I hurled the spear at the Saxon who stood triumphantly at the top of the barricade and was preparing to jump down. It hit him squarely in the chest and he fell, knocking over another three who were trying to climb on the top. I did not stop but used the Saxon body before me to gain some height. I swung Ragnar's Spirit at face height. One

Saxon reared back and tumbled to the ground but the next warrior was not so quick and my sword tore across his cheek, into his nose and his eye. He fell back screaming. From my vantage point I could see Aclea. The three brothers were surrounded. They had no barricade and it was shield wall against shield wall.

Standing there I became a target for the Saxons. One threw a spear at me. Unlike the Saxon I had slain I had quick reactions. I flicked it away with my shield. I shouted, in Saxon, "I am Jarl Dragonheart of the Land of the Wolf! I have the sword which was touched by the gods! Fear me Saxons!" I lifted my head and howled.

I saw the Saxons before me recoil. It was not me they feared, it was the pagan in me. It was the fact that I had something which was magic. Saxons had only been Christians for a short time. Most warriors did not embrace Christianity easily. At heart they were still superstitious and they too believed in the power of a magic sword. The Saxons made good swords. Before they had become Christians, they had woven spells into them. I was the embodiment of a past they had lost.

Galmr shouted, "Enough, Jarl Dragonheart! We need you here in the line!"

He was right and I descended. However, my outburst had stalled the attack. I saw the Saxons regrouping. Priests began to chant their prayers.

I shouted, "Throw the bodies over the top."

In twos, my men picked up the bodies and hurled them over the top. They would slow up an attack. Their hacked bodies would show what they could expect if they met us sword to sword. Snorri Haraldsson came up to me, "How long can we hold on, jarl?"

"As long as we have to. Have your men sharpen their swords. Pick up the Saxon weapons. These warriors wear no mail. We can hurt them. We can make them fear us and afraid to attack us. I know not how many men attack us but I think that more are fighting the brothers. We hold on until dark."

I saw a thegn, dressed in mail, organising his men into a shield wall. I knew what was coming. They were going to demolish the barricade by charging it with the bodies.

"Jam these broken spears and discarded weapons into the barricade. Put them at head height. Then have the men ready to form a two-deep line."

"You can see the future, jarl?"

"No, Snorri but I have fought for many years and I know that if you have superior numbers you use them. They will try to batter us down. I want men with mail in the front rank. Wait for my command!"

"Aye Jarl."

I could see the priest blessing the hundred or so men who were about to attack us. I took out my whetstone and put an edge and a tip on Ragnar's Spirit. I had just finished when I heard a roar and the Saxons ran at us. They were thirty men wide and three men deep. I shouted, "Shield wall!"

I stood and waited for them to form up around me. We were just eight paces from the barrier. Siggi Long Face and Galmr flanked me. We had just thirty-two men, a threttanessa crew. This would not be easy. "Lock shields." Our shields touched. "When they break down the barrier their lines will become disorganized. The ones at the back will push hard. Step forward with me. Aim for the faces. We are better warriors and today we will prove it."

There was a crash and a crack as they hit the barricade. Intermingled with it were the screams of men who had been rammed into the swords and spears we had left there. The barrier, which was not as substantial as the one at the northern end of the road collapsed.

"Now!"

We took three strides and the sprawling Saxons who had broken through and survived were now on their knees. Ragnar's Spirit sliced into the skull of the first Saxon. As Galmr and Siggi killed the next two I raised my sword and, taking one more step, brought it down on the helmet of the next Saxon. I split his skull in two. I saw the third man in the line. He was slightly above me for he stood on the body of one who had been impaled by a spear. I broke my own rule and disobeyed my own orders. I left the line and rammed the sword up between his legs. He fell screaming. As I pulled out the sword I swung it backhand and it bit into the back of another in the second rank. One quick witted Saxon jabbed at me with his spear. It slid off my shield. He made the mistake of following through and I punched him in the face with the boss of my shield. I took one more step and felt Galmr and Siggi's shields lock with mine.

The Saxon thegn shouted, "Reform! God is on our side!"

Just then an arrow flew over my head and struck the thegn in the throat. As he fell back I shouted, "Drive them back!" I brought my sword over from my right and swept it into the shoulder of the Saxon fighting

Galmr. The Saxons still outnumbered us but they were leaderless. I had weakened their line in front of me and Galmr, Snorri and I began to advance into their line. When the three at the rear of their line fell, we turned to begin to attack the sides of the lines. The rout began. The Saxons turned. They had had enough. They trampled over their own dead and dying. They tumbled over the last of the barricades. We had defeated them. I looked up at the sun. It was barely past its zenith. We still had half a day to hold on. It would not be easy.

Seven of Snorri's warband had died. We took their bodies and covered them with cloaks. I looked around and saw, at the northern barricade, Haraldr as he raised his Saami bow. I now knew who had made the kill. I raised Ragnar's Spirit and shouted, "Your father is in Valhalla, Haraldr Leifsson and he is telling the Allfather that his son is a warrior!"

Some battles are over in the blink of an eye. One side breaks and flees. The other holds the field and robs the dead. This was different. We were an army trapped by a larger army. The King of Wessex was obviously not going to negotiate for he could just slaughter us all and then take our ships. Men cannot fight as we had done without a rest. Both sides were so weary that the battle stopped. I had no idea what the Danes would do but I knew what we had to do.

"Half the men repair the defences! The other half eat, drink and sharpen your weapons. Ulfheonar, to me!"

I saw that even Olaf Leather Neck, the warrior who never tired showed the effects of the battle. His axe was nicked. His helmet was dented and his mail had been cut. He took off the helmet, looked at it and said, "These Saxons die hard!"

I nodded, "They will break through when next they attack and they could do that at any point. I will see Haraldr in a moment. Those defences appear to be holding."

"He has done well." Haaken pointed south. "How goes it there?"

"Bloody! It is shield to shield. We can do nothing about the brothers. The web is spun and we must follow the path the Sisters have chosen for us. We have half a day to survive and then we risk a break out. I do not think that all of us will survive but so long as some get home then this tale will be told. Be ready to fall back to the ditch. I leave the judgement to you two. We may have to make our perimeter smaller." They nodded. "I want three warriors from each of you. I want good men with swords."

Haaken cocked an eye at me, "You do not intend to go out into the woods, do you? That would be fatal. You are tired."

"No, Haaken One Eye, the opposite. I intend to have ten men with me. When they break through I will take my ten men and we will eliminate the threat."

The both seemed satisfied. "Good for I have more than enough stories for a thousand voyages. We could sail to the edge of the world and I would still have tales to tell."

I went to Snorri, "I need two men from here. I am going to have a reserve to meet any Saxons who break through."

He nodded, "And they will break through. That is clear. I find it hard to believe why we still stand here. They are the grains of sand on the beach. There are too many to count. The last ones to attack had not fought us before." He held up a sword. It was a short one and poorly made but it had no marks upon it. "This sword fell from one of the first to attack. It is unused."

"And that gives me hope for they will be running out of warriors who have yet to face us. We have a short time to hold on. Eat, drink and sharpen weapons. We are stronger than the Saxons. When I give the command then fall back and we will make a last stand near our dead. I hope it does not come to that but it may do."

I headed up to the northern barricade. I noticed that those men who had drunk and had eaten now went to relieve their brothers who were repairing the damage done to the defences. Bodies were being removed. I saw that Haraldr had not lost any men. He handed me some cheese and a piece of ham.

"Where did you get these?"

"When we checked the bodies of those just on the other side I found them on a warrior."

"You went amongst them?"

He shrugged, "We needed the arrows. We found twenty we could use again. That gives us three each left to use."

I chewed on the ham and pointed south, "That was an arrow which turned the tide. I thank you."

He handed me his ale skin and I drank. "They had retired here and when I looked around to see how you fared he seemed an inviting target."

The ale was needed more than the ham. I was tempted to drink more but I knew we would need it during our escape. "I need four of your men. You have lost the least. I need men who are good with swords."

"That would be me then!"

"No Haraldr, you have shown to me that you can be a rock. You must hold here. Once you run out of arrows then these men will need someone to lead them."

"Thank you for your faith in me."

"You have earned it. If the rest have to fall back I want you and your men to hold this barricade. It is our most solid defence. When I command the rest to fall back you hold."

"Yes, Jarl Dragonheart."

I went back to the centre. The bodies of our dead lay there. I had a plan to have them serve us still. Looking around I saw that we had just over one hundred men who were unwounded. Six or seven had wounds and would slow us down when we left. The Saxons had lost more men. I had examined the bodies as I had walked around. Few had been the warriors. We had faced the fyrd. Their King would have used his better warriors against the greater number: the Danes. I took out my whetstone and began to sharpen my sword, dagger and seax. Ragnar's Spirit looked the worse for wear. It took me some time to return the edge and the tip. During that time my men arrived. As I sharpened I spoke with them. "You have all eaten, drunk and sharpened your weapons?" They nodded. "Good, then we are going to be the last resort. You will stay by me. We will be a wedge which charges whoever breaks through. If the dam bursts then we plug it. We kill the Saxons and then come back here to our dead. Their spirits will help us this day. Form yourselves up."

I sheathed my weapons and examined my shield and helmet. My helmet had a couple of scratches and dents but I had been lucky. I had avoided any serious blows. My shield, however, showed damage. The leather cover was ripped and torn. My wolf looked a little worse for wear. The shield would still work but edged weapons could now begin to chip away at the wood.

I heard a shout from Olaf, "They come!"

I shouted, "We are Vikings and we are brothers this day! I am not yet ready to go to Valhalla! Let us send these followers of the White Christ to their lamb in the sky! Odin!"

My men all began banging their shields and chanting, "Odin!" We were not yet beaten.

I felt the two shields of the men behind me as the wedge formed up. I had seen a pattern to the Saxon attack. The Saxon king was using his thegns to lead the men who worked his land to attack us. That explained why some attacks had been more successful than others. The last thegn who had attacked, the one killed by Haraldr, had had better armed men and that was why he had almost succeeded. We had defences which had been repaired but they were still slightly weaker than they had been. The bodies of the dead Saxons were still the greatest barrier.

It was hard to just stand and watch the men I led fight and die while we waited. It was not my way. The first attack was beaten off without us having to move but I saw method in the attack. The Saxons did not try to scale the barricades, they pulled at them. Without arrows and with few spears we could not hurt them as much. We killed but a few Saxons. The thegns had been given clear orders for after they had lost one or two they withdrew and the next band attacked the defences. The weak points would be the woods.

It was on Haaken's side that they broke through. Erik Cold Blade fell. Two of his oathsworn went to his aid and they were slain too. Haaken did not have enough men to hold them. I raised my sword and led my wedge. The thegn and the eight men who had broken through thought they had won the battle for their king. With my shield before me, we charged into them. The thegn saw us and shouted, "Shield wall!" It was a lifetime too late. We were running. I had ten men behind me. I rammed my sword into the open mouth of the thegn. I tore it out of the side of his skull. Behind me, my men hacked and chopped the Saxons. We kept moving. Erik and two of his men had fallen in the ditch. I used their bodies as a bridge and entered the wood.

The wedge I had formed was now broken. The Saxons had broken down the defences we had made. A fresh thegn, emboldened by the success of the first led his men towards me. I blocked his sword on my shield and, spinning around, brought Ragnar's Spirit into his back. One of the fyrd lunged at me with his spear. Bagsecg's mail saved me as the poorly made head slid along the oiled links. My sword took his head. The death of the thegn and the sudden appearance of my wedge made the fyrd fall back. I shouted, "Wedge withdraw!"

Our attack had allowed Haaken to reorganise his men. As I passed I said, "Withdraw to the ditch. We shrink the area we have to defend!"

"Aye jarl. Erik died well. I liked him."

I turned to my men when we reached the cloaked dead. "Fetch the three dead and lay them here."

"Aye Jarl Dragonheart." Two of Erik Cold Blade's men went to collect the bodies.

My men had all survived unscathed. I saw that one had no mail. I said, "Lars Snorrison, go and strip the mail from the dead thegn. It is yours!"

He grinned, "Aye, jarl. I felt naked amongst the rest of you!"

One of his shield brothers said, "Perhaps you ought to try that Lars. When they see what passes for your manhood they would die laughing!"

The banter was a healthy sign. We might be outnumbered and we might have to bury dead but we had yet to be defeated. The Saxons had been soundly beaten in every attack. Those yet to be sent into the fray had seen warriors leave full of the joy of battle and then the remnants returned defeated.

I saw that the Saxons were about to launch attacks at the two barricades once more. Lars managed to squeeze into the mail just as an attack began at the southern barricade. This time they tore the remnants down. I shouted, "Snorri, fall back and form a shield wall. "

"Aye Jarl."

"Olaf, fall back to the ditch!"

"Aye jarl." We would be closer together and better able to defend each other. If we had to then we could move all the way back to Haraldr and the carts. That would be our last stand. Our sudden move took the Saxons by surprise. Some of those at the front thought we had routed and came charging after our men. Vikings do not like to retreat. I saw Snorri Haraldsson and his men butcher the twelve men of Wessex who foolishly approached too close. To my left Olaf Leather Neck waited until all of his men were across before he sauntered back. For two of the Saxons it was too much and they hurled themselves at his seemingly unprotected back.

Fótr Firebeard shouted out a warning but it was unnecessary. Olaf knew what he was doing. He took one stride across the ditch and then, without even looking, began to swing his axe two handed. It hacked into the side of one of the men and, as he fell to the ground Olaf twisted it from the man's body and brought it up to smash into the skull of the second. Then he stepped back over the ditch and joined the men he led.

Haaken and his men were busy fighting off the Saxons who came from the west. Although, as Olaf had shown, a man could step across it, he could not do so while our warriors slashed and stabbed at them. I heard Haaken shout, "Push their bodies from the ditch!"

The men trying to get at Snorri had the remains of the barricade to negotiate and that ensured that they could not make a shield wall. The braver ones ran at Snorri and his men. Man for man they could not compete with us. A horn sounded and the Saxons stopped. They were going to do something. A horn always meant something. I said to the wedge, "Be ready to move in an instant."

They all murmured, "Aye jarl."

The Saxons were just waiting. They knew we had no arrows. For some reason, they had not bothered with slingers and they just stood. Then I saw men appearing. They did not run, they just stood behind the men who already faced us. Then a third row appeared. I could only see the ones to the south clearly but a glance left and right told me that they were preparing for a final assault.

"They will be coming. When they do Snorri, you and you men fall back to allow my wedge to hit them!"

"Yes, jarl."

I began to bang my shield and to step in time with it. My wedge emulated me. I said, "We are going to charge and hit the centre of their line. We are weakest here. No one goes beyond me! When I say '*fall back*' then do so!"

Perhaps the Saxons thought it made no difference that they had signalled their intent so clearly. They had sent more men but there were still just seventy-five or so before us. The bulk of their men had to be engaged with the brothers. We were an annoyance. They were a threat. I stared at the thegn at the rear of the Saxons. He was on a horse. That made him one of the commanders. I watched him counting his men to make certain that they were in the right formation. When he seemed satisfied I saw him turn to speak to the man with the horn.

"Snorri, ready?"

"Aye jarl."

I shouted, "Move just as the horn sounds." As soon as Snorri and his men moved I saw that there were eighty paces to the wrecked barricade. The front rank had formed there. Even before they began to move I shouted, "Now!" The Saxon line was moving but they were travelling slower than we were. I had no doubt that Haaken and Olaf faced the same threat but they still had the ditch before them. Snorri had nothing. I held Ragnar's Spirit over the top of my shield. There were one or two mailed men before us but only one or two. We hit them just as the third rank cleared the wrecked barricade. I ignored the spears which were jabbed at us. We had three good shields and they shattered the spears. My men had shields with metal studs. They were not just simple willow boards. They were a weapon and we used them well!

Viking Warband

As a spear scraped off my helmet I punched with my sword. Sometimes the Allfather takes a hand. He guided mine and my sword entered the eye hole of the full-face helmet and was only stopped by the helmet at the back. The man was dead and the weight of the men behind carried the dead body, like a battering ram, into the two ranks behind. The warriors behind me were using their swords too and our wedge forced itself into the heart of the Saxons. When Bolli splits logs for the strakes of a ship he uses wedges, which look too small for the task but they always do the job. We were like a small wedge. We were eleven men hitting seventy-five but our point and tip had all of our power behind it. The Saxons had locked shields and the whole three lines were dragged back. As they were Snorri and his men laid about them and the flanks were attacked.

   I was through their lines and the thegn on the horse stood obligingly close. I did not have the death wish but I did gamble. "Hold here!" He was ten steps from me and I hopped and sprang over the wrecked barricades. His eyes seemed to be on Haaken and his men. The Saxon with the horn shouted a warning but by then it was too late. I brought my sword across the horse's neck. Blood spurted. Its front legs collapsed and the thegn landed, awkwardly at my feet. I raised my sword and brought it down on the back of his neck. His helmet fell from his skull. I reached down and lifted it up by the hair. Swinging it, I hurled it at the Saxon with the horn. He shouted and tried to get out of the way. That was the last straw for the Saxons we had attacked. They fled. When they left the ones attacking the other three sides joined them. I reached down and took the chain of office from the headless corpse. The man I had slain had to be an Eorledman. They were the rank below the King. I had hurt them. I stood there as the Saxons ran past me. They gave me a wide berth. As I turned all of my men began banging their shields and shouting, "Dragonheart! Dragonheart!" I climbed onto the horse's carcass to get a better view of Aclea. To my dismay the fighting was further away. The Danes were about to lose and when they did then we would face the full force of King Æthelwulf. I looked at the sky, night was less than a couple of hours away. It was time to tell my men of my plan.

Viking Warband

Map showing: Mersea Island, Foulness Island, Lundenwic, Tamese, Canvey, Isle of Grain, Isle of the Sheep, Hrofecester, Cantwareburh, Aclea, Seouenaca

Chapter 15

I spoke to my Ulfheonar and the remaining three Norse leaders. The rest of the men were standing to and watching the Saxons. "I want the men well fed. Eat all that we have. When it is dark I want the Saxon dead propping at the two barricades and along the woods. Make it look as though they are still alive. I want them to think their own dead are our men watching. Then we gather all the spare kindling we can find and we will burn our dead. They died well and I would not have their bodies despoiled by Saxons. In death they will be fighting for us still."

"How so, Jarl Dragonheart?"

"While the fire burns, Fótr Firebeard, we will head east through the Saxon lines. The men I led the other night will clear a passage."

"But our ships are north of here!"

"They will be watching there. The best way to escape them is to head east and then turn north east. When you reach the river then you head west. They will not expect you from that direction."

"You say you as though you will not be with us."

I shook my head, "My drekar waits at the Isle of the Sheep. We will wait there three days for you. If you cannot get a ship then head there and we will take you with us."

Harald Iverson nodded, "We came for treasure and now the only treasure we take is our lives."

Haaken shook his head, "Not so. There is the mail, swords and helmets your men took. All of us took coin from the dead and there are three hundred laden drekar in Lundenwic. Some will have been retaken and others will have fled but there will still be ships there. Do not be precious about your own ship. Take whichever ship you can."

"Aye."

Some of the Saxons had had food with them. We also had a dead horse to butcher. We lit a fire and roasted it in small pieces so that they would cook quickly. It all added to the illusion that we planned to stay and fight another day. The funeral pyre was built close to the food fire. As soon as it was dark dead Saxons, including the headless Eorledman, were propped by the ditches and barricades. Broken spears and shields were arranged to make them look, in the dark as though we had sentries. Four of my men slipped out after eating and slit the throats of the nearest

Saxon sentries. There would be more but the alarm would not be given while we were still close to the road.

Before we set fire to the pyre we killed our dead warrior's swords. We put them in the crook of a tree and bent them. No Saxon would use them. I had the men move into the woods to the east of the road. When all was quiet I set the fire alight with Snorri, Harald and Fótr. Before it had taken hold the four of us, with shields on our back and helmets hung from our swords, moved into the woods. My knife men would be moving ahead of us. The Saxons who watched the flickering flames would die silently. I was at the rear. Every so often I would turn and listen. When I did turn I saw the flames leaping higher into the sky. The Saxons would be watching too. The wood crackled and burning wood floated, like stars into the night sky. It was fitting for it was like the warriors were flying to Valhalla. I saw my men's handiwork as we kept heading east. We used the stars ahead and the fire behind to stay on course. When the Saxons discovered our ruse, they would pursue us but not before the Danes had been killed.

As we headed through the forest which seemed to stretch for miles I reflected that I had done the Norn's bidding. I had led the Danes and they had died. I still had no idea why they were being punished or if this was just part of some grander plan. For me it meant that my land and my clan would not be cursed.

When we left the forest, we might be in trouble but, from the marks Atticus had put on the map he had given me, there were not many areas of high ground between us and the Temese nor were there any Roman Roads. We had one night to disappear and then the Saxons would search for us. Eighty-four of us entered those woods. When dawn broke we were close to the edge. I decided that we ought to rest before we moved on. Tired men made mistakes. It was we were waiting that we discovered there were only eighty of us. Four men had become separated in the night. If they were just lost then we would not be hurt but if they had been captured it could change everything. The plan to head east was known to all. I spent an anxious hour with Haaken and Haraldr staring into the woods. Suddenly we heard the sound of men approaching. We sheltered behind trees and waited. When we heard Norse, we stepped out. However, it was not just our four lost sheep we found, they had with them five Danes.

"Where did these come from?"

One Dane, with a bandaged arm spoke for them, "Jarl Dragonheart, we were at Aclea. We were part of Guthrum Saxon Slayer's warband. He is dead. All of our oar brothers are dead. Halfdan Ragnarsson fled south with four hundred of his men and we were left behind. We lay amongst the dead until the Saxons had passed. We tried to go north but the men of Wessex have horsemen out hunting for us. We heard the sound of swords clashing, horses screaming and men dying. There are just five of us left."

"Are the rest of the Danes dead?"

"Hvitserk Ragnarsson is dead. Sigurd Snake in the Eyes is still in Aclea. The last of the army are gathered with him. There cannot be more than five hundred. with him." He shook his head. "Three days since I would not have believed that so many could have fallen! We fought hard. There is a ring of dead Saxons around the village. They cannot get close to them but they are doomed."

"How so?"

"We ran out of food yesterday and when we came through the forest we saw men gathering wood. They are going to burn them. That is why we headed north and east. Your men found us two miles back."

I waved them to the others. "Now Haaken, here is a puzzle. Where has Halfdan gone? There is nothing for him south but it might work to our advantage. If the Saxons follow him and try to burn out Aclea we might have a chance."

"Perhaps but you know the Sister's webs are complicated. There will be twists and turns before we see the Land of the Wolf once more."

We left the forest. We now had eighty-nine men. We were a formidable force but we had to remain hidden. We needed to put as much distance between us and King Æthelwulf. Sigurd would not surrender. It was Halfdan Ragnarsson who interested me. I knew he was clever. Was he doing as we were doing? Was he going in one direction to later change it and to throw off his pursuers?

I led for I had the maps. We followed the tiny threads of red which were Atticus' roads. They looked like the threads of a spider's webs. Was that a sign? Now that the sun was up it was easier to check our direction. I headed north and east. We were heading for the valley of the Darent. Atticus had put the blue line there. I could not read the name but he had, patiently, explained the names of the different places he had written. We would have water and be sheltered from prying eyes. The rest could follow it to the Temese but my warriors would leave it at Seouenaca. Atticus had said there was a chapel there. There was also a hall. He knew that for he had journeyed there with his master to buy horses. It was another reason I had devised this plan. The last thirty or forty miles would be easier if we had horses. Seouenaca was still a day away.

By late afternoon, when the sun was dipping in the west, we left the forests behind. We slipped out into the open countryside. We were in country dotted with farms. The farms had fields with growing crops in them. There were a few animals dotted about. Then we would be in copses and thickets again. We passed through a particularly lush thicket of hawthorn, rowan and ash. I was at the front and I smelled the village. It was a mixture of wood smoke, animals and dung spread on fields. I could not see anything for the undergrowth hid it but I trusted my senses. I waved my hand for my men to take cover. "Galmr, come with me."

Dropping our shields and drawing our swords we ran through the barley, keeping as low as we could. I heard the noise of people chatting. It was a village. There were two choices. Take the village or retrace our steps and try to find a way around it. If we chose the latter then we were inviting disaster. We had spent half a night and half a long day putting distance between us and the men of Wessex. The last thing we needed to do was to go back towards them. They would be hunting for Danes and spreading their net ever wider. We bellied up through the barley. It was not a flat field. I lifted my head and saw that the village was on a slightly higher piece of ground. There were six huts. It looked to be a collection of farms.

We slid back down. "Go and fetch the men. Haaken can bring half through the field. I want Olaf Leather Neck to go along the road and try to approach from the far side. I do not want any to escape."

He disappeared through the barley. I marked his progress by the swaying cereal as he passed through it. To any in the village who happened to see it, it would have appeared like the wind. I crept a little closer to the edge of the barley. I could not see any younger men. I spied women, children and a couple of white beards. I wondered if the men had been called to follow their thegn. That would make sense and would make our task easier. I heard the rustling of barley as Haaken and half of my men approached.

I spoke to Haaken, "I do not think there are any men. If we can stop any escaping this might be a perfect place to lie up for the night. There will be food and shelter."

"We will have to guard the women and children... or kill them."

I shook my head, "That is not my way and you know it. If any escape then it is the will of the Norns. We will give Olaf a little while longer. He is not getting any younger."

There was a sudden shout in the distance. I stood and raised my sword. "We want prisoners!"

Forty men rising in a long line from the field of barley came as a real shock to the villagers. They screamed. Children ran to their mothers. Old men grabbed wood axes and stood protectively in front of the women and children. Those on the far side ran. I saw Olaf and the rest of my men appear. It stopped the flight. The shoulders of the women dropped in resignation and they held their children a little tighter to them.

I shouted, in Saxon, "Drop your weapons and you will live. I swear that you will not be harmed."

One of the six old men shouted back, "And why should we believe you, Viking?"

Haaken said, "Because we could cut you down and not even notice old man! Do as the Jarl Dragonheart says. He does not lie!"

The old man looked around. Seeing eighty men he realised the futility of resistance. "Do as the heathen says!"

"Fótr, find a building which can be guarded and put the old men in it. Find another for the children."

He nodded, "And the women?"

"There will be no need to watch them. If the children are guarded they will not do anything to risk their lives. They can prepare food, under supervision, of course." I sheathed my sword and followed the old men who were shepherded by Fótr's men. I knew if I asked direct questions I would not be given truthful answers. I decided to be devious. "Old man, your fyrd fought well against us but they were still defeated."

The one who had spoken looked at me. He was shocked, "How could a small band such as this defeat so many men? When they passed through here it took a day for them all to do so. I have never seen as many men before."

"We are part of the warband. Did you not know that Vikings fight in small warbands? We just joined together."

"Then where are the rest?"

I shrugged, "I know not. Cantwareburh is not far away is it?"

He said nothing but scowled, "God will punish you if you touch our churches!"

"We have taken many already. I think he does not care."

"Blasphemy!"

Fótr's man said, "Here Jarl Dragonheart. This has just one door."

"Then guard it well. You will be relieved."

As we headed back to the others Fótr asked, "What was that about Cantwareburh?"

"Nothing. When we leave they will run to tell others of the Viking warband and they will look to Cantwareburh. They will try to be clever and catch us there. You will be safe and heading north. The land around Cantwareburh is boggy and marshy. It will take them a long time to search it."

"How do you know such things?"

"I have men in my land who are curious and they gather knowledge like I gather white hairs. They make me maps. We just try to outwit the enemy if we have not the numbers to defeat him."

Snorri shook his head as we headed back to the others, "I thought we had enough men this time. Did you not think so too?"

"I thought we had enough men but they were not the right men. As soon as the brothers allowed their men to rampage we were lost but I believe that this venture was doomed from the start. You cannot recruit three hundred and fifty ships and not expect your foe to know what you plan. We should have marched to meet the army of Wessex. If we had defeated that then we could have raided Lundenwic, Cantwareburh and even Wintan-Caestre without fear of opposition."

As we neared the camp an older woman, I could see streaks of white flecked in her golden hair, stood defiantly with her hands on her hips. "Where are our children and our fathers?"

"They are being guarded. I promised the old one that they would not be harmed and I will keep my word."

She nodded and then said, "Eorledman Edgard and the King will come for you. You are many miles from the sea and you are on foot. You will all die."

A thought struck me. I took out the seal I had taken from the dead Saxon. "Is this the seal of Eorledman Edgard?"

She could not hide her horror. Her hand went to her mouth and she gasped, "He was a good man! Where is he? Where are our men of the hundred?"

"He is dead and so I imagine that, in your religion, he is in heaven. As for your men?" I shrugged, "Some were killed but not all. No one is coming to hunt us. Prepare food for us and tomorrow we will be gone and you can tell the tale of how the barbarians came and you survived."

I nodded to Beigaldi Bergilsson, "Go and watch the women. Make sure they do not taint the food. Tell them the same food we eat will be fed to their children."

The campaign thus far had taken its toll of me. I felt weary and yet we still had a long way to go. The ale we found had been prepared, I guessed, for a victory feast. There was plenty of it. We would all have enough in our ale skins to keep us going when we left. There was also enough for us to drink to the dead. The food was hot and that, in itself, was like a feast. There was plenty of it. Again, they had supplies in ready to celebrate. I was an old soldier and knew that you thanked the Allfather for such bounty. You knew not when another one might come along.

Harald, Fótr and Snorri joined me and my Ulfheonar as we sat around the fire. "We part tomorrow, Jarl Dragonheart?"

"Some time tomorrow, Harald. Seouenaca is to the north of us. I know not who long it will take us but you will need to go north. I would offer you all an oar on *'Red Snake'* but she is a threttanessa."

"We have decided to heed your advice. There seems little point in trying to extract our ships. They were in the middle of the fleet. We will take whichever ships we can from the ones which remain."

Haaken said, quietly, "From what those Danes said, resistance at Aclea was over yesterday. The Saxons will be hunting. You may find them waiting for you at the Temese."

I saw the three heads droop. "You forget, Haaken One Eye, that others will have escaped. We know that Halfdan and his warband are loose in the land. There will be others. I do not think there will be a band as big as ours. The Saxons need to hunt and then to kill. None of us liked fighting alongside the Danes but even I admit that they are warriors. They will not submit without a fight. What I do say, is that you must move quickly. Do not tarry. Looking at the map it is not a long way from Seouenaca to the river. Once you reach the river you are in the hands of the Allfather."

Haaken said, quietly, "And the Norns."

We all clutched our amulets. He was right. They were not yet finished with us.

We left before dawn. The old men and women still looked at us fearfully as though we might go back on our promise. I led the men east. That was to maintain the illusion that we were heading for Cantwareburh. I had Haraldr hide a mile from the village to discourage any who sought to follow us. His long legs made short work of the run and he caught up with us to tell us that none had followed. We turned north. I kept us to the folds and hollows upon which the ancients had built their trackways. We followed, after a few miles, the stream which seemed to be heading north. When we reached the river, I knew that Seouenaca would not be far away. Every warrior had taken food from the village. We had our ale skins and we had our weapons. We were still a dangerous foe. Once we reached Seouenaca we would divide and then the danger would begin.

Galmr was the scout who found the tiny village. "Jarl Dragonheart, it is over the next ridge."

I nodded, "Then, my shield brothers, this is where we part. We will wait. You have three days from now. If we do not see you again then it has been an honour to fight alongside you. If you survive then visit the Land of the Wolf. If we do not live through this then you can tell our families the tale of the end of the Dragonheart and his Viking warband."

Snorri said, "You will survive." He clasped my arm, "Farewell."

There were many such goodbyes for when you have fought alongside other warriors there is a bond which lasts a lifetime and beyond, to Valhalla. The Danes we had found chose to follow Snorri and the others. That made sense. There were Danish ships and crews at the river. It meant that I led just sixteen men to Seouenaca. If we could I would avoid the people. Now that there were just seventeen of us we could not afford a pitched battle.

The land through which we were travelling had fields cleared amongst hedges and woods. It was rolling land. I could see why they bred horses, cattle and sheep. It would be easier than ploughing. We followed the greenways which wound north and east. Atticus' maps had served their purpose. We were now two days from the Isle of the Sheep. We had just crossed a small beck when Haraldr, who had sharp ears, picked up the noise of the horses. We spread out in a line and left the trail to move through the scrubby undergrowth. I waved the men down and we bellied up to the field which lay before us. There were animals grazing. Six horses shared the field with four cattle and a small flock of sheep. There had to be a shepherd.

I waved Ráðgeir Ráðgeirson over and pointed to the field. I made the sign to scout and then drew my finger across my throat. He nodded and slipped along the edge of the field. We could not afford to have the alarm raised. Six horses were not enough. Ráðgeir could have been an

Ulfheonar. He lived by hunting and to stalk a shepherd was easy. As there were horses and cows the shepherd did not have a dog. Had he had one he might have been alerted. He died silently and we slipped into the field. In the war gear we all carried we had lengths of rope and we fashioned them into halters. The top of the farm could be seen, smoke spiralling from the roof but we were in dead ground and hidden. We led the horses down the slope and rejoined the greenway.

Once we were out of sight I had six of my men mounted, "Ride in threes and see if you can find more horses. Another six would do. Some of us can ride double."

Haaken said, "And see if you can find a giant one for Haraldr!"

"We will continue on this trackway. It heads in the right direction. It would be better if you could avoid being detected."

The six rode off and Ráðgeir and Galmr acted as scouts with Haraldr bringing up the rear.

"Where next, Jarl Dragonheart? You seem to have a plan in your head but we are not aware of it. You do not mean us just to head north and east, do you?"

"No, we have to avoid Hrofecester. That lies at the mouth of the Medway. Atticus told me that the Romans had a fort there and the men of Cent refortified it. That means we must cross the river soon. Bridges will have people close by them. We need a ford and that means crossing upstream somewhere." Atticus and Aiden had done their best but the finer details we needed were not on the map. We would have to waste time searching out a ford.

My six men appeared to be away a long time. The ground over which we travelled was sloping down towards the river. It did not appear to be a steep valley. That meant there would be many loops in the river. The fact that the fyrd had been called to give battle made our task easier. There were few men working the fields. Old men and boys could be seen in the distance. Walking in the greenway meant we were hidden from view. We saw them through the gaps but they would not notice us; I hoped. It was after noon when we heard hooves and we slipped into the undergrowth. It was easier now that there were fewer of us. It was Karl Olafsson with the other horsemen. They had with them eight horses. Three men would have to ride double. We would be easier to spot and to track but we now had the ability to travel further and quicker.

"Did you have any trouble?"

"No, Jarl Dragonheart. These eight were penned in two different fields. They had gates. We were not seen."

Once mounted we made much better progress. When we reached the road, which led due east I took it as a good sign and we followed it for a mile or so. It descended steadily. I saw smoke in the distance and the light shining on the river. Where there were houses there would either be a bridge or a ford. There would also be people. When I saw a track leaving the road I joined it. The track headed south but it then began to turn east. It was heading down to the river. Once again, I saw smoke but this time it was a single hut. I decided to risk it. The track twisted and turned and ended up at the river. There was a hut but I saw no one. We would have made noise as we approached. If anyone was in the hut they would hide. Horsemen would not be welcomed. The river was just forty paces wide. It was hard to tell the depth.

"Haraldr. Let us see how deep this is. Begin to walk across."

Haaken laughed, "I do not think you thought you would be a walking measuring stick eh Haraldr?"

Alarmingly the water was deep at the bank. It came up to his waist. He began to wade across. The water came up to his chest. He was half way across and it had got no deeper. He was almost at the other side when he disappeared from view. A hand came up and grabbed a handful of grass on the other bank. A spluttering Haraldr raised his head and waved. He pulled himself up.

"We have our answer. Let us ford."

Once on the other side we ate and we drank from our ale skins. Haraldr dried himself as best he could. "Jarl Dragonheart, I will run rather than ride for a while. It will dry me off." I cocked my head to one side. "I will not slow you up. The Allfather gave me long legs for a purpose. I can run.

Olaf said, "I am sure I spied a movement at the hut."

I nodded, "The smoke told me someone was in there but there is no horse and it will take time to get to the settlement with the bridge. We will have disappeared by then. We head due east to make them think we go to Cantwareburh and after dark head due north. I wish us to reach those fishing boats the shepherds use."

As we headed north and east the land became even more sparsely populated. It was boggy and filled with twisting little streams and tarns. At one point Haraldr sank to his waist in a particularly deep pool. We were grateful for the horses. As darkness fell I estimated that we were not far from the sea. We could smell it. The horses were struggling and it seemed foolish to blunder around in the dark. We did not want to risk losing one more of our number. We were all acutely aware that we had lost fewer men than any other warband. I was proud of that and I wanted to take all sixteen men to join the others on the drekar.

We could have risked a fire but that would have meant finding dry wood. Besides we had nothing left to cook. We were on the dried food we saved for such emergencies. The last of our ale made it palatable. We hobbled the horses and almost collapsed into a weary stupor. Haaken and I were awake longer than the others. He knew I had things on my mind.

"You are worried about Sámr are you not, Dragonheart?"

"I am. We have both seen how events can turn out differently. I did not think the Danes would lose as many men as they did."

"Where did they go wrong?"

"They did not listen to me nor to their own common sense. They believed that sheer weight of numbers would win the day for them and they were wrong. We had enough men to have controlled the Temese. Knowing that the Saxons were ready for us could have been used to our advantage."

"How?"

"The farms we raided had no men. They were away fighting us. If we had not given them the chance to fight us they would have drifted back to their farms and their army would have been smaller. The sons of Ragnarsson did not exercise enough control over their men. I can see a day when another Viking army will come and the next time they will conquer this land!" I was silent and stared north east as though my eyes could penetrate the dark and see the Island.

"But you still worry about Sámr."

"I still worry."

"The dream showed him a man. You have done all that you could. He will be there."

"I hope so and I hope that we are not being tricked!"

We awoke to a grey day. We woke to rain filled clouds scudding from the north east. That was always a bone chilling cold wind. It found gaps in cloaks and mail. I was just glad that we did not have far to travel. The rain did not help the journey and Haraldr was travelling as fast as we were. It took us half a day to cover the ten miles to the estuary of the Temese and the Medway. The river was just a mile away as we climbed to the top of an island of dry ground. Before we even saw it, we saw the burning drekar. There were twenty or thirty of them and they were between the Isle of Grain and the Isle of the Sheep. I knew they were Danes but the sight of those beautiful ships filled me with sadness. That sadness was replaced by fear almost instantly. Who had burned the ships? What about **'Red Snake'**? I could see that they had been set alight in the estuary and the wind had blown them to the southern shore. When the tide went out they would be blackened skeletons.

I shouted, "Dismount. We lead the horses. I do not wish to be seen."

I put my shield around my back and hung my helmet from my sword. I needed to be able to see and to hear. The grey murk made visibility difficult. Had the ships not been on fire we would have struggled to see them. They looked to be close inshore. The wind must have blown them there. We probably did not need the horses but I kept them anyway. I gave the halter to Haraldr and I drew my sword. I led. I spied the fishing village with the boats. It was about two miles away. In the murk and the drizzle, it was hard to be accurate estimating such distances. Once I had located it we dropped down into the lower ground. I did not want to be seen. There was urgency in my footsteps now. I had thought that evasion was all that was needed and now I saw that we had taken too long. My ship and great-grandson were in danger. A little less sleep and we might have already been on the island. Old Ragnar's voice came into the head, *'Do not dwell on the past you cannot change it. The future is not yet written. Do something about that!'*

I almost made the mistake of rushing and moving too quickly. I was about to climb a drier piece of land when I heard voices. I held up my hand to halt the others and bellied up. I saw that there were twenty Saxons. They were armed and standing close to the sea. The boats were being readied. They were going to the island! In the distance I saw the banners of more men. They were hard to make out but I estimated that they were a mile away. The twenty men had been sent to secure the boats. They were going to the Isle of the Sheep.

I returned to my men. "There are Saxon warriors. More are coming. I want ten of you to take the horses. The rest of us will make our way to the shore. When I give the howl of the wolf then make the horses stampede towards the village. Follow up. We have to strike quickly and decisively. We must take the fishing boats before the others reach the village."

Any other warriors would have had a dozen questions. These were the best of my men and they just nodded. I swung my shield around and headed for the water. I did not look who followed me. They were all good. The sound of the water breaking on the shore to our left would mask the jingle of armour and leather. I hurried. As soon as I saw that the boats were less than forty paces from me I howled. I did not wait for the horses I ran. The sound of the horses from my right sounded like Odin's thunder. The Saxon warriors were confused. They had heard a howl, from the sea, and then they heard horses. Was this witchcraft?

The first Saxon was looking at the horses as I tore my sword across his middle. I punched a second in the face with my shield and Haraldr ended his life. Speed was all that mattered. I rammed my sword into one side of a Saxon and it came out of the other. I saw the horses trample three warriors and four of the fishermen who had been standing nearby. The horses just panicked and galloped hard to get away from my men. Olaf Leather Neck swung his axe and a head flew. Haraldr had become a skilled swordsman. He knew how to use his height and reach. None could get near him. Even as my men rushed after the horses the Saxon warriors lay dead or dying.

Folki Siggison shouted, "Jarl, the banners! They are getting closer!"

There were ten fishing boats. We needed four. "Olaf wreck six of the fishing boats. The rest of you get aboard and get to the island."

Galmr said, "What is the hurry, Jarl Dragonheart, the Saxons are dead?"

I pointed east. The Saxon banners were coming. I saw them moving quickly along the beach from the east. "But they are not!"

Olaf Leather Neck needed no second urging and he began to hack and smash into the bottom of the boats. Haaken had grabbed the ale skins from the dead Saxons and my other men had taken random items. It was in our nature. The first three boats had left and the Saxons were just four hundred paces from us when Olaf had finished and the three of us and Haraldr climbed aboard the last boat. We hoisted the sail. The wind was from the north east but it would take us away from the Saxons. We would be able to land on the western side of the Isle of the Sheep. It was not a big island. The other three boats were ahead of us. I let Haaken steer and I stared at the burned drekar. Most were on the beaches. They were like black skeletons. Three of them had not made the shore. They now blocked the channel to the Medway. Their masts poked forlornly above the water. As Haaken turned us to steerboard to make a landfall I wondered how so many ships could have been destroyed. Once ashore we dragged the fishing boats high above the high-water mark. None of us said a word but we knew that if our drekar was not there then we would have to sail home in the fishing boats. That would be a voyage that was the stuff of legends.

We took all that we had collected and we headed towards the inlet in the north. The murk had brought evening on sooner. It was not nightfall but we would have an interminable east coast dusk. I My drekar would be well hidden. She would have her mast on the mast fish and my crew would have disguised her. I hoped she was there but I had been expecting to see her almost as soon as we landed. That was not to be.

Haraldr had sharp eyes, "Jarl Dragonheart. There are two Saxon ships heading for the inlet."

I now knew what had burned the Danes. The Saxons had ships in the estuary and they were heading for *'Red Snake'*. Bizarrely that gave me hope for it meant she was still there. The fact that they were heading to shore also told me that we were close.

"Drop what you carry! We need to get to our drekar or be doomed!"

I was carrying nothing. I donned my helmet and slung my shield. I drew my sword and I ran. If I died protecting my great-grandson I would be able to face my son in the Otherworld. I would have died saving his grandson. I knew we would not make it in time. The ships were just two hundred paces from shore and we were still three hundred paces from them. Then hope filled my heart. The drekar was not at the mouth of the stream. I saw her shape and she was eighty or so paces from the sea. There was a chance, a slim one but I would take any chance!

Chapter 16

I heard my men on the ship as they began to hurl curses at the Saxons. They all had bows and there were using them. My men all knew the value of arrows descending upon a ship. Men could not row and hold a shield. The more arrows you sent the more men you hit and the fewer you would have to fight. I heard a roar from the leading Saxon ship as it ground ashore. They had eighty paces to run. We were sixty paces from them. They had not seen us and we would hit them in the flank. The second ship might cause us a problem but I would worry about that later. First, we had to break up the attack by the forty Saxons.

Their shields were on their left arms. We would be hitting their sword arms. Our shields would protect us and theirs would not. These are little things but they save lives. The Norns were spinning. My men were spread out in a long line. Some were ahead of me but that did not matter. I hit a warrior in the middle of the line. I swung my sword from my right and I timed it perfectly. He wore no mail and my sword bit into his chest. I knocked his body away with my shield and lunged at the next Saxon. My sword went through his shoulder and into his side. I tore it out and it made the mortal wound worse. We had broken into the centre of the Saxons and I shouted, "Back to back shield wall!"

If we could hold off the second boat load of Saxons then my crew had the chance to bring their arrows to bear and there was a chance we might survive. It was a slim chance but a warrior took any chance the gods gave him. Haraldr was on one side of me and Olaf on the other. I could not see Haaken. It felt strange to be fighting without my oldest friend at my side. We fought the Saxons while we jostled into two lines. We had had surprise on our side. Arrows from our drekar slew others too. Men began to run back to the Saxons from the second ship.

We had barely locked our shields when the second boat load hit us. They did not do so together and they wore no mail. I blocked the spear thrust and brought my sword from on high. The Saxon tried to block it with his shield but it was a simple willow board and a small one at that. My sword slashed it to kindling and ripped through his arm. I backhanded the man next to him. He blocked my sword with his own but Haraldr rammed his through the middle of the Saxon. Arrows, from our drekar, flew over my head and I knew that my men had read my thoughts. Or perhaps I had trained them well.

There had been eighty Saxons. Half that number lay dead or dying. The prospect of facing our arrows and our wall of steel proved too much and they turned and ran back to their ships. We saw the first one leave the beach and head west. We had taken them by surprise but they had numbers on their side. They could sail to the fishing village and pick up another forty men. They had been the ones who had almost caught us. It was not over yet but we had survived. If nothing else I could speak with Sámr again.

"Finish off the wounded. Strip the bodies. Haraldr, take some men and fetch what we dropped. We may need it."

Leaving my men to do as I had bid I hurried to the drekar. To my relief I saw Sámr. He peered over the side and grinned at me. My other men had all survived too. We were now in a better position to defend ourselves. Sámr had grown and he had become a warrior but the boy in him ran to me and threw his arms around me, "Great Grandfather, we thought you lost!"

Sweyn Alfsson nodded, "He is right Jarl Dragonheart." He pointed to the west. "Those ships which were burned were attacked by the Saxons. The Saxons lost two ships but all the crews of the Danish drekar were slaughtered. Forty ships escaped and followed us down the river but that was days since. What happened?"

I put my arm around Sámr, "That is a long tale. It is best told around a fire with food. Have you any food?"

Sámr nodded, "We chased away the shepherds two days ago. We had taken the sheep from close by us and Sweyn decided to use the larger flock for food."

I did not openly criticise for we could not change the past but that had been a mistake. The shepherds had returned to the mainland and they had summoned help. Had we arrived back just a few hours later then my ship would have been burned too.

I smiled, "Good, then let us eat mutton."

Night had fallen completely. I could not see the Saxons attempting to attack us at night. We would have a night to rest and to decide what to do. We ate and I let Haaken tell the story. I knew that he would be composing the chant for the drekar. The bloody battles would become heroic contests. It was good for the dead would be remembered that way. When he had finished Sámr and the crew asked about the ones who had not returned. We told them. We had not lost many but they would be in Valhalla.

Olaf Leather Neck said, "And we must stay here until the end of tomorrow for the Dragonheart promised those that fought with us that we would do so." There was the hint of criticism for making such a promise but having given it I could not go back and renege on it.

"It will take tomorrow to prepare the ship for sea. We have to get her back into the estuary and step her mast. We need food preparing for the voyage home."

Haaken said, "And you think that the Saxons will just let us do that?"

"Haaken One Eye, we do one job at a time. If they come, then we fight them. If we defeat them then we carry on with our preparations and if not…"

"If not does not bear thinking about for this story would not be told. We will make sure that we do defeat them!"

That night we slept aboard the drekar. The island was a damp, boggy place. The drekar was drier. The deck also reminded me of home.

When we rose, the drizzle had gone but it was still a grey day. The wind still came from the north and east. We would struggle to use the sail when we left. After we had eaten we began the task of moving the drekar. My crew had done well to move her. It would not take us as long to put her back into the sea. The tiny stream beneath her keel would enable us to pull her. We took away the disguise. Now there was no need. The men of Wessex and Cent knew where we were. We stripped down to our kyrtles and used ropes to haul it down the little stream to the estuary. Once she floated we tied her off and washed the mud from ourselves. Stepping the mast was not hard but the yard and the sail took time. My men were warriors and not lithe ship's boys who could scamper like squirrels up the masts and the rigging. Sámr had to do most of it. Haraldr proved to be of great use. Sámr was able to stand on his shoulders and rig the fore and back stays. It saved time but, even so, we were not finished when, just after noon, Sámr shouted from the masthead. "Four Saxon ships to the west!"

I looked west but could not see them. They would have to row and that would take time. We had not yet rigged all of the stays. That had to be done before we could sail. We would have to fight the Saxons on the land. I would not be able to break my word, even if I chose to.

"Arm yourselves. Sámr keep rigging the ship. When they come then use your bow. Snorri and Leif, you help Sámr and use your bows too." I began to prepare for battle. I donned my mail. I had not oiled it since the last battle near Aclea. It was still covered in Saxon blood. I had sharpened my sword before I had slept. I looked at my helmet. It had been a good thing that Bagsecg had made a new one for me. It now looked old for it was battered, dented and scratched. I could not even remember most of the blows. When I looked over at my men I saw that they too bore the marks of battle. It was only Haraldr's helmet which looked untouched. That was because few weapons could reach his head but his leather vest was cut and slashed. If he reached home then he could lay it to rest with honour for it had served him well.

By the time I was ready I could make out the Saxon ships as they beat up the river towards us. There were four of them. The Saxons were getting better at ship building but they were not dragon ships. They did not have our lines nor our speed. They looked to have a crew of about thirty in each. They would outnumber us but we could choose the ground on which we fought. The land close to the drekar was marshy and boggy. If we fought there we would die. Just thirty paces further south was a small piece of dry ground. It was where we had camped and cooked. The fire had dried out the ground a little more. Before it was a patch of water and bog. It also had a large pool which, although it did not look deep, looked to be muddy and would slow down an attacker. It was hard to see where the stream began and the pool ended. To get to the drekar the Saxons would either have to travel further south or come across the boggy ground. There would be twenty-three of us who would be contesting the ground.

"To the fire. We make a three-deep shield wall. Seven is a good number. Sámr fly my standard from the masthead. Let them know that they fight the Wolf of the North!"

The cheer from my men told me that they did not think that we were beaten yet! As we arrayed ourselves in our usual formation, Haaken and Olaf flanking me and Haraldr towering behind me, I stared at the approaching ships. They knew the coast for they were not landing at the boggy part close to our ship. They were heading for the beach where we had left the fishing ships. They would have almost eight hundred paces to reach us. If they were well led then they would wait until all four crews had landed. We would struggle to overcome such a large number. However, we were not dead yet and the day was young.

Haaken said, "The Norns, it seems, have not yet finished with us. Do they want every Viking dead?"

"You know better than any Haaken that it does not do to try to fathom the plots of the sisters. We are warriors. We have helmets and mail. Our swords are sharp and these are Saxons we fight. You know that if they have come by ship they will not wear mail."

The first ship had landed and I saw the thirty men disembark. The next ship was some forty paces from shore and the other two were further astern. The leader of the thirty raised his sword and they came towards us. They saw a handful of men on a small lump of earth. Our third rank was almost hidden for they were on the back side of the hummock. The Saxons must had seen just fourteen of us. Haraldr's bulk also hid those behind him. They could not come at us in a line. The ground was too boggy for that. The men had to watch their feet as they ran towards us. Ráðgeir laughed as two Saxons sank into a pool which was deeper than they had expected. Already they were weakening their chances of success. Those who were fleet of foot would reach us first. They would be the youngest. They would be the most reckless.

"Lock shields!" The Saxons might be fools but we were not. A wall of shields would be our defence; our swords, peering over the top of them, our attack. Eight of them had outstripped the rest. One was their leader and I saw that he was young. He had on a leather jerkin studded with metal plates. He had an open helmet and he, alone out of his men, faced us with a sword. The others used spears.

"Death to the pagans! For St Edmund and Essex!"

Even as I blocked his blow on my shield I was running his words through my head. The King of Wessex had raised the fyrd from the land south of Temese. The reason there were ships was that this was the army of Essex. They came from north of the river and they were allies of Wessex. I rammed my sword at the young Saxon's head. His shield came up and my blade slid along his cheek. It opened a bloody wound. It was not life threatening but I could see, from his eyes that it had startled him. My men despatched the spearmen next to him as I took another blow on my shield. The young Saxon was strong and my arm shivered.

Olaf growled, "Finish him Jarl Dragonheart!"

I feinted with my sword. He brought his shield up to protect his head. I rammed my knee between his legs. As he doubled over I plunged my sword into the back of his neck. I kicked his body to the ground. Four more of the Saxons had proved to be over eager and Olaf Leather Neck's axe took the head of one. Ráðgeir Ráðgeirson's sword a second while Galmr and Sweyn took the other two. The survivors were young and they were reckless but they were not fools. They knew that they would die if they attacked. They decided to wait for the others. That wait cost four of them their lives as Sámr and the men on the drekar sent their arrows into stationary targets. Shields came up and they cowered. They wore no mail and our archers aimed at legs. The four who were unwounded fled. The wounded ones crawled and limped away. Two were hit in the back as they did so. We had eliminated a quarter of our enemies and not suffered a wound. The next fight would be harder. I saw the thegn or eorledman who led them. He was a veteran warrior. He would attack us in a more organized way.

He halted his men beyond bow range and waited for them all to arrive. He waved his sword and half of them headed to our left. They were going to try to outflank us. They would have to negotiate the pool. Obviously the thegn did not know of the obstacle. He organised the other half, fifty men into a line ten men wide and five men deep.

Olaf Leather Neck laughed, "I will bare my arse in Windar's Mere if he can keep that formation all the way here!"

Haaken said, "If you do that the sun will disappear! Keep your breeks on!"

The thegn had his men march towards us. They had shields above their heads and before them. Sámr and the archers on the drekar just aimed for their legs. The arrows and the uneven ground made gaps appear in the line. As soon as there was a gap then the shield wall ceased to function. It only worked if the shields of all protected all. The men we had already slain were another obstacle. The dead were not as deep as at Aclea but they still had to be negotiated. The result was that the ten wide line was no longer ten warriors wide. They would not lap around our flanks.

"Charge!" When they were twenty paces from us they ran. Two warriors slipped and tripped. The thegn also fell. As the rest of the front rank tried to climb the small hill I slashed my sword in an arc. I sliced through the nose of one and smashed into the side of the helmet of a second. Haaken rammed his sword up under the shield of a third. Olaf's axe smashed the shield and arm of a fourth. This time, however, the weight of men from the rear was brought to bear. Those in our second rank brought over axes and swords to batter the shields which were intended to protect those fighting us. I punched with the boss of my shield and with the hilt of my sword. They were too close for us to swing. Men began to die.

I shouted, "Third rank, push!"

As the weight of the nine men in the rear pushed we began to move the shields down the slight slope. Slick with blood and bodies they began to lose their footing. As they fell to the ground we sank swords into backs and necks.

The thegn shouted, "Fall back!"

Some of the young warriors were so eager to obey that they turned and, in doing so, presented their backs to my archers and to those of my men with a long reach. Seven men fell before the shields were reorganised. I saw that they had lost twenty-one of their number. I looked to my left. The other half were now wading through the pool. We had a dilemma. They would reach us and I needed to have men ready to fight them.

"Haraldr, have half of the men turn to face the second warband. The rest of you we fight in a single line."

"Aye Jarl Dragonheart."

Haraldr and his nine men would have to hold off those on our flank. That left ten of us and our archers to deal with the twenty odd men who remained. The thegn saw that we were weakened by our formation change and he organised a second shield wall. Lack of numbers meant that this one was just three lines deep. The front rank matched ours. It was ten men wide. Man for man we were better than they were. We had a chance of winning. Even as I allowed that thought to flit across my mind I heard the Norns spinning and Sámr shouted, "Jarl Dragonheart! Another two Saxon ships approach and I can see three more vessels behind them."

Haaken began to sing. He sang the song of my battle with the Saxon champion, Sigeberht.

The Dragonheart looked old and grey.
He fought a champion that cold wet day.
A mountain of a man without a hair
Like a giant Norse snow bear
Knocked to the ground by Viking skill
The Saxon stood and struck a blow to kill
Saxon champion, taking heads
Ragnar's Spirit fighting back
Saxon champion, taking heads
Ragnar's Spirit fighting back
Knocked to the ground by Viking skill
The Saxon stood and struck a blow to kill
Saxon champion, taking heads
Ragnar's Spirit fighting back

Viking Warband

Saxon champion, taking heads
Ragnar's Spirit fighting back
Old and grey and cunning yet,
The Dragonheart his sword did wet
With Ragnar's Spirit sharp and bright
He sliced it down through shining light
Through mail and vest it ripped and tore
Saxon Champion, champion no more.
As he sank to the bloody ground
Dragonheart's blade whirled around
Sigeberht's head flew through the air
Dragonheart triumphant there
Saxon champion, taking heads
Ragnar's Spirit fighting back
Saxon champion, taking heads
Ragnar's Spirit fighting back

As we banged our shields in time with the chant I saw the Saxons slowing. Their thegn began berating them. He shouted, "They sing their death song! They know they are going to die! You are not afraid of eleven barbarians, are you? We are the men of Lothuwistoft! Our brothers will join us soon!"

The arrows of my archers began to pick holes in the advancing Saxons. They were running out of arrows, I knew that. Soon they might have to join us and fight with sword and seax! This time we had no extra weight behind us. This would be down to us. I slipped my seax into my left hand. Their spears were fewer in number this time and I knew that the Saxon swords would be shorter than mine. Olaf struck the first blow. He stepped forward and with no one behind him was able to swing his axe one handed. It smashed through the helmet of the leading Saxon as though it was made of wood and not metal. It sliced into the skull. It split his head in two. The men behind visibly recoiled. It was like the bursting of a dam for all of us stepped forward and brought our swords and axes down on the Saxons while they were still trying to get close to us. One managed to ram a spear at my side. It broke some mail links but then my sword smashed his helmet. I did not break the metal but my blow broke his head. He fell dead.

Sámr shouted, "The two Saxon ships have landed! There are sixty more men coming."

Olaf Leather Neck bellowed, "Then I will need to sharpen my axe! Saxon heads are thicker than I remember!"

The thegn saw his chance to get at me. Flanked by two oathsworn who had mail shoulder protectors, the three came at me. One of the bodyguards discovered that Olaf's axe still had an edge as he was hacked in two. I blocked the blow from the thegn's sword on my shield. He held his shield high and I slashed my sword across his thigh. Haaken One Eye head butted the second oathsworn and as he reeled back ripped his sword across his neck. I punched with my shield at the thegn. The men behind him were struggling to keep their feet and he had no shield to support him. As he flailed his arms I used the tip of my sword. I rammed it towards him. He wore leather mail with metal plates but my tip found a gap. I twisted as I pulled it out and I saw the guts gripping Ragnar's Spirit. He was a dead man. As he fell the Saxons lost heart. They ran.

I heard a shout from behind. It was Haraldr, "These Saxons are fleeing too, jarl!"

"Then reform behind us we have fresh men to face. Galmr, Sweyn go amongst their dead and retrieve any usable arrows and spears." If we had had more time then I would have moved the bodies to make a barrier but the two Saxon ships had landed and another thegn was shouting at those who had fled. They halted. They were eight hundred paces from us and I could not hear what they were saying but I guessed that he was rallying them. It took some time and we used that time to gather what we could from the dead. We needed arrows! Then they began to march. This time they came in one long column, six men wide. Galmr ran to the drekar and threw the twenty arrows they had retrieved. Sweyn had taken the spears and he handed them to the men in the second rank. We would use them to throw when the enemy were close. These, too, had no mail.

As they marched I saw that mist had begun to form on the water. I could barely see the Saxon ships. If the Allfather sent it to help us then he needed to send it quicker. It was coming too slowly for my liking. If it had come quicker then we could have used it to our advantage. The Norns! The Saxons came slower than their companions had. This time their leader was ensuring that the column hit us as a solid mass. The men at the front had their shields held high. There were shields to protect them from our arrows. My archers had a mere twenty arrows left. None could be wasted. They would use them on the legs of the front rank just before they hit us.

We had fought a long time. We were all dry and had no voice to sing but we still banged our shields in defiance. The Saxons outnumbered us but we were not yet beaten. When they were twenty paces from us my archers sent their arrows. There were only three of them and I knew that Sámr must be tiring but the arrows flew and men fell. They were not dead but wounded legs do not make it easy to fight. As their shields dropped the three archers were able to send their arrows into the bodies. Two men fell mortally wounded and another was wounded in the leg. My archers now had to send the arrows into the side of the column but they had done enough. When we threw our spears, there were gaps in the Saxon lines and warriors fell. We had killed or wounded ten but there were eight times that number who remained.

I rammed my sword over the shield of the first Saxon. Perhaps he was watching his feet and not me but whatever the reason my blade came out of the back of his neck. Then the second rank rammed their spears at us. Those further back threw their spears. This Saxon thegn had used his head. I heard a cry and saw Sweyn rip a spear from his chest. The whole head was bloody. It was a deep wound. Then Olaf Leather Neck gave a roar. I glanced down and saw that he had been speared in the thigh. I punched with my shield and blindly swung my sword before me. I hit a helmet and the Saxon was stunned. Haaken slashed at him. I turned my shield slightly so that the seax in my left hand could be used. I lunged forward. A sword scraped along my cheek opening it up. The look of joy on the Saxon's face was replaced by horror as my seax tore into his side and eviscerated him.

When Galmr gave a grunt and dropped to one knee I feared the worst. There were three men wounded already. My archers had used all of their arrows. We were going to lose. I lifted my sword and shouted, "Ragnar's Spirit! Let us make this a glorious day for the Clan of the Wolf!"

Suddenly, from my right came a roar. Out of the mist appeared Snorri Snorrison, Harald Iverson and Fótr Firebeard. They were leading their warriors. I had no idea how many men they brought or whence they had come but we now had a chance for the Saxons were taken by surprise as the Viking warband plunged into their side. The thegn made the mistake of turning to see who his new enemies were. It was his last mistake. I hacked at his bare neck. The edge had gone from my sword but I still had enough of one to rip through his throat. We then began to butcher the Saxons. It took but a heartbeat for the Saxons to break and to flee. They ran through the mist to their ships. Harald Iverson's men chased after them. We were too tired.

I saw Haaken bending over Olaf Leather Neck. "Does he live?"

Olaf snorted, "Of course I live! It is a scratch!"

Haaken shouted, "Fetch fire or he will lose the leg." He nodded to Sweyn, "Galmr will live but Sweyn is gone to Valhalla. He died well. He took three with him."

I saw that his body had been cut several times. He had died hard. I would have expected nothing less.

Sámr ran with the flint and kindling. He began to make a fire. "I thought the ships looked like two drekar, Jarl Dragonheart but I lost them in the fog. I am sorry I did not make a better lookout."

Haraldr ruffled his hair, "You were the best of lookouts!"

Fótr came over to me, "We hoped you would still be here but when we saw the Saxon ships we feared the worst."

"Your timing was perfect. Lundenwic?"

He shook his head, "The drekar are gone. They were burned. We were lucky. We came across these two drekar not far from Earhyth. They had been damaged and their crew had pulled them into the shore. We came upon them as the last Dane was being put to the sword. We fell upon the Saxons and took the ships. The last Dane told us that only Halfdan Ragnarsson and three hundred men escaped. They had taken as many ships as they could."

I pointed into the mist. "Some of them are there, caught and burned."

"We will need to repair our ships."

"I do not think that all of the Saxon ships will escape. Take one of those. They will have spare tackle, pine tar and sails."

Ráðgeir asked, "What if more Saxons come?"

"Then we fight them but I do not think that they will."

We spent the next two days helping our rescuers to repair their ships. We slaughtered and salted more sheep and loaded our drekar with our plunder. We burned the enemy dead. It was to stop the smell and the carrion. We saw Saxon ships. There were only one or two and I think that they came just to make sure we had not begun to raid again.

We clasped arms with our friends. "I hope this is not farewell, Jarl Dragonheart. We have each helped the other and that means that our threads are twisted."

"Aye, Fótr, we will meet again. You are warriors and I am proud to have led you."

I did not know for certain that we would meet again but they were richer for the raid. We had relied on each other and we had succeeded. Thousands of others had died across Wessex, in Lundenwic and beneath the waters of the Temese. We had survived.

Chapter 17

With our wounded warriors we had twenty oars to use when the wind was not with us. The Allfather kept the wind from the north and east. We had a short way to row until we rounded the headland and the port of Dwfr. The wind whipped us along at a healthy pace. Sámr spent more time at the steering board with me. He had grown during the voyage both from within as well as in height and size. I realised that, as the summer had passed, he was that much older. The down on his cheeks would turn to a beard in another two years. He was almost a man. A Viking grew up quicker than others. I taught him all that I could about steering a drekar. I knew that my time was running out. I was getting older. The new scar on my cheek blended with the others. Haaken joked that it now looked like a map drawn by Aiden! The wind was a steady one and it afforded me much time to talk with Sámr. I told him how to tell if a man was lying. I gave him advice on dealing with women. I taught him about the wind, how it could be used both on land and at sea. He just soaked it all up. He listened. He in turn told me things about himself. Even though I had known him since he was born there was much I did not know. He liked to compose songs. He was shy about it at first but eventually he told me some of them. Haaken would have been proud of them. I felt embarrassed for most of them were about me. The voyage was perfect and then we reached Syllingar.

It had taken five days to reached the dreaded isles. The wind had veered from north east to south east but, as we approached the witch's lair it turned into a storm from the south and west. At this time of year, Tvímánuður, they could be worse than any winter storm. The wind would not be cold but the winds could be so fierce that a ship could be blown over completely. That was when I feared for Sámr's life. He was the only ship's boy and he had to scamper up the mast and reef the sail. I had to use all the skills I had learned over the years to keep us afloat. We were pushed out in to the vastness of the seas which led to the edge of the world. We spent a whole day and night in that vast emptiness. Even with reefed sails it seemed that the Allfather was pushing us on to the rocks. I did not know if it would be Syllingar, Om Walum or even Hibernia. It was all I could do to keep us upright. When we eventually turned, from the open ocean to head north east, it was as though the Allfather himself was pushing us. It felt like **'Red Snake'** was a wild horse who had never been tamed. I hung on to the steering board and I prayed that we would come through this alive. The sail was reefed until it was as small as it could be and yet we still flew.

The coast of Om Walum is renowned for its rocks and those teeth seemed eager to rip out our hull. I breathed a sigh of relief when we neared the Sabrina. The coast of Dyfed was only slightly less frightening but there were beaches there. It was pitch black and the storm showed no sign of abating but we had to land. Haraldr went to the prow and it was he who saw the flash of white which told us there was a beach ahead of us. How we made it ashore without tearing out our keel I will never know but we managed it. I would worry about getting us off the beach the next morning. We were all exhausted and we needed food. The crew jumped ashore and tied us to the land. Sámr was exhausted and in no condition to do it alone.

We managed to get a fire going and we cooked up a stew made with the salted mutton and shell fish we collected from the rock pools. We had no ale left and had to resort to water. None wished to stay aboard. If the Allfather took the drekar then so be it. We wanted earth beneath our bodies. Sámr slept curled up next to me. My seal skin cape covered us both and kept us dry.

When we woke the storm had abated slightly. It was still a strong wind but it was not the wild stallion it had been the previous day. It was a frisky colt! I checked the hull and it appeared to be sound. What was worrying was that some of the sheets and stays had become a little frayed. We had a couple of spares, which we used but if more were damaged then we would be in trouble. Surprisingly enough the wild storm had made the crew more determined than ever to get home. Our hold was filled with the treasure we had taken in Lundenwic. When we reached Whale Island every man, Sámr included, would be rich. The trick would be to get home.

When we sailed I let out a couple of reefs. We still sailed swiftly but it was not the wild ride of the previous days. The men had not had to row but there was still plenty to do. With only one ship's boy every one of the crew had to work. We turned north and west to take us around Ynys Môn. I was not going to risk the straits! The wind helped us. It was as we neared the coast of Gwynedd that danger burst upon us. I was standing well off from the coast. I did not wish to risk damage on the rocks there. Three Welsh ships put out from the port of Aberffraw. That was where the Welsh king lived. We had raided it once. They saw us not as a wolf but as a lamb to the slaughter. Three to one were not good odds. I saw a beacon light burning too and wondered what it meant.

"To the oars!"

My men took to the oars. We would show the Welsh who were the better sailors. We were close enough to Wyddfa to recall my ancestor and Haaken chose the right chant. It was a chant which invoked the power of the spirits of a long dead ancestor and the most powerful wizard ever to have lived.

> *The wolf snake-crawled from the mountain side*
> *Hiding the spell-wight in cave deep and wide*
> *He swallowed him whole and Warlord too*
> *Returned to pay the price that was due*
> *There they stayed through years of man*
> *Until the day Jarl Dragon Heart began*
> *He climbed up Wyddfa filled with ghosts*
> *With Arturus his son, he loved the most*
> *The mouth was dark, hiding death*
> *Dragon Heart stepped in and held his breath*
> *He lit the torch so strong and bright*
> *The wolf's mouth snarled with red firelight*
> *Fearlessly he walked and found his kin*
> *The Warlord of Rheged buried deep within*
> *Cloaked in mail with sharp bright blade*
> *A thing of beauty by Thor made*
> *And there lay too, his wizard friend,*
> *Myrddyn protecting to the end*
> *With wolf charm blue they left the lair*
> *Then Thor he spoke, he filled the air*
> *The storm it raged, the rain it fell*
> *Then the earth shook from deep in hel*
> *The rocks they crashed, they tumbled down*
> *Burying the wizard and the Rheged crown.*
> *Till world it ends the secret's there*
> *Buried beneath wolf warrior's lair*

We soon began to outpace them. When we turned north east and the wind came from over my shoulder, we positively flew and that was when the Welsh sprang their surprise upon us. Two more ships were waiting for us and they were ahead of us. Now I understood the beacons. They had sent a message to trap us. The other three were ten lengths behind us. The two ahead planned on closing the door on us. It is at such times that you make quick decisions. The Saxons had tried the same when we had raided Wihtwara. Like the Welsh they did not know that we were fearless! I shouted, "Ready to withdraw oars!"

Sámr was next to me, "What do you intend to do Jarl Dragonheart?"

"Simple, we aim for the bow of the one on the right. I hope he turns into the wind to avoid us then we row for our lives."

"But if he does not turn?"

"Then we hit him and we will see how good we are at swimming!"

I saw that the leading ship was preparing to turn into the wind. If we were going to avoid the second one then it would be the right thing to do. But I was not planning on doing that. I saw that the Welsh ships bristled with warriors. If they appeared on either side of us then we would be doomed. When I saw the bow of the second Welsh ship begin to turn to join its consort in trapping us I put my steering board over and aimed for his bow.

"Withdraw oars!"

My men slipped their oars inside the oar holes and I moved the steerboard the opposite way. I thought we were going to miss both ships but the Norns were spinning. We struck the nearest Welsh ship to the steerboard side of her bow. The snake figurehead on our drekar tore through her fore stays. Our whole ship shivered. As we ground along her side I saw that the torn forestays had weakened her mast and it fell, with a crash to the deck. She would not be pursuing us. As soon as we were past her I shouted, "Out oars!"

My men cheered but it was premature. The ship did not feel right. We had sprung something. Even worse the other Welsh ship had turned and was now gaining on us. We were fighting a losing battle. The wind and my men kept the Welsh ships astern of us. I saw the coast of Mercia ahead. There were two rivers we could use but both of them were guarded by burghs and Mercian warriors. They had no love for us.

Sámr looked astern, "She is catching us."

"I know. We have sprung strakes. We are taking on water. The faster we go the more water we ship and yet we cannot slow up for we would be caught."

So long as we were afloat we had a chance. Then I noticed that the rowers had slowed. They were hard men but even they were tiring. This had been a long race. Already the sun was dipping in the west. Would darkness save us?

"They are two lengths behind us."

They would catch us. "Are the others in sight?"

"No, Jarl Dragonheart."

"In oars. Get your weapons. We fight!" I turned to Sámr, "Take the steering board and head for the coast. Do not turn. Do not stop, no matter what happens." I took out Wolf's Blood. "Use this. May the Allfather be with you."

I saw that the Welsh ship was heading for our larboard side. I did not bother with my mail. It was too late for that. I took out Ragnar's Spirit and my seax. "Haraldr, with me! The rest of you, stop them coming aboard."

I wanted to be as close to Sámr as I could. The only chance we had of escaping was to damage their steering board. I had a plan but it was filled with risks. I would have a young boy steering my drekar. I would have an old man leaping across the sea to land on a moving ship. There were more things that could go wrong than could go right!

"Haraldr, when we board you watch my back. I will cut their withy and then we return here."

He grinned, "Aye, jarl!"

He was far too happy about what might be suicide for my liking.

The Welsh boat was higher at the prow and that was where they could board by jumping down on to my ship. The majority of their men were there. There were six men at the steering board. Four were armed and they were not expecting us. As we edged closer and I grabbed the back stay ready to jump, Haraldr suddenly leapt across the gap. He had long legs and he made it but he landed heavily. I had to follow him even though the gap was greater than I might have liked but I made a better landing. Landing on my feet I ripped my seax across the throat of the helmsman and hacked into the back of the man next to him. Even though he had landed heavily, Haraldr was slashing with knife and sword. There was a tangle of bodies and I could not help Haraldr. Blood was spurting and I could not tell whose it was. I picked up one of the axes the Welsh had held. I hacked through the withies and then through the steering board. The axe was sharp and I put all of my effort into the blow. I went to the back stay and chopped through it before going to the larboard side and doing the same there. The men at the bow had seen me and began to come down the ship. I saw that Haraldr was wounded.

I shouted, "Back to our ship." I sheathed my sword and seax. I would need both hands.

He was struggling. His leg had been cut and he was bleeding heavily. "Leave me Jarl Dragonheart!"

"I leave no man." I stood on the gunwale and grabbed the flapping back stay. I put my other hand out and pulled him up. Hang on!" A sudden gust of wind caught the Welsh sail and the mast began to creak and crack. As Haraldr put his arms around my waist I jumped across the yawning gap. It was Haraldr's size and weight which saved us. We swung over the grey, black water and landed heavily on the deck close to our steering board.

"Haaken!" Haaken disengaged himself from the Welshman he had been fighting. Olaf slew him. I saw that the Welsh who had boarded us were dead and the rest were back aboard their stricken ship. "Haraldr is wounded. See to him!"

"Aye jarl!" He shook his head, "After all these years you can still surprise me."

I nodded and ran to the steering board. "She is sluggish, great grandfather!"

"We are sinking! Back to the oars! Row for all you are worth!"

Olaf Leather Neck began the fast chant. This was the one we used when we wished to fly across the sea!

Push your arms
Row the boat
Use your back
The Wolf will fly

Ulfheonar
Are real men
Teeth like iron
Arms like trees

Push your arms
Row the boat
Use your back
The Wolf will fly

Ragnar's Spirit
Guides us still

Viking Warband

Dragon Heart
Wields it well

Push your arms
Row the boat
Use your back
The Wolf will fly

I pushed the steering board over a little. I could see white sand. From my memory I took it to be the desolate land north of the Maeresea. A Viking from Man had landed there. He had named the beach and the village after himself, Fornibiyum. He and his people had been wiped out by the Mercians. Although he was long dead, we remembered the name and we recalled that it was a safe place to land for the tide went out a long way. I could see that the sea was almost at our gunwales. The men were pulling as fast and hard as they could.

I turned to Sámr, "Throw the bodies of the dead overboard. Throw anything over the side which is not treasure."

He laughed, "Great Grandfather, travelling with you takes me to a world I did not know!" He ran down the ship to do my bidding.

Haaken looked up. He had staunched the bleeding. "He is not just Wolf Killer; he is Wolf Killer and Dragonheart in the same body. This is a warrior I would follow."

Haaken One Eye was right. Sámr was special. He had been chosen by the gods. It suddenly came to me. That was the reason we had been saved. It was not for us. It was for Sámr. He had become not only a warrior but he had learned what it took to be a leader. My men had told me that on the Isle of the Sheep, it was Sámr who had kept them together.

We were no longer in imminent danger. The discarded bodies had helped a little. We made a few more paces towards the beach. Water was lapping around the upper strakes but it was not pouring over any longer. When I felt the keel grind upon the sand I silently thanked the Allfather.

"Get the wounded off the ship and them empty the treasure. We have found land. We have not found the Land of the Wolf. This is Mercia and every man's hand will be turned against us." I donned my mail and took my shield. I picked up my helmet. *'Red Snake'* was dying. She had had a bad start but, at the end, she had proved herself. We had sixty miles to travel to the Land of the Wolf. The men did not hang around. They worked feverishly. We had to lift the deck to get the treasure and the chests we had stored there. We had to remove the sacks of grain we had taken. It all took time. The sea was sucking at *'Red Snake'*. The tide was turning. Njoror wanted to take her down to his home! I placed all the maps inside the leather case and slung it around my neck. I put my shield upon my back. I waited until everyone else had left the drekar and then I went to the prow. I stroked the figurehead as I left her. "I cannot burn you, as you deserve. Njoror will take you out and you will sink. You will always be in our hearts." I jumped into the sea. The tide was on the ebb. The drekar would be taken out to sea and she would die.

By the time I reached the others the drekar was already drifting out to sea. My men and all that we had saved were gathered on the beach. Haraldr looked a little pale and the other three wounded men might be a problem. A Viking looked for solutions. "Whatever we do not wish to take home, we leave here. We have two hard days of marching. We need food. We can find water but food cannot be created!"

Some of the things we had brought seemed unimportant. We made a pile. Sámr said, "Why not bury what we cannot take. We are sixty miles from the Land of the Wolf. We can come back for it."

"Dragonheart reborn!" Haaken's words were genuine and well meant. When all had been sorted we found a place in the sand dunes and dug a hole. I went to the nearest tree and carved Sámr's name in the bark. We would find it. I looked out to sea as the last chest was buried. I saw *'Red Snake'*, she was slowly sinking beneath the waves. Of the Welsh ship there was no sign. I suspect that the damage I had done meant they had no control over her. If she drifted close to Man then they would incur the wrath of the Vikings there. I cared not. We had made land. We had lost no one.

It was dark. I did not wish to risk becoming lost by travelling at night time. And we were all exhausted. "We camp here and march in the morning. Can we make thirty miles?"

Ráðgeir Ráðgeirson shouted, "We can make Norway it you ask, Jarl Dragonheart!"

We made a cheery camp. There were no rock pools for shellfish and most of our food had already been eaten but we lit a fire and we huddled together. We were just grateful to be alive.

I ached when I woke. I was getting too old for this. We had chests to carry. The strongest men carried the chests with the coins and the sacks with the food. Sámr joined the Ulfheonar and me at the front of the column, Ráðgeir Ráðgeirson and Galmr brought up the rear. There were twenty-six of us and we had lost irreplaceable men. We struggled on, in their memory. We reached the river the Romans called the Belisima. As much as we wanted to rest we had to cross it. We headed upstream and found a ford. We managed another three miles and could go no further. We camped and drank water and ate the last of the mutton. It was on the edge of being rancid.

Haraldr did not look good. Haaken had a worried look upon his face. "What is amiss Haaken?"

"I fear there is poison in the wound. I would open it."

"You need fire."

"I need fire."

"Then light one. He deserves that." I set sentries and a fire was lit. Haraldr was brought before the fire and I retrieved Wolf's Blood from Sámr. I placed the knife in the fire. When the fire was hot enough Haaken placed his blade in the fire. He nodded to me. I took my blade and slit open the wound. Pus poured out of it. Haaken waited until it ran red with blood and then used his sword to seal it. Sámr held Haraldr's hand. The wounded warrior's back arced and then he relapsed, unconscious.

I put my arm around my great-grandson, "You did well."

"Will he live?"

"That is in the hands of the Allfather."

When we woke Haraldr had a better colour and an appetite. I felt hopeful as we headed north. We had raided this land before. Sigtrygg Thrandson had been jarl here until he had fallen to the Danes. We were almost home. The Norns are like a cat with a mouse. They like to tease and to torment. By the middle of the afternoon we were approaching the Lune when Galmr, who was scout, reported enemies to the north, at the river. "Jarl, there are Saxons at the ford."

I knew we could head upstream but that would just bring us into even more danger. The ford was the shortest way home. We were less than twenty miles from home. I looked at my men. I had twelve who were fit. "Galmr, how many men contest the crossing?"

"Twenty."

"Mercians?"

"Yes, Jarl Dragonheart,"

"Then we take them." I pointed to the men who I would lead. "You come with me. The rest stay here. If we fail…. Make your own way home and remember us well."

Sámr ran to me, "No!"

Haaken said, "Sámr, this is *wyrd*. We throw the bones and see where they fall. It has been a good life and I would not miss one moment of it for I have followed the Dragonheart!"

I nodded to Sámr and drew my sword. "We want to get home to our families and twenty men stand in our way. They are Saxons. We are Viking!" I nodded to Siggi Long Face who led us over the top of the ridge and through the undergrowth. As soon as we crested the rise I saw the Saxons. They had horses and they were camped by the river. They were a border patrol. The Lune marked the northern border of Mercia. They had fishing lines out and some were stretched out sleeping. We ran down the slope. I thought we were making noise but obviously they did not hear us. We were less than fifty paces from them when they spied us. I still had my shield around my back and I swung my sword two-handed at the middle of the surprised Mercian. My blade tore him in two. I lifted it and brought it down on to the skull of the warrior next to him. I did not feel like a greybeard. I felt like the young warrior who had stood with Old Ragnar and Haaken and fought our enemies. I dropped to one knee and lunged upwards as the Mercian swung his sword at my head. My blade split him from the crotch to the throat. I had brought just eleven fit men with me. We were outnumbered but the Saxons had been enjoying a day fishing. It was an unequal contest. Olaf Leather Neck and Haaken were by my side. We hacked, slashed and stabbed at any Saxon who came within range of our blades. And then it was over. They were all dead.

While Sámr and the others came over the ridge to join us I mounted one of the Saxon horses and forded the river. Once on the other side I kissed the ground. "Allfather, you have brought us back to the Land of the Wolf. I thank you." We were almost home.

Epilogue

It was some moons later that we heard the whole story. We had many goods to sell in Dyflin and Bruggas. We sent our knarr escorted by two drekar to do so. The Welsh attack had been a warning. My ships stayed in the ports to trade and to hear news. Both ports were full of the stories. Some were true; I recognised those parts which I had witnessed. Others were, patently, exaggerations. The Saxons had been the victors and they had written the stories. It was Aiden and Atticus, along with Haaken and me who pieced together the whole story. We eliminated the lies and assessed the rest.

Thousands of Danes had died in the battles of Lundenwic and Aclea. The Saxons said that their God had saved them. I knew that was wrong. The Danes, Halfdan Ragnarsson, said that they had been betrayed by Jarl Dragonheart and faithless Norsemen. My people knew that was not true but the story was told and retold. As a result, it was the dead brothers, Hvitserk and Sigurd who were accorded all the glory. Halfdan had returned to their family's lands and, so I heard, was planning an even bigger raid. It seemed that the raid had only whetted his appetite. I was not finished with Halfdan Ragnarsson but I would not raid for a while. I had young to train. The survivors of the raid were rich but we all felt that there was something unfinished. We had achieved something great and yet there were still enemies who remained unpunished. The gold we had taken would be put to good use. The next time we went to war it would be with a warband who all had mail and helmets. We would take so many arrows that their flight would make day night. The survivors of the raid came back changed men. They came back determined men.

The biggest change was in Sámr. His parents noticed it. Ulla War Cry was desperate to emulate his big brother. He had Ulfheonar as friends and the warriors who had sailed with him now spoke of him as a warrior. He became totally focussed on becoming the best warrior that he could be. He had seen death and he had survived. He had seen men die and he had lived. He had witnessed treachery and deceit as well as honour and sacrifice. He now looked like a man. The raid of the Viking warband had changed him from a child to a warrior. Ragnar would lead after I died but when he fell Sámr would ensure that the Clan of the Wolf lived on. It was *wyrd*.

The End

Norse Calendar

Gormánuður October 14th - November 13th
Ýlir November 14th - December 13th
Mörsugur December 14th - January 12th
Þorri - January 13th - February 11th
Gói - February 12th - March 13th
Einmánuður - March 14th - April 13th
Harpa April 14th - May 13th
Skerpla - May 14th - June 12th
Sólmánuður - June 13th - July 12th
Heyannir - July 13th - August 14th
Tvímánuður - August 15th - September 14th
Haustmánuður September 15th-October 13th

Glossary

Afen- River Avon
Afon Hafron- River Severn in Welsh
Àird Rosain – Ardrossan (On the Clyde Estuary)
Aledhorn- Althorn (Essex)
Alpín mac Echdach – the father of Kenneth MacAlpin, reputedly the first king of the Scots
Alt Clut- Dumbarton Castle on the Clyde
An Lysardh - Lizard Peninsula Cornwall
Balley Chashtal -Castleton (Isle of Man)
Bardanes Tourkos- Rebel Byzantine General
Beamfleote -Benfleet Essex
Bebbanburgh- Bamburgh Castle, Northumbria also known as Din Guardi in the ancient tongue
Beck- a stream
Beinn na bhFadhla- Benbecula in the Outer Hebrides
Belesduna – Basildon Essex
Belisima -River Ribble
Blót – a blood sacrifice made by a jarl
Blue Sea- The Mediterranean
Bondi- Viking farmers who fight
Bourde- Bordeaux
Bjarnarøy –Great Bernera (Bear Island)
Breguntford – Brentford
Brixges Stane – Brixton (South London)
Bruggas- Bruges
Brycgstow- Bristol
Burntwood- Brentwood Essex
Byrnie- a mail or leather shirt reaching down to the knees
Caerlleon- Welsh for Chester
Caer Ufra -South Shields
Caestir - Chester (old English)
Cantwareburh -Canterbury
Càrdainn Ros -Cardross (Argyll)
Cas-gwent -Chepstow Monmouthshire
Casnewydd –Newport, Wales
Cephas- Greek for Simon Peter (St. Peter)

Chape- the tip of a scabbard
Charlemagne- Holy Roman Emperor at the end of the 8th and beginning of the 9th centuries
Celchyth - Chelsea
Cherestanc- Garstang (Lancashire)
Cil-y-coed -Caldicot Monmouthshire
Colneceastre- Colchester
Corn Walum or Om Walum- Cornwall
Cymri- Welsh
Cymru- Wales
Cyninges-tūn – Coniston. It means the estate of the king (Cumbria)
Dùn Èideann –Edinburgh (Gaelic)
Din Guardi- Bamburgh castle
Drekar- a Dragon ship (a Viking warship) pl. drekar
Duboglassio –Douglas, Isle of Man
Dun Holme- Durham
Dún Lethglaise - Downpatrick (Northern Ireland)
Durdle- Durdle dor- the Jurassic coast in Dorset
Dwfr- Dover
Dyrøy –Jura (Inner Hebrides)
Dyflin- Old Norse for Dublin
Ēa Lōn - River Lune
Earhyth -Bexley (Kent)
Ein-mánuðr - middle of March to the middle of April
Eoforwic- Saxon for York
Falgrave- Scarborough (North Yorkshire)
Faro Bregancio- Corunna (Spain)
Ferneberga -Farnborough (Hampshire)
Fey- having second sight
Firkin- a barrel containing eight gallons (usually beer)
Fornibiyum-Formby (near Liverpool)
Fret-a sea mist
Frankia- France and part of Germany
Fyrd-the Saxon levy
Ganda- Ghent (Belgium)
Garth- Dragon Heart
Gaill- Irish for foreigners
Galdramenn- wizard

Gesith- A Saxon nobleman. After 850 AD, they were known as thegns
Glaesum –amber
Glannoventa -Ravenglass
Gleawecastre- Gloucester
Gói- the end of February to the middle of March
Gormánuður- October to November (Slaughter month- the beginning of winter)
Grendel- the monster slain by Beowulf
Grenewic- Greenwich
Gulle - Goole (Humberside)
Hagustaldes ham -Hexham
Hamwic -Southampton
Hæstingaceaster- Hastings
Haustmánuður - September 16th- October 16th (cutting of the corn)
Haughs- small hills in Norse (As in Tarn Hows)
Hearthweru- The bodyguard or oathsworn of a jarl
Heels- when a ship leans to one side under the pressure of the wind
Hel - Queen of Niflheim, the Norse underworld.
Here Wic- Harwich
Hersey- Isle of Arran
Hersir- a Viking landowner and minor noble. It ranks below a jarl
Hetaereiarch – Byzantine general
Hí- Iona (Gaelic)
Hjáp - Shap- Cumbria (Norse for stone circle)
Hoggs or Hogging- when the pressure of the wind causes the stern or the bow to droop
Hrams-a – Ramsey, Isle of Man
Hrofecester -Rochester (Kent)
Hundred- Saxon military organisation. (One hundred men from an area-led by a thegn or gesith)
Hwitebi - Norse for Whitby, North Yorkshire
Hywel ap Rhodri Molwynog- King of Gwynedd 814-825
Icaunis- British river god
Issicauna- Gaulish for the lower Seine
Itouna- River Eden Cumbria
Jarl- Norse earl or lord
Joro-goddess of the earth
kjerringa - Old Woman- the solid block in which the mast rested

Viking Warband

Karrek Loos yn Koos -St Michael's Mount (Cornwall)
Knarr- a merchant ship or a coastal vessel
Kyrtle-woven top
Lambehitha- Lambeth
Leathes Water- Thirlmere
Legacaestir- Anglo Saxon for Chester
Ljoðhús- Lewis
Lochlannach – Irish for Northerners (Vikings)
Lothuwistoft- Lowestoft
Lough- Irish lake
Louis the Pious- King of the Franks and son of Charlemagne
Lundenburh- the walled burh built around the old Roman fort
Lundenwic - London
Maeldun- Maldon Essex
Maeresea- River Mersey
Mammceaster- Manchester
Manau/Mann – The Isle of Man(n) (Saxon)
Marcia Hispanic- Spanish Marches (the land around Barcelona)
Mast fish- two large racks on a ship designed to store the mast when not required
Melita- Malta
Midden- a place where they dumped human waste
Miklagård - Constantinople
Mörsugur - December 13th -January 12th (the fat sucker month!)
Njoror- God of the sea
Nithing- A man without honour (Saxon)
Odin - The "All Father" God of war, also associated with wisdom, poetry, and magic (The Ruler of the gods).
Olissipo- Lisbon
Orkneyjar-Orkney
Pecheham- Peckham
Pennryhd – Penrith Cumbria
Pennsans – Penzance (Cornwall)
Poor john- a dried and shrivelled fish (disparaging slang for a male member- Shakespeare)
Þorri -January 13th -February 12th- midwinter
Portesmūða -Portsmouth
Pillars of Hercules- Straits of Gibraltar

Prittleuuella- Prittwell in Essex. Southend was originally known as the South End of Prittwell
Pyrlweall -Thirwell, Cumbria
Ran- Goddess of the sea
Roof rock- slate
Rinaz –The Rhine
Sabrina- Latin and Celtic for the River Severn. Also, the name of a female Celtic deity
Saami- the people who live in what is now Northern Norway/Sweden
Samhain- a Celtic festival of the dead between 31st October and 1st November (Halloween)
St. Cybi- Holyhead
Scree- loose rocks in a glacial valley
Seax – short sword
Sennight- seven knights- a week
Sheerstrake- the uppermost strake in the hull
Sheet- a rope fastened to the lower corner of a sail
Shroud- a rope from the masthead to the hull amidships
Skeggox – an axe with a shorter beard on one side of the blade
Seouenaca -Sevenoaks (Kent)
South Folk- Suffolk
Stad- Norse settlement
Stays- ropes running from the mast-head to the bow
Strake- the wood on the side of a drekar
Streanæshalc- Saxon for Whitby, North Yorkshire
Stybbanhype – Stepney (London)
Suthriganaworc - Southwark (London)
Syllingar Insula, Syllingar- Scilly Isles
Tarn- small lake (Norse)
Tella- River Béthune which empties near to Dieppe
Temese- River Thames (also called the Temese)
The Norns- The three sisters who weave webs of intrigue for men
Thing-Norse for a parliament or a debate (Tynwald)
Thor's day- Thursday
Threttanessa- a drekar with 13 oars on each side.
Tinea- Tyne
Tilaburg – Tilbury
Tintaieol- Tintagel (Cornwall)

Thrall- slave
Trenail- a round wooden peg used to secure strakes
Tynwald- the Parliament on the Isle of Man
Tvímánuður -Hay time-August 15th -September 15th
Úlfarrberg- Helvellyn
Úlfarrland- Cumbria
Úlfarr- Wolf Warrior
Úlfarrston- Ulverston
Ullr-Norse God of Hunting
Ulfheonar-an elite Norse warrior who wore a wolf skin over his armour
Vectis- The Isle of Wight
Veisafjǫrðr – Wexford (Ireland)
Volva- a witch or healing woman in Norse culture
Waeclinga Straet- Watling Street (A5) Windlesore-Windsor
Waite- a Viking word for farm
Werham -Wareham (Dorset)
Western Sea- the Atlantic
Wintan-ceastre -Winchester
Withy- the mechanism connecting the steering board to the ship
Wihtwara- Isle of White
Woden's day- Wednesday
Wulfhere-Old English for Wolf Army
Wyddfa-Snowdon
Wykinglo- Wicklow (Ireland)
Wyrd- Fate
Wyrme- Norse for Dragon
Yard- a timber from which the sail is suspended
Ynys Enlli- Bardsey Island
Ynys Môn-Anglesey

Maps and drawings

Stad on the Eden - a typical Viking settlement

A wedge formation (each circle represents a warrior)

```
         0
        0 0
       0 0 0
      0 0 0 0
     0 0 0 0 0
    0 0 0 0 0 0
   0 0 0 0 0 0 0
```

The boar's snout formation
A boar's snout had two wedges and up to five ranks of men behind.

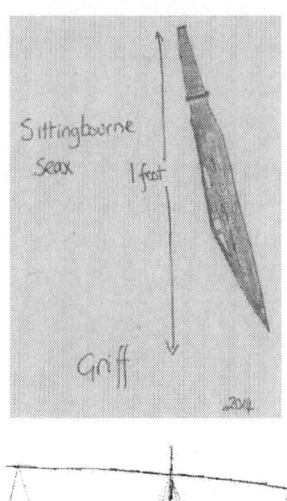

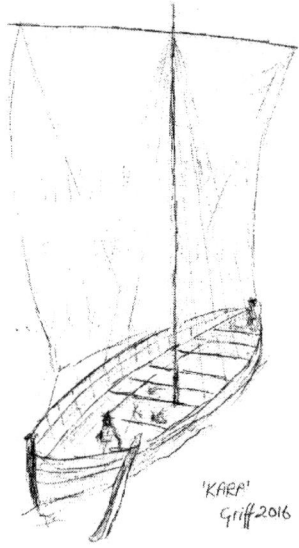

A knarr (reproduced from the Hrolf series- same design)

Historical note

The Viking raids began, according to records left by the monks, in the 790s when Lindisfarne was pillaged. However, there were many small settlements along the east coast and most were undefended. I have chosen a fictitious village on the Tees as the home of Garth who is enslaved and then, when he gains his freedom, becomes Dragon Heart. As buildings were all made of wood then any evidence of their existence would have rotted long ago, save for a few post holes. The Norse began to raid well before 790. There was a rise in the populations of Norway and Denmark and Britain was not well prepared for defence against such random attacks.

My raiders represent the Norse warriors who wanted the plunder of the soft Saxon kingdom. There is a myth that the Vikings raided in large numbers but this is not so. It was only in the tenth and eleventh centuries that the numbers grew. They also did not have allegiances to kings. The Norse settlements were often isolated family groups. The term Viking was not used in what we now term the Viking Age beyond the lands of Norway and Denmark. Warriors went a-Viking which meant that they sailed for adventure or pirating. Their lives were hard. Slavery was commonplace. The Norse for slave is thrall and I have used both terms.

The ship, '*The Heart of the Dragon'* is based on the Gokstad ship which was found in 1880 in Norway. It is 23.24 metres long and 5.25 metres wide at its widest point. It was made entirely of oak except for the pine decking. There are 16 strakes on each side and from the base to the gunwale is 2.02 metres giving it a high freeboard. The keel is cut from a piece of oak 17.6 metres long. There are 19 ribs. The pine mast was 13 metres high. The ship could carry 70 men although there were just sixteen oars on each side. This meant that half the crew could rest while the other half rowed. Sea battles could be brutal. The drekar was the most efficient warship of its day. The world would have to wait until the frigates of the eighteenth century to see such a dominant ship again. When the Saxons before Alfred the Great tried to meet Vikings at sea it ended in disaster. It was Alfred who created a warship which stood a chance against the Vikings but they never really competed. The same ships as Dragonheart used carried King William to England in 1066.

The length of the swords in this period was not the same as in the later medieval period. By the year 850 they were only 76 cm long and in the eighth century they were shorter still. The first sword Dragonheart used, Ragnar's, was a new design, and was 75 cm long. This would only have been slightly longer than a Roman gladius. At this time the sword, not the axe, was the main weapon. The best swords came from Frankia, and were probably German in origin. A sword was considered a special weapon and a good one would be handed from father to son. A warrior with a famous blade would be sought out on the battlefield. There was little mail around at the time and warriors learned to be agile to avoid being struck. A skeggox was an axe with a shorter edge on one side. The use of an aventail (a chain mail extension of a helmet) began at about this time. The highly-decorated scabbard also began at this time.

 A wedge was formed by having a warrior at the front and then two and so on. Sometimes it would have a double point, boar's snout. A wedge with twenty men at the rear might have over a hundred and fifty men. It would be hard to stop. The blood eagle was performed by cutting the skin of the victim by the spine, breaking the ribs so they resembled blood-stained wings, and pulling the lungs out through the wounds in the victim's back.

 I have used the word saga, even though it is generally only used for Icelandic stories. It is just to make it easier for my readers. If you are an Icelandic expert, then I apologise. I use plenty of foreign words which, I know, taxes some of my readers. As I keep saying it is about the characters and the stories.

 It was more dangerous to drink the water in those times and so most people, including children drank beer or ale. The process killed the bacteria which could hurt them. It might sound as though they were on a permanent pub crawl but in reality, they were drinking the healthiest drink that was available to them. Honey was used as an antiseptic in both ancient and modern times. It was also the most commonly available sweetener. Yarrow was a widely-used herb. It had a variety of applications in ancient times. It was frequently mixed with other herbs as well as being used with honey to treat wounds. Its Latin name is Achillea millefolium. Achilles was reported to have carried the herb with him in battle to treat wounds. Its traditional names include arrowroot, bad man's plaything, bloodwort, carpenter's weed, death flower, devil's nettle, eerie, field hops, gearwe, hundred leaved grass, knight's milefoil, knyghten, milefolium, milfoil, millefoil, noble yarrow, nosebleed, old man's mustard, old man's pepper, sanguinary, seven year's love, snake's grass, soldier, soldier's woundwort, stanchweed, thousand seal, woundwort, yarroway, yew. I suspect Tolkien used it in The Lord of the Rings books as Kingsfoil, another ubiquitous and often overlooked herb in Middle Earth.

    The Vikings were not sentimental about their children. A son would expect nothing from his father once he became a man. He had more chance of reward from his jarl than his father. Leaders gave gifts to their followers. It was expected. Therefore, the more successful you were as a leader the more loyal followers you might have. A warrior might be given battle rings by his jarl. Sometimes these were taken from the dead they had slain. Everything would be recycled!

    The blue stone they treasure is aquamarine or beryl. It is found in granite. The rocks around the Mawddach are largely granite and although I have no evidence of beryl being found there, I have used the idea of a small deposit being found to tie the story together.

    There was a famous witch who lived on one of the islands of Scilly. According to Norse legend Olaf Tryggvasson, who became King Olaf 1 of Norway, visited her. She told him that if he converted to Christianity then he would become king of Norway.

    The early ninth century saw Britain converted to Christianity and there were many monasteries which flourished. These were often mixed. These were not the huge stone edifices such as Whitby and Fountain's Abbey; these were wooden structures. As such their remains have disappeared, along with the bones of those early Christian priests. Hexham was a major monastery in the early Saxon period. I do not know it they had warriors to protect the priests but having given them a treasure to watch over I thought that some warriors might be useful too.

    I use Roman forts in all of my books. Although we now see ruins when they were abandoned the only things which would have been damaged would have been the gates. Anything of value would have been buried in case they wished to return. By 'of value' I do not mean coins but things such as nails and weapons. Many of these objects have been discovered. A large number of the forts were abandoned in a hurry. Hardknott fort, for example, was built in the 120s but abandoned twenty or so years later. When the Antonine Wall was abandoned in the 180s Hardknott was reoccupied until Roman soldiers finally withdrew from northern Britain. I think that, until the late Saxon period and early Norman period, there would have been many forts which would have looked habitable. The Vikings and the Saxons did not build in stone. It was only when the castle builders, the Normans, arrived that stone would be robbed from Roman forts and those defences destroyed by an invader who was in the minority. The Vikings also liked to move their homes every few years; this was, perhaps, only a few miles, but it explains how difficult it is to find the remains of early Viking settlements.

Lundenwic/Lundenburh

I know that there may be some confusion about these, apparently, similar sounding names. Lundenwic was the name of the sprawl of houses and farms just outside the Roman walls. It is the area now known as Central London. Lundenburh equates to London City (St. Pauls and the area around the Bank of England. It is the old Roman city of Londinium. There was a Roman wall around it and, in the centre was a Roman fort. Between the city walls and the fort were houses. When the Saxons began to defend against Viking raids they made burghs/burhs. They cleared houses to give a good field of fire and they built ditches. The raid I describe was one of the first ones on London. In 871, some years after this novel is set, the Vikings camped within the city walls and controlled the city until Alfred evicted them. The Viking raids began in the 830s.

King Egbert was a real king who did indeed triumph over King Coenwulf. He founded the power base upon which Alfred the Great built. When he defeated the Mercians he became, de facto, High King of Britain. It was also at this time that the Danes came to take over East Anglia and Yorkshire. The land became, over the next 50 years, Danelaw. Its expansion was only halted by Alfred and was finally destroyed when King Harold defeated his brother and King Harald Hadrada at Stamford Bridge in 1066. Until Alfred the Danes were used as hired swords. They fought for gold. It was a mistake for more often than not, as with the first Angles invited over, Hengist and Horsa, they stayed and conquered.

I have made up Elfrida and Egbert's marriage to her but the kings of that time had many liaisons with many women. Some kings sired up to twenty illegitimate children and many legitimate ones. The practice continued into the late middle ages. Wives were frequently taken for political reasons. The inspiration for the abduction comes from the story of the Welsh Princess Nest (Nesta) who, in the 12th century had two children by King Henry 1st and was then married to one of his friends. She was abducted by a Welsh knight who lived with her until her husband recaptured her and killed her abductor. The Danish raids on the east coast began in the late 700s. However, the west coast and Hibernian were raided by Norse and Rus warriors who also went on to settle Iceland. There is less recorded evidence of their raids, attacks and settlements. The records we have are the Anglo-Saxon Chronicles and they tend to focus on the south and east of what was England. The land that is now the Lake District was disputed land between Northumbria and Strathclyde however the Norse influence on the language and its proximity to the Isle of Man and Dublin make me think that the Norse there would not have been part of what would become Danelaw.

I have used the word Welsh even though it is a modern word. The words used by Vikings and Saxons to describe them were similar to each other and both originated from the Proto-Germanic word Walhaz which means foreigner. Ironic as the Danes, Saxons, Norse and Germans were all the foreigners and the Welsh or Celts were the natives of Britain.

The Vikings had two seasons: summer and winter. As with many things a Viking lived simply and his world was black or white! There was no room for grey or any shades save the dead!

Viking Warband

Other books by Griff Hosker

If you enjoyed reading this book, then why not read another one by the author?

Ancient History

The Sword of Cartimandua Series
(Germania and Britannia 50 A.D. – 128 A.D.)
Ulpius Felix- Roman Warrior (prequel)
The Sword of Cartimandua
The Horse Warriors
Invasion Caledonia
Roman Retreat
Revolt of the Red Witch
Druid's Gold
Trajan's Hunters
The Last Frontier
Hero of Rome
Roman Hawk
Roman Treachery
Roman Wall
Roman Courage

The Wolf Warrior series
(Britain in the late 6th Century)
Saxon Dawn
Saxon Revenge
Saxon England
Saxon Blood
Saxon Slayer
Saxon Slaughter
Saxon Bane
Saxon Fall: Rise of the Warlord
Saxon Throne
Saxon Sword

Medieval History

The Dragon Heart Series
Viking Slave
Viking Warrior
Viking Jarl
Viking Kingdom
Viking Wolf
Viking War
Viking Sword
Viking Wrath
Viking Raid
Viking Legend
Viking Vengeance
Viking Dragon
Viking Treasure
Viking Enemy
Viking Witch
Viking Blood
Viking Weregeld
Viking Storm
Viking Warband
Viking Shadow
Viking Legacy
Viking Clan
Viking Bravery

The Norman Genesis Series
Hrolf the Viking
Horseman
The Battle for a Home
Revenge of the Franks
The Land of the Northmen
Ragnvald Hrolfsson
Brothers in Blood
Lord of Rouen
Drekar in the Seine
Duke of Normandy
The Duke and the King

Viking Warband

Danelaw
(England and Denmark in the 11th Century)
Dragon Sword
Oathsword
Bloodsword
Danish Sword

New World Series
Blood on the Blade
Across the Seas
The Savage Wilderness
The Bear and the Wolf
Erik The Navigator
Erik's Clan

The Vengeance Trail

The Reconquista Chronicles
Castilian Knight
El Campeador
The Lord of Valencia

The Aelfraed Series
(Britain and Byzantium 1050 A.D. - 1085 A.D.)
Housecarl
Outlaw
Varangian

The Anarchy Series England 1120-1180
English Knight
Knight of the Empress
Northern Knight
Baron of the North
Earl
King Henry's Champion
The King is Dead
Warlord of the North

Viking Warband

Enemy at the Gate
The Fallen Crown
Warlord's War
Kingmaker
Henry II
Crusader
The Welsh Marches
Irish War
Poisonous Plots
The Princes' Revolt
Earl Marshal
The Perfect Knight

Border Knight
1182-1300
Sword for Hire
Return of the Knight
Baron's War
Magna Carta
Welsh Wars
Henry III
The Bloody Border
Baron's Crusade
Sentinel of the North
War in the West
Debt of Honour
The Blood of the Warlord
The Fettered King

Sir John Hawkwood Series
France and Italy 1339- 1387
Crécy: The Age of the Archer
Man At Arms
The White Company
Leader of Men
Tuscan Warlord

Lord Edward's Archer
Lord Edward's Archer

Viking Warband

King in Waiting
An Archer's Crusade
Targets of Treachery
The Great Cause
Wallace's War

Struggle for a Crown
1360- 1485
Blood on the Crown
To Murder a King
The Throne
King Henry IV
The Road to Agincourt
St Crispin's Day
The Battle for France
The Last Knight
Queen's Knight

Tales from the Sword I
(Short stories from the Medieval period)

Tudor Warrior series
England and Scotland in the late 14th and early 15th century
Tudor Warrior
Tudor Spy

Conquistador
England and America in the 16th Century
Conquistador
The English Adventurer

Modern History

The Napoleonic Horseman Series
Chasseur à Cheval
Napoleon's Guard
British Light Dragoon
Soldier Spy
1808: The Road to Coruña

Viking Warband

Talavera
The Lines of Torres Vedras
Bloody Badajoz
The Road to France
Waterloo

The Lucky Jack American Civil War series
Rebel Raiders
Confederate Rangers
The Road to Gettysburg

Soldier of the Queen series
Soldier of the Queen
Redcoat's Rifle

The British Ace Series
1914
1915 Fokker Scourge
1916 Angels over the Somme
1917 Eagles Fall
1918 We will remember them
From Arctic Snow to Desert Sand
Wings over Persia

Combined Operations series
1940-1945
Commando
Raider
Behind Enemy Lines
Dieppe
Toehold in Europe
Sword Beach
Breakout
The Battle for Antwerp
King Tiger
Beyond the Rhine
Korea
Korean Winter

Viking Warband

Tales from the Sword II
(Short stories from the Modern period)

Other Books
Great Granny's Ghost (Aimed at 9-14-year-old young people)

For more information on all of the books then please visit the author's website at www.griffhosker.com where there is a link to contact him or visit his Facebook page: GriffHosker at Sword Books

Printed in Great Britain
by Amazon